I0640366

STUNTED

By

Breanna Hughes

2018

Stunted © 2018 Breanna Hughes
Triplicity Publishing, LLC

ISBN-13: 978-0999737095
ISBN-10: 0999737090

All rights reserved. No part of this publication may be reproduced, distributed, or transmitted in any form without permission.

This is a work of fiction. Names, characters, places, and incidents are the product of the author's imagination and are used fictitiously. Any resemblance to actual persons, living or dead, business establishments, events of any kind, or locales is entirely coincidental.
Printed in the United States of America

First Edition – 2018
Cover Design: Triplicity Publishing, LLC
Interior Design: Triplicity Publishing, LLC
Editor: Miranda Campbell - Triplicity Publishing, LLC

Thank you to Triplicity Publishing and my amazing editor Miranda Campbell. To Jaymi, Allisa, and Rikke for your unconditional friendship. And to my parents for your endless support.

This book is dedicated to Clexa fans everywhere.

Chapter 1

The moment Jessie Knight stepped out of the car, the hot and dry desert heat greeted her like a swift backhand to the face. It was a vast contrast to the air-conditioned town car, and the offensive triple-digit heat nearly knocked her on her ass. It was barely nine a.m. She grabbed her bag and headed towards the closed movie set. Not that it really needed to be "closed." No one in their right mind would be dumb enough to brave this heat in the middle of the Nevada desert unless they were getting paid, which Jessie was. After checking in with security and showing them her ID, the second assistant director greeted her and showed her to her trailer. She snapped a quick photo of the sign on her trailer door: Jessie Knight, stunt double - *Best of Enemies.*

Once inside, she was thankful to feel relief in her air-conditioned trailer and wanted to soak in an ice bath for an hour to keep cool. Whose idea was it to film in the middle of the desert in the dead of summer anyway? She really shouldn't mind too much though. It was a well-paying gig and now she knew why. She'd worked in pretty intense weather conditions before, but nothing like this. She knew better than to complain. There were several crew members who'd been here much longer and worked much harder in the searing heat building sets, fixing lights, and setting up shots. Jessie's job was relatively easy compared to theirs. Sure, there weren't many people who could do the job she did, but she loved it. It was fun, adventurous, a little bit dangerous, and it paid well. But that was mainly because she was damn good at it.

Jessie had been working as a stunt double in films for about three years now. Her childhood friend, Peyton, was the one who actually got her into it. Peyton moved out to Los Angeles a few years back and had a friend who was a stunt coordinator looking for a girl who fit Jessie's description. He was looking for someone experienced in mixed martial arts and who knew how to handle weapons. Jessie fit the bill perfectly. She was looking for a change, so she moved out to Los Angeles from Colorado and met with him. He was immediately impressed with her skills. She was only needed for a quick scene, but it came so naturally to her, she decided to pursue it as a career. She took stage combat classes, weapons classes, brushed up on her fight skills, took racing lessons with the top stunt drivers in the country and started to make a name for herself in the industry. It'd gotten to the point where she didn't need to submit her name for consideration. Stunt coordinators sought her out. She'd always been a bit of a thrill-seeker and loved the fact that now she got paid for it.

She found her wardrobe hanging in the closet of her trailer and changed into it. Upon looking in the mirror, she shook her head. Tight black leather pants and a matching tank top. *Really? Were they trying to kill her?* At least she looked good in the pants. They seemed to breathe a little bit, but the heat could very well prove to be a problem. Thank God for hazard pay.

She slathered on some sunscreen and headed out to the set. Her call time was in 20 minutes, and she still had to get hair and makeup done. Her face was never shown close up on camera, but she was still required to wear some makeup for each scene.

When she stepped outside she was already sweating, but she was ready to work. She spent the past week practicing all the stunts with the stunt coordinator, along with the actress—Hayley Carhart—she was doubling for. That was very different, though. All of those rehearsals were done on a soundstage in Los Angeles in a much cooler, more intimate atmosphere.

When she got to the set, she was glad to find that she knew a couple of crew members from past films she worked on. They all gave her a friendly hello as she walked by. Jessie always made it a point to be kind to the crew. They worked 10 times harder than anyone else on the set and were always the first to arrive and the last to leave. While she was friendly, she also made it a point to keep her distance from everyone and maintain only professional relationships, not wanting to get too close. Her job was the most important thing in the world to her. She had to keep her concentration and avoid any distractions.

Nate, the assistant director on the film, came up to greet her.

"Jessie! Welcome to hell."

They shook hands.

"How's everyone holding up in this heat?"

Nate shrugged. "We have a few air-conditioned tents over there, so people have been taking breaks to cool off. We've got ice cold water over there and of course, the trailers have AC. But yeah…pretty much everyone wants to die."

Jessie laughed. "Well, I know how efficient the director is. Very big on just one or two takes, so maybe it'll be a quick shoot."

"That's the plan." He looked over to the young woman approaching them. "Jessie, you remember Hayley, right?"

"Of course. Good to see you again." Jessie looked down at her own wardrobe and then at Hayley's black leather pants and tank top. "How embarrassing. We're wearing the same thing."

Hayley chuckled and greeted Jessie with a high five. "I'm gonna have to fire my stylist."

They spent a large part of last week together, so Jessie felt comfortable enough to act more informal around Hayley. That tends to happen when you're working with someone, tediously rehearsing blocking and landing your mark over and over again. Hayley only had to worry about a few minor stunts since Jessie was doing all the dangerous work, but the director insisted the actors worked with their doubles so they could hit their marks perfectly, no matter who was filming the scene. Getting along with Hayley was fairly easy, and Jessie seemed to be the perfect double since they were both petite brunettes. They were the same height with the same hair length, but where Hayley was a bit more ample, Jessie was more lithe and practically all muscle.

Principal filming started two days ago, and the director wanted to get the difficult scenes out of the way. This meant all the scenes with heavy stunts would be at the front end of filming.

"Ready to kick some ass?" Hayley asked.

"Always."

"Hayley, you're needed in makeup," a production assistant informed her. "Jessie, you'll be needed for light makeup in a few minutes."

Jessie nodded as Hayley headed off to makeup. She took this moment to look around the set and noticed a dilapidated bridge they built specifically for the film. She smiled upon realizing this was the bridge she'd jump off of at some point today. First, they were filming combat scenes which was the easiest thing for Jessie; she could do it all. Her fight skills were second to none. After three years in the business, she was also quite good with knives, swords, gymnastics, and parkour. She had excellent stunt driving skills, knew how to handle a prop gun, and was particularly good at falling and landing. She had yet to find a height or apparatus she couldn't wait to jump from. At 26-years-old, she was one of the most sought-after stunt women around.

After familiarizing herself with the set, she grabbed some water from one of the coolers and took a swig from the bottle as she watched what was going on in front of the camera. She swallowed hard when she noticed a beautiful blonde girl talking to the director. Her mouth hung open as she watched the girl going over some blocking. The blonde's brow furrowed as she concentrated on repeating the movements the director showed her. She laughed. The sound traveled all the way to Jessie's ears, filling her with something vaguely familiar, but she was too entranced to figure out what the feeling was.

Suddenly realizing how thirsty she was, she took another swig of water and watched as the blonde left the director to walk over to the designated makeup area. She cast a glance in Jessie's direction. The blonde quirked an eyebrow and gave her a smile, as if catching Jessie staring at her. Jessie snapped out of it immediately and looked away. She'd never been caught off guard quite like that before and didn't intend for it to happen again.

"Is that the legendary Jessie Knight?"

Jessie turned around and saw a familiar face walking up to her. The girl was dressed in dark jeans and a skin-tight red top.

"Kat! It's good to see you again." She pulled her into a hug.

"You too! I haven't seen you since that race car project. What was that, like a year and a half ago?

"Yeah, I think so."

"Wow, you look good. Who are you doubling for?"

"Hayley Carhart." She looked around for Hayley, but didn't see her.

"Oh yeah? How's that going?"

"It's good. She's actually pretty cool." Jessie tugged lightly at Kat's hair. "Nice hair. I don't think I've ever seen you this blonde."

"Hey, I'm a natural blonde. I just had to go a few shades lighter. Got to look the part when I'm doubling for Elliot Chase. You've heard of her, right?"

Jessie shrugged. "Can't say I have."

Kat looked at her incredulously. "Why am I not surprised? I swear for someone who works so consistently in this industry, you really have no knowledge of it."

"Hey, I have the knowledge I need. I know how to do my job."

"Try reading a gossip magazine or watching *Access Hollywood* for once."

"I get to know the people I double for really well. That's enough for me. Hayley and I are at a place where we can actually joke with each other," Jessie protested.

"Well, that's better than the actress you doubled for on the race movie. You wouldn't even talk to her unless it was work related. The poor girl was terrified of you."

"I didn't like the way she treated the crew. She was rude and demanding and disrespectful."

Even though she worked with famous people on a daily basis, Jessie often made it clear she had no desire for fame herself. She wasn't into the whole celebrity thing. She liked her life the way it was. Why bother adding the inconvenience of fame to it?

"Fair enough," Kat relented.

Jessie looked around once more. "Is this your first day on set, too?"

"No," Kat responded. "I started yesterday. I think Elliot's character has a few more action sequences than Hayley's. I think they're playing enemies or something."

"You didn't read the script?"

"I know my stunts. That's all I need."

"Why am I not surprised?" Jessie chided.

"Let me guess, your script is full of notes and blocking."

"It doesn't hurt to be prepared. I'm glad we'll be working together again."

"I know. It's been too long. We need to catch up."

"Definitely."

"You'll have to introduce me to Hayley Carhart. That girl is all kinds of hot."

Jessie cocked her head. "I'm sorry, don't you have a boyfriend?"

"Oh, we've got a lot to catch up on. I am super single now."

"Well, I'll introduce you, but no hitting on her. It's unprofessional."

Kat rolled her eyes. "Always so proper. Oh, you should totally meet Elliot. She's an absolute sweetheart, and she might actually appreciate meeting someone who doesn't know who she is." Kat turned and motioned toward someone.

Jessie's body went stiff. Her throat suddenly felt very parched again when she noticed the blonde she'd been so captivated with earlier waving to Kat and walking toward them. She hadn't noticed it earlier, but Elliot was dressed the exact same way Kat was dressed, and it certainly wasn't helping Jessie's very obvious physical reaction to her. She tried to control her eyes and keep them from blatantly looking the girl up and down, but failed miserably and could only hope she didn't notice. The smirk on the blonde's face told her otherwise.

Kat gestured to Elliot.

"Elliot, this is Jessie. We've worked together a couple times in the past. She's Hayley's stunt double. Jessie, this is Elliot Chase."

Elliot held out her hand and flashed the sweetest smile. Jessie straightened her posture and took her hand, paying no attention to how amazing it felt against her own. She also made it a point to ignore how stunning Elliot looked in triple-digit temperatures. Jessie was sweating through every piece of material she wore, but Elliot merely looked like she radiated something otherworldly instead of sweating profusely.

She steeled herself. She could do this. It was just another actress. She'd dealt with so many over the years, and Elliot was no different.

"It's nice to meet you, Elliot."

"You too, Jessie."

Before allowing herself to stare too long into Elliot's strikingly blue eyes, she ended the handshake and cleared her throat.

"I'm due in the makeup chair. I'll see you guys later."

She walked away without looking back. But God, did she want to.

*

Ten minutes later, Elliot and Hayley were rehearsing the close-ups for their fight scene. She tried to listen to the director as they adjusted the lighting, but was too preoccupied scanning the area for the girl that Kat introduced her to. She had to be nearby since the doubles were needed once they wrapped the close-up scenes, but she didn't see her anywhere. The girl took off so quickly, Elliot barely had a chance to talk to her. It was like she couldn't get away fast enough. Elliot was too struck by the girl's beauty and sparkling green eyes to say anything other than the words "you too, Jessie."

How the hell had Hayley not told her about Jessie? Her friend had spent a week going over stunts with the most gorgeous woman she'd ever seen, and Hayley didn't even bother telling her? That simply would not stand.

"So…your stunt double seems nice. I met her for a second."

"Jessie? Yeah, she's cool. Very good at what she does. A consummate professional."

"Right. Professional." Elliot was lost in thought as she saw Jessie walk out of one of the air-conditioned tents with Kat.

She wanted to ask Hayley more about her but decided against it. That girl was never good at keeping secrets and definitely didn't know what it meant to be discreet about something. Of course, Hayley knew of

Elliot's proclivity for women, and Elliot knew she'd never tell anyone, but the girl did have a tendency to spill other secrets, especially to their friend, Morgan. Morgan would be pissed Elliot hadn't told her about it and drama would ensue.

She loved her friends and trusted them with everything, but they acted like babies if one of them knew something before the other. She either had to tell them both about Jessie or tell neither, but she'd just have to worry about that later.

The three of them moved out to Los Angeles together after high school. Elliot and Hayley were determined to make it as actresses and surprisingly enough, they defied the odds. Even more impressive was the fact that they both managed to succeed without the other's help. Hayley made a name for herself after being cast in a popular teen drama television series. After several commercials and portraying roles like "party-goer number five," Elliot landed a key role as a rebellious high school student opposite Drew Barrymore's inspirational teacher. From there, the offers started pouring in for both of them. This film was actually the first time the two of them had been cast in something together. It was Elliot's first ever action role, so she was nervous but excited she'd get to work alongside her friend. Actually, both of her friends.

"So are we going to blow some shit up or what?"

Elliot heard Morgan's voice over the radio and looked up to the custom built bridge to find her friend waiting very impatiently with a detonator in her hand.

When Morgan moved out to LA with them, she chose to work on the production side of the industry and found her niche in working with pyrotechnics and explosives for action films. It all seemed to work out perfectly for them—an unlikely success story.

Nate replied to her over the radio. "We'll be ready for you in about an hour, Morgan. Hang tight up there and make sure everything is set."

In the meantime, Elliot and Hayley cleared the way for the doubles to come in and film the wide shots. Elliot couldn't take her eyes off of Jessie. She was in complete awe watching her ninja-quick fight moves, hitting every single mark perfectly. The girl was a machine, performing backflips, jump kicks, and taking hits from Kat with so much grace it almost seemed like a dance. As part of the script, Jessie was knocked onto her back and then jumped back up using only her hands as leverage. Elliot always wanted to do that but was never able.

They finished the scene in two takes, and then it was time for Elliot and Hayley to film their close-ups. She was a little flustered, especially as she watched Jessie walk past her, dripping with sweat. Her scenes with Hayley required much less physical exertion, and she almost felt embarrassed. She smiled at Jessie as she walked by, but Jessie simply nodded in return and kept walking.

However, that didn't deter Elliot. Her scenes with Hayley took much longer to film because of the dialogue, but she noticed Jessie had stayed behind to watch the scene even though she wasn't needed again for at least another half hour. Kat had long since gone back to the tent, but Jessie stayed in the blistering sun, downing a cold bottle of water. She didn't head back to the tent until the scene was wrapped.

"Cut! Great job. Let's set up the shot for the bridge!"

Since this was Elliot's first foray into action films, she wasn't exactly used to the extremity of certain scenes. When she found herself up on the bridge built specifically for this shoot, she was a little wary. First of all, she wasn't expecting it to be so high up. Secondly, she didn't realize how windy it'd be, and she could feel the bridge move slightly with each gust of wind. It was built to look like a long-deserted freeway overpass, but to her, it felt like a rickety suspension bridge about to give out at any minute. She made it a point to stay by the edge near the railing until it was time to film her scene. This was the big chase. Her character was supposed to chase Hayley's character across the bridge, and she couldn't allow herself to look terrified on camera. Her character was supposed to be a badass. Unfortunately, Elliot herself was somewhat scared of heights.

She looked over to see Morgan with Kat testing out the squibs on a vest hidden by her shirt. Elliot hadn't expected the squibs to actually go off, and when they did a gust of wind happened to blow at the same time, causing the bridge to jolt. Elliot jumped at the noise and stumbled, trying to find her balance as the bridge continued to shake. Suddenly, she felt two strong arms come up behind her and catch her as she stumbled backward.

"Whoa. Careful there," warned Jessie. "You're okay. It's just a bit chaotic up here."

Elliot's breath hitched at the thought of knowing Jessie's arms were wrapped around her. Her chest was pressed against Elliot's back in an effort to steady her as the wind continued to blow. She could've sworn she felt

Jessie's arms tighten as her hands gripped her hips. She felt a chill when Jessie whispered in her ear.

"Don't worry. It's completely sturdy up here. You're safe."

And then she was gone. Jessie's arms were no longer around Elliot, even though she could still feel them there long after.

*

As they set up for the scene, Jessie got fitted for her harness. They attached the cables and tested the wires to make sure everything worked perfectly. She didn't have to look to know that Elliot was watching her. Elliot seemed to have been watching her all day, and she wondered if this was a common occurrence for the actress. She tried her best to ignore it, to forget just how good Elliot felt in her arms when she caught her. She tried not to look back at her, but caught herself eyeing Elliot a couple times. Each time, Elliot seemed to conveniently look away when Jessie looked over. Apparently they were back in grade school.

She shook the thoughts from her mind and went over the moves precisely. She peered over the edge of the bridge to find the mark where she'd land. Her goal was to land directly on the X clearly marked on the inflatable stunt jump on the ground. She'd done the move many times before, but she always made sure her marks were memorized. She couldn't take any chances. She knew that even one inch off could not only ruin the shot, but be very dangerous for her.

The prop master handed her a prop handgun as other crew members adjusted her harness and cables. She chanced another glance at Elliot and noticed a bit of apprehension on her face. She was still a bit shaky.

"Guys, sorry. Can I take these off for a second?" She gestured to the cables connected to her harness.

"Sure, no problem." They removed the cables, and Jessie headed over to where Elliot stood.

"Hey."

"Hi." Elliot did her best to sound like nothing was wrong. Jessie didn't buy it.

"Let me show you something," offered Jessie. Without another word, she ran down the entire length of the bridge, then turned and ran all the way back to Elliot.

"See? You've got nothing to worry about. Completely sturdy. You'll do fine." She ducked her head to meet Elliot's eyes, needing her to see she was serious and that there was no reason for her to be scared. She hoped it worked.

Elliot nodded and smiled. "Thank you."

Jessie nodded in return and started to walk back.

"What if I fall?"

She turned and faced Elliot. "I'm on cables. I'll jump off after you and catch you."

"You really have no fear, do you?"

"Sure I do. Just not in a physical capacity." They eyed each other for a moment before she turned and walked back to get her cables re-connected. "Good luck, Elliot."

A few minutes later, Jessie watched as Elliot pulled off the scene without any sign of trepidation. She chased Hayley down the bridge as Hayley threw an explosive behind her, just in front of Elliot, before the director yelled cut.

*

Having successfully completed the scene, Elliot stayed and watched as Jessie and Kat tested their harnesses one last time.

The director got on the radio. "This is a take, everyone! I want to do this in one shot, otherwise it'll take the rest of the day to set up again. Morgan, cue it up! Here we go!"

Once cameras rolled, the slate board clamped down, and the director called "action!" The wide shot for the scene started, and Elliot moved around to get a better view. She watched as Jessie ran across the bridge, and Kat chased after her.

"Go for fire!"

Morgan hit the detonator, and the explosion went off halfway down the bridge. Elliot felt the heat from the fire and could only imagine how much hotter it felt for Jessie who was right in the thick of it. She watched with excitement as Jessie outran the explosion and leapt off the bridge with a ball of fire hot on her trail. Elliot ran to the side of the bridge to watch the girl's jump. The cables allowed her to move her arms and legs perfectly before landing in the dead center of the stunt jump.

"Cut! That was perfect! We managed to do it in one take! Great job, everyone."

She watched as Jessie raised her fist in celebration, and Elliot smiled. She couldn't help but be charmed by it.

When Elliot made her way back down from the bridge, she looked around for Jessie. She wanted to congratulate her, but couldn't find her anywhere. She grabbed the AD as he walked by.

"Hey, Nate, have you seen Jessie?"

"Oh, she's done for the day, so I think she's heading back to the hotel. She said something about needing a shower and a long nap, but she might still be in her trailer."

"What hotel is she staying in?"

"Same as us."

Elliot thought for a moment. "Okay, thanks."

*

The next day, Elliot's call time was way too early, and she relied heavily on coffee to get her through it. She had another action scene with Hayley later that day, but had to film a few scenes with other actors—the ones who played members of Elliot's squad—before that. Today was their first day on set and Elliot wanted to be there to greet them. She'd worked with Drew Dorsey before on an HBO original movie. He was nice enough, but made her uncomfortable with the amount of times he hit on her. He backed off after a while though, which she was thankful for. Once he stopped, they got along fairly well. He was set to play her love interest in this film, which she wasn't too happy about. Mainly because she felt like her character had far more important things to worry about than having a boyfriend. She didn't write the script though, so she had to do her job. At least she'd worked with him before, so they knew each other well enough.

She'd seen a few of Ashton Hanson's films, but had never met him. She greeted him, straining her neck to look up at his hulking, six-foot-five frame. She'd known James Carhart since she was a kid seeing as how he was Hayley's cousin. He moved out to Los Angeles 10 years ago to work as an actor. She'd only seen him a handful of times since then because he was always on location filming something.

He had yet to land any lead roles, but he consistently worked. She'd only met the other actors briefly at the table read, but didn't have much time to talk to them.

She found them all in one of the tents, trying to keep out of the heat. Drew noticed her right away and greeted her with a hug.

"Well if it isn't my favorite blonde princess."

She offered him a one-armed hug and a smile.

"Nice to see you, Drew. Hey, James! She hugged him and re-introduced herself to the rest of the actors.

"Where's Hayley?" asked James.

"She's not due on set for a couple hours."

"She can't even come early to see her cousin? I haven't seen her since Christmas."

"We had a long, tiring, and very hot day yesterday. You won't believe this heat. It's insane. I can't wait to get back to the soundstage in LA."

"Oh man, I really want to meet Hayley," Drew interjected. "Tell her to get to set early."

"Dude, that's my cousin. Knock it off."

Drew put his hands up. "Hey, I was just joking. Elliot will tell you. I like to joke around."

Elliot whispered to James. "Don't worry. He's harmless. He's a nice guy, just sometimes a bit misguided."

"If you say so."

Filming that morning went fairly smoothly, and Elliot was excited to film the motorcycle chase scene. Not because she'd be driving a motorcycle—her agent made sure it was in her contract that she wasn't required to drive one—but it meant that she'd be able to watch Jessie drive a motorcycle. And that appealed to her way more than it should.

Jessie had only just arrived on set and was already dreading this. Yesterday was bad enough with the heat, but today would be way worse because she knew she'd have to sport a leather jacket for the motorcycle scene. It'd be brutal, but she was determined to get it done. It was her only scene for the day, so she wanted to get in, get out, and get back to the comfort of the hotel. She spent the previous night thinking way too much about a certain blonde actress, and Jessie couldn't have that kind of distraction. Not only was it wildly inconvenient, but it also went against her own code. She didn't get involved with actresses, and she definitely didn't get involved with people she worked with. It was around three a.m. when she decided she needed to ignore Elliot and get through the rest of this shoot the way she would any other: with the utmost stoicism and professionalism.

After changing into her outfit, she exited her trailer and immediately caught sight of Elliot, who gave her a little wave. Jessie nodded and went to find Kat so they could go over the notes with the stunt coordinator.

"Hey." Kat greeted her by tossing her a water bottle, which Jessie easily caught. "Where's your leather?"

Jessie scoffed. "That thing is not going on my body until the cameras are rolling. It's too damn hot. Where's yours?"

"Same."

"Shall we do a test run? I need to familiarize myself with this model bike."

"Yeah, I informed Nate. He's getting the keys."

Jessie noticed as Elliot made her way over to the makeup area. They locked eyes before Jessie tore her gaze away.

"She asked me about you," informed Kat.

"Who?"

"Elliot. She asked me about you yesterday after you left."

"Oh." Jessie absolutely didn't want to know what she asked. She didn't have time for this. She honestly didn't even care. "What did she ask you?"

Damn it, Jessie.

"She just wanted to know how long I've known you and how long you've been doing this. She seemed really impressed with everything you did yesterday."

"Well, I don't blame her. I'm quite impressive." Jessie tried to brush it off and decided to ignore the feeling she got in her stomach at the thought of Elliot asking about her. No big deal. She probably asks about a lot of people.

Nate arrived with the keys, and Jessie was thankful for his timing. She and Kat did a test run with the bikes on the empty road where they planned on filming. It only took five minutes for her to fall in love with the bike. It rode so smoothly and could turn on a dime. She'd have to remember that since she was thinking of buying a motorcycle at some point. She couldn't handle the LA traffic in her car anymore.

She pulled up next to Kat and took off her helmet. Her hair fell around her shoulders as she shook it out. Kat nodded over to Jessie's left. She turned to find Elliot watching them before suddenly turning around as if she'd been caught staring.

"What's going on there?"

Jessie wasn't in the mood for this. "Literally nothing. Now let's run it one more time. Bump it up to 80 since that's how fast we'll be going in the scene."

Kat nodded and put her helmet back on.

Jessie turned to see Elliot in the distance talking to Hayley. She was laughing at something, and Jessie had to fight the smile that threatened to break out across her face. There was something about the girl's laugh that filled Jessie's chest with something new. Something she hadn't felt in quite some time. She put her helmet on and revved up the engine, knowing it would catch some people's attention. As she sped off down the road, she found herself reluctantly hoping Elliot was one of those people.

*

Once Jessie's scene wrapped, she jumped off the bike. Elliot wasted no time in greeting her.

"Nice moves on the bike."

"Thanks."

The girl looked her up and down.

"Nice leather, too."

Jessie smirked at her. "You're into leather? Good to know."

She wanted to slap herself. *Why would she say that?* That counted as flirtation, which was a no-go area for her. But the look on Elliot's face kind of made it worth it. The girl was speechless, so Jessie decided to leave on a high note.

"See you later, Elliot."

Jessie walked away hoping to remain relatively unscathed.

Chapter 2

By the end of the following day, Elliot was a little grumpy and rather annoyed. It wasn't because she had just put in a 14 hour day; she was used to that. It was because she barely had any interaction with Jessie. Every time she tried to watch one of her stunts or tried to strike up a conversation, something interrupted her.

Now that they were nearly done shooting for the day, Elliot saw another opportunity to talk to Jessie. She was by herself at the craft services table, mulling over a rather brown-looking banana. She smiled, watching as Jessie examined the withered peel, even going so far as to smell it.

"Don't do it," warned Elliot. "It looks rather questionable."

Jessie smiled. "I guess that's what happens to a good piece of fruit when it sits out in the brutal heat for hours."

Elliot grabbed an apple and handed it to Jessie.

"I think this is a safer choice."

Jessie took the apple. Elliot opened her mouth to say something when her co-star James came up behind her out of nowhere.

"Hey!"

Elliot jumped and squealed, immediately embarrassed by losing her cool in front of Jessie.

"Don't do that!" She playfully swatted at James, trying to recover.

"Sorry. My cousin was looking for you."

"Tell Hayley if she wants to talk to me, she can come here. I'm not about to seek her out."

"She's in her trailer. Said it was an emergency. Girl problems or something. I didn't feel like getting the details."

Jessie smiled at her and shrugged as she left the craft services table, apple in hand. "I should probably go see if they need me for anything else."

Elliot sighed and closed her eyes. "I can't catch a break."

*

"This better be good," proclaimed Elliot as she stormed into Hayley's trailer.

"Oh good, you're here!" Hayley peeked her head out of the bathroom. "Are you wrapped?"

"Pretty sure. I haven't heard final word yet though."

"Do you know if Ashton is wrapped?"

"Ashton? How would I know? And why would you ca—oh, don't tell me."

Hayley looked at her sheepishly before disappearing behind the bathroom door again.

"What?"

"You're into Ashton?"

"What's not to be into? Have you seen the guy?"

Hayley did have a point. The guy didn't talk much, but he didn't have to. Standing at six feet tall and practically shirtless for most of the shoot, Ashton was a rather impressive looking specimen. She shouldn't be surprised by Hayley's crush.

"Does this look too slutty?"

Hayley stepped out of the bathroom in a tight, short, revealing crimson dress. Elliot had to physically stop her jaw from dropping.

"Too slutty for what? Prostitution?"

"I just want to make a good impression."

"We're just going back to the hotel and taking shots with Morgan. We're not going clubbing."

"Yeah, but if Ashton sees me in this for even five seconds, it'll be worth it."

"I think it's safe to say you'll catch his attention. And everyone else's."

"Good. Let's go see if we're wrapped."

*

Back at the hotel that night, the three girls were gathered in Morgan's room, already on their third drinking game. This one involved a deck of playing cards and several shots of tequila. Hayley wanted to move the gathering to her room, but Morgan insisted that the "talent" be subjected to the basic accommodations of the lowly film crew. Elliot and Hayley both knew it was futile to try to argue with Morgan. She was always too good at proving her point.

After being forced to take another shot, Elliot admitted defeat.

"Okay, I've had my fill. I don't want to be hungover tomorrow."

"Chase, that's only your third shot."

"Such a lightweight."

"Sad but true," Elliot agreed.

Morgan scoffed. "Something tells me it's not so much a hangover you're worried about, but wanting to look fresh and beautiful for a certain someone."

"Oh Jesus, here we go." Elliot rolled her eyes.

"Did I strike a nerve there?"

"Shut up."

"What? I've spent the last couple days being subjected to watching you two blatantly eye-fuck each other. It's painfully obvious," Morgan informed her.

"Oh God." Elliot turned to Hayley. "Is it really that obvious?"

Elliot got her answer when Hayley hummed and refused to make eye contact.

"Look, it's not like that. I just want to get to know her."

"You want to get in her pants."

"No, I'm just curious about her."

"About what she's like in bed."

"Oh my God, you have to stop."

Elliot playfully threw a few playing cards at Morgan.

Morgan laughed, unfazed by Elliot's little outburst. It was a common occurrence for them to tease each other about potential love interests. Morgan and Hayley used to always try to set Elliot up with people, but were often met with emphatic refusal.

Hayley decided to help defend her friend against a well-meaning, but antagonistic Morgan.

"Looks like Elliot can finally land a girl without our help."

"Maybe the girl will land on *her*. Elliot, you should lay on the stunt jump and break her fall."

Elliot wanted to hide her face in embarrassment, but she refused to be bullied by her friends. "Guys, I don't even know her. She just seems really cool."

"Oh, she is. And she just oozes sex appeal. It's almost offensive how hot she is," affirmed Morgan.

"Can we bring the objectification down to a minimum please?"

"You want me to talk you up, Chase? Put in a good word with her?" asked Hayley. "And wow, are you so unable to admit your crush on me that you have to go for the girl playing my double?"

"I hate you."

"You love me. Just try to control yourself around her. I'm sure it'll be difficult."

Morgan threw a pillow at Hayley.

"Oh please! Like you haven't been drooling over Ashton? I thought I was going to have to follow you around with a diaper rag."

"What? He's hot."

"I definitely agree. Could you imagine if Ashton hooked up with Jessie? How gorgeous and physically fit would those babies be?"

Elliot felt a nagging in the pit of her stomach. Perhaps it was the idea of picturing Jessie with someone else.

"Please don't even joke about that," begged Hayley.

Elliot wanted to protest as well. Instead, she took one more shot to satisfy her friends before switching to beer to slow her pace. She wasn't as much of a partier as they were.

Morgan laid on her back, her head hanging upside down over the side of the bed.

"Can you turn the air conditioning up? It's boiling in here."

"I think that's just the alcohol."

"Why did we have to film in the middle of the desert? It's dry and hot and doing disastrous things to my skin," Hayley complained.

"Just keep moisturizing." Morgan rolled over onto her stomach. "I need some water. Is there more ice?"

"I think we're out. I'll go grab some."

Elliot grabbed the ice bucket and headed out of the room down the hall, thankful for the brief respite away from her teasing friends. She loved them dearly, but sometimes they were a lot to handle. The three of them were all vastly different. Hayley had always been the boisterous one—cute, sweet, popular, and easy to get along with. She was also a bit naïve, which made it rather easy for Morgan to get under her skin. Morgan was always more loud, snarky, abrasive, and unapologetic. Since she was a whiz with explosives and a computer genius, they always joked that Morgan would ditch them for MIT or Cal Tech to become a rocket scientist or something akin to that. But her passion for explosions and aversion to school led Morgan to where she is now.

Elliot was somewhere between the two polarizing personalities, which often made her the peacemaker, always having to diffuse escalating matters between Morgan and Hayley. They loved each other fiercely and were unconditionally supportive and protective of one another, but at the moment they were too much for Elliot to deal with. She welcomed the opportunity to escape.

At the end of the hall, Elliot rounded the corner and was surprised to find Jessie filling up multiple ice buckets. Elliot eyed her curiously as she filled up her fifth bucket.

As if sensing her presence, Jessie acknowledged Elliot with a nod and an explanation.

"Ice bath. I think I pulled something in my leg today."

Elliot raised her bucket.

"Alcohol. My friends enjoy getting drunk and teasing me relentlessly."

"Sounds more fun than shocking my body with subzero temperatures."

"Wanna trade?"

"You want to take an ice bath while your friends make fun of me?"

Her tone was light and playful, leaving Elliot wanting more. *She was flirting. This was flirting, right?*

"Or I could just join you and we can leave Hayley and Morgan to roast each other."

Jessie smirked at the suggestion, then paused for a moment as though seriously contemplating the offer. She finished filling up her last bucket and stacked it on top of the others.

"Have a good night, Elliot."

She backed away, her eyes lingering on Elliot.

Unable to think of anything clever to say, Elliot gave her a thumbs up and managed to choke out, "see you tomorrow."

She decided it was best to not mention this interaction to her friends. She'd never hear the end of it, especially the awkward thumbs up.

*

Jessie spent most of the day trying to avoid Elliot. As drawn to her as she was, she couldn't allow herself to be distracted on set. The last thing she expected was running into her at the ice machine. She thought Elliot's room was on the top floor, but realized Morgan's room was on hers.

Flustered and clad in her tight-fitting workout shorts and sports bra, she poured the last of the ice into the tub and hesitated only a moment before getting in. She hissed at the shock of the cold water hitting her feet, her shins, and finally her thighs as she slowly lowered herself into the icy water. Her skin immediately pebbled with goosebumps as she waited impatiently for her body to adjust to the freezing temperature. She had to focus on her breathing until she felt numb enough to allow her muscles to loosen.

She heard her phone go off next to her and noticed a text from Kat.

Are you icing?

Jessie took a picture of her goosebump-covered arm and sent it back to Kat as proof.

A moment later, she got a text back in the form of a picture of Kat huddled in a blanket with a caption that read: *Just finished mine. Off to bed. Big day tomorrow.*

Jessie sent a quick *good night* text before suffering through the rest of her ice bath.

20 minutes later, Jessie dried off and put on some sweats and a hoodie to warm up when her phone rang. Peyton was calling to video chat. She threw her hair up in a messy bun and answered the phone. Before she could even say "hello," Peyton bombarded her.

"I know that look. You look pale and unhappy, so I'm assuming you just had an ice bath?"

"Stop knowing me."

"Stop being so predictable."

Jessie leaned against the headboard of her bed and made herself comfortable amongst the pillows.

"To what do I owe the pleasure of your call?"

"Just wanted to check in and see how it's been going. I'm sure it's been unbearable with the heat."

"I must've lost five pounds in water weight alone. I've been sucking down sports drinks like crazy. Other than that, it's actually been okay." Her thoughts immediately went to Elliot.

"What was that?"

"What?"

"That smirk."

"What smirk?"

"You're smirking."

"I don't smirk."

"That's your 'I saw a hot girl' smirk."

"Will you please stop analyzing my facial expressions?"

"Sorry, but you're not as stoic as you think you are. So what's her name?"

"I'm hanging up now."

"Jess, come on. It's okay to have a crush. It doesn't mean you have to fall in love with the girl. Is it Elliot Chase? It's her, isn't it?"

Jessie felt her jaw tighten. Her eyes grew wide.

"And that's the 'oh shit, I'm caught' look."

Jessie rolled her eyes.

"You need to seriously stop." She paused for a moment and took a deep breath. "How did you know it was her?"

"Because she's insanely hot and totally your type."

"She's very sweet. Honestly not what I expected her to be."

"You gonna go for it?"

"And here I thought you knew me so well."

"Why won't you? Your stupid rule?"

"That's exactly why, and it's not stupid. I can't have any distractions on this shoot. There's too much on the line here. Some of these stunts are next level."

"Fine. Go live your boring, rule-laden life."

"I perform death-defying stunts for a living. I hardly call that boring."

"When was the last time you went on a date?"

"I'm hanging up now."

"Bye, bitch."

"Bye."

Jessie tossed her phone onto the nightstand and turned on the TV hoping to fall asleep to old episodes of *Friends.*

Chapter 3

The wind was particularly harsh today, and it made things on set a little tense. Jessie knew they might have to shut down production for the day. Not only could it damage the very expensive equipment, but performing any kind of major stunts in these conditions could be extremely dangerous. Still, the director insisted they wait it out a bit. Jessie hung out in her trailer in full wardrobe, ready to go at a moment's notice. She knew she could socialize with the others in the tents, but felt it was smart to avoid Elliot as much as she could. She let herself get a little too carried away with the girl yesterday, and she couldn't let that happen again.

Unfortunately, boredom got the best of her, and she headed out to see if she could find Kat or Hayley. It was a difficult walk just to get to the tents, but once inside, it was much calmer and a bit cooler. They were made to withstand high winds and high temperatures, but there were a lot of people crammed inside each one. Jessie knew she'd have no choice but to socialize, and that was just fine. She could do this. No problem.

She found Kat sitting at a table playing with her phone, so she sat down next to her on the bench.

"Hey."

"Hey." Kat barely looked up. "Do you get service out here? I can't get anything on my phone."

"Nope. I've pretty much given up trying. My phone's back at the hotel."

"Not a bad place they've got us set up at, huh? I thought it would be a dump since we're in the middle of nowhere."

They heard someone scoff at the table next to them and turned to see a shorter brunette in full wardrobe and makeup.

"That hotel is a joke. It's 90 minutes from set, the rooms are subpar, and the room service is shit. It may as well be a rent-by-the-hour shithole."

"It's the only five-star hotel in the area. I'm pretty sure it's 90 minutes away because every hotel within a 50 mile radius of here actually *is* a rent-by-the-hour shithole." Kat was clearly not impressed with this girl.

"Well, you're obviously not used to the finer things in life. I suppose that's why you're a double and not the real thing."

"Excuse me?" Kat stood up, ready to get in this girl's face. Jessie tried to diffuse the situation.

"Kat, stop. Just let it go."

"No." She looked back at the girl. "What's your name?"

The girl stood up. "Cassie Ryan."

"And what do you do here? Are you one of the extras?"

That evidently pissed Cassie off. "I'm one of the leads."

"There are only two leads that I know of in this film, and you're not one of them."

"Fine. Whatever. I'm a second lead. I was supposed to be cast as the lead. Doesn't change the fact that you're just a double."

"Just a double?" Kat was ready to start swinging.

Jessie stood up and grabbed Kat's arm to pull her back down.

"Kat, look. I think you finally have service on your phone. Use it now before you lose it again."

Kat shot the girl one last glare and finally complied.

"I'm gonna go make a call," informed Kat. "I'll be back."

Cassie whispered rather loudly at the girl sitting next to her.

"You know, they should really have one tent for the actors and one tent for the expendables."

Jessie rolled her eyes and mumbled under her breath. "Fucking actors."

When she turned back around, she noticed a presence next to her holding something in front of her face.

"Red vine?"

Jessie looked up and saw Elliot holding out some red vines with a big smile on her face. She took a couple, not wanting to seem ungrateful for the gesture.

"Thanks."

"No problem." Elliot sat down next to her with her legs straddling the bench. She was dressed identical to Kat—a new outfit today—in a tight, deep blue v-neck with multiple rips and tears along the front, and very tight fitting jeans. One of the holes in Elliot's shirt just near her navel caught her attention. Well, that and the rather ample cleavage that was noticeable in the low cut shirt. *God bless whoever invented the v-neck.*

When Jessie realized she was staring a bit too long, she looked back up to see Elliot sucking on a red vine in the most seductive way possible, quirking her eyebrow. Jessie swallowed hard and turned to look straight ahead, gnawing on the sweet licorice Elliot had brought her.

"How was the ice bath?"

"Cold."

"Did it help?"

"I think so. I'm not as sore as I was."

"So, today's kind of a drag, isn't it?"

"Yeah, but I've been in worse situations. I've had to wait out snow storms, rain storms. Even a tornado once, which is one of the reasons I'm not a fan of filming in the Midwest."

"I thought nothing scared you."

"I wasn't scared of the tornado. I'm just not a fan of waiting." Jessie gave Elliot a quick glance and noticed she was still staring at her shamelessly. Jessie averted her eyes once more.

"You just wanna go, go, go, don't you? Can't just sit and relax?"

"Not when I know there's work to do. A bridge to jump from, an explosion to outrun…" She looked back at Elliot and bit her lip. "A motorcycle to ride."

Elliot pulled the piece of licorice she'd been sucking on out of her mouth.

"Do you like working on films? You enjoy being a stunt double?"

"I wouldn't be here if I didn't. What about you?"

Elliot smiled. "I love it. I make pretty good money while being able to follow my passion. I get to travel the world and…meet new and interesting people. Plus, it's kind of cool when everyone knows who you are."

Jessie grabbed another red vine from Elliot's hand. "And who are you?"

"I'm Elliot Chase. World-renowned actress and soon to be action star."

Jessie's eyes locked on Elliot's. She knew she shouldn't be doing this. She should get up and walk away. In fact, she's going to do just that. Right now. Any minute.

"Who are you really, Elliot?"

She could see the smile on her face falter, but only for a moment.

"Um...I should go." She looked over Jessie's shoulder at Cassie. "Oh, and don't let her get to you. I actually begged the casting director not to cast her, but he owed her agent a favor or something. I think she's just bitter. Hayley and I always seem to edge her out for certain roles."

"She didn't get to me."

Elliot laughed as she continued to suck on the red licorice. "Yes, I suppose nothing ever does."

With that, she got up and left. Jessie's eyes were immediately drawn to the girl's backside. As she walked away she tried not to think about the fact that never had she wanted a piece of red licorice so badly in her life.

Right. Nothing ever gets to her.

*

Elliot didn't know what had come over her in the last few days. Her career was flourishing, and this movie would bump her from star status to superstar status. She knew how important it was for this movie to be perfect, but all thoughts of memorizing lines and going over blocking seemed to take a backseat to thoughts of the drop dead gorgeous stunt woman that somehow made her body ache in ways she didn't even think possible. She'd never been so attracted to someone she'd only just met, and the attraction seemed to grow by the hour. The fact that Jessie seemed somewhat immune to her charms one minute while making suggestive remarks the next had Elliot's head reeling.

Red flags were practically draped all over this situation. Jessie sent mixed signals yet seemed focused on maintaining a professional decorum. Not to mention the fact that Jessie just so happened to be a woman, and Elliot was very much not out to the public. Plus, there was the whole "no time for a relationship" thing. Elliot wasn't really a relationship girl. She really couldn't be. Her schedule wouldn't allow it. She tried in the past, but it only ever ended badly. She was hardly in one place long enough to really make something last, and it was starting to take its toll. She was lonely. Sure, she was surrounded by friends and co-workers, and being famous, pretty, and 25 didn't exactly make it difficult to find someone to share her bed with when she needed it. But she craved intimacy. Which is why she knew it was stupid to have a silly crush on Jessie. She didn't seem like the type of girl who did "intimacy." Elliot knew it was best to keep her distance no matter how much pull she felt toward the woman.

She stepped outside the tent and was met with a large gust of wind that nearly blinded her from loose, upturned sand. She trudged on, trying to make her way to her trailer, unaware of the brunette following her.

Once Elliot made her way to the trailer and closed the door, she welcomed the calmness and took a deep breath to collect herself. She hoped they'd call it a day so she could go back to the hotel and lay by the pool, unless it was just as windy over there. Then she'd just have to settle for a bath, some television, and absolutely no thoughts of a certain stunt woman. It was just a crush. It would go away. It had to.

The knock on her door pulled her out of her thoughts. She opened it and was met with green eyes and wild, wind-blown dark hair.

"Can I come in?"

Elliot nodded and stepped aside to let Jessie into her trailer before closing the door.

Elliot turned to ask what she wanted, and Jessie was just inches from her. She could feel her breath on her face.

"Jessie...what—"

"I can't do this."

Elliot swallowed thickly. "Do what?"

"You know what." Jessie's voice was just above a whisper.

Elliot had to tamp down the desire she felt deep inside, but found that she couldn't. Not when Jessie was this close to her. Not when the girl was in the midst of confessing whatever it was she was trying to say.

"Then why are you here?"

The question seemed to catch the other girl off guard. She faltered for a moment before responding.

"To tell you that I can't do this with you."

Jessie's face inched closer to Elliot's. Elliot took a step back, but Jessie only followed her. She took another step back until Jessie backed her into the wall. She remained as stoic as possible when she felt the brunette's hand on her hip. She stifled a moan when Jessie pushed her body up against her own and gazed down at her lips. Jessie's other hand came up to brush a few strands of hair out of Elliot's face. She straightened her posture, trying her hardest not to look insanely turned on, which was exactly how she felt. She wanted to challenge her. Jessie seemed like a girl who never backed away from a challenge, so she pressed her luck.

"If you can't do this with me, then leave." Her voice was confident which was a far cry from how she actually felt. She was a withering mess, desperate to keep Jessie as close as possible.

The other girl smirked ever so slightly.

"I'm afraid I can't do that either, Elliot."

Before she could respond, Elliot felt Jessie's lips against her own. There was nothing tentative about it. Jessie was all confidence as her lips surged forward against Elliot's, poor Elliot doing her best to keep up. She felt the kiss absolutely everywhere. The glide of Jessie's tongue against her own brought an uninhibited moan out of her, which Jessie seemed to like. Soft lips sucked gently against her lower lip as she brought her hands up around the small of Jessie's back and pulled her closer. Jessie took complete control of the kiss, delving her tongue deep into Elliot's mouth, bringing out another moan. Her hand moved behind Elliot's neck to bring them even closer together, and Elliot boldly moved her hands down to grasp Jessie's hips. The noise from the brunette's throat was proof that she enjoyed having Elliot's hands on her, so she repeated the action. She wasn't sure if it was the howling wind outside or if Jessie made the high-pitched sound in response. By this point, she was desperate for more contact. She started a slow grind with her body, causing Jessie to push even further into her while removing Elliot's hands from her hips and forcing them against the wall above her head.

Elliot took pleasure in the feeling of her wrists being pushed up against the wall, relinquishing all control. Jessie moved her lips down to Elliot's neck, sucking and biting along the way.

Elliot loved every second of it, but knew she had to be careful.

"Just...just don't leave a mark," she panted. She didn't feel like explaining a sudden hickey to the makeup department.

Jessie grunted and made her bites much softer. Elliot closed her eyes and indulged in the feeling of those plump lips all over her. She wanted this moment to last forever. Unfortunately, being on a movie set meant that permanence was non-existent.

Just when Jessie's hands made their way down Elliot's arms towards her chest there was a knock on the door. Jessie immediately pulled away, putting at least five feet of distance between the two of them.

"Miss Chase? We're wrapped for the day!" the second AD yelled through the door. The wind won't die down until tonight, so we're going to reconvene tomorrow morning."

"Okay! Thank you!"

Jessie closed her eyes, looking somewhat pained. When she opened them again, Elliot knew what was about to come out of her mouth, but before she could protest, Jessie spoke.

"I'm sorry. I shouldn't have done that. That was irresponsible on my part. I should go." She stopped at the door and looked at Elliot one last time. "I'm sorry. It won't happen again."

And that was the problem. Because Elliot definitely wanted it to happen again.

*

The next morning, Jessie waited in the lobby of the hotel for her hired driver to take her to the set. She sat in a comfortable chair going over the stunt coordinator's notes for today's shoot. She needed to keep herself busy and keep her thoughts away from the actress infiltrating her mind. The lobby was rather busy for a Thursday morning. It seemed multiple families were checking in, which wasn't surprising. The area was a bit of a tourist destination for anyone who enjoyed camping or hiking over the summer.

She heard murmuring among the guests in the lobby and looked up to see Elliot stepping off the elevator. A few of the guests immediately ran over and asked for autographs and photos with her. Jessie thought it was somewhat presumptuous and rude of them, especially this early in the morning, but Elliot handled it like a pro. She smiled and talked to each and every one of them, posing for pictures and signing autographs. It made Jessie smile despite herself. She almost forgot that Elliot was a well-known actress, and she really couldn't understand how she could walk around with zero anonymity. It took a special kind of person to be able to endure that kind of fame.

She realized she was staring again and immediately chastised herself. She needed her car to get here. It was a long drive to the set, and she planned on napping for a bit on the way. Anything to keep her from thinking about that kiss in Elliot's trailer yesterday. That was quite possibly the stupidest thing she'd ever done. She wanted to blame the actress for being so damn forward and blatant in her flirting, but in the end it was Jessie's choice to follow her. It was Jessie that pushed her into the wall and kissed her.

Once the crowd around Elliot disappeared, Jessie saw her heading in her direction. At that moment her car decided to show up, so she took full advantage and ran out the door into the car.

*

On set, Jessie found herself in full wardrobe and makeup, looking up at the tower she'd soon climb and fall from. The sun was bright, and her sunglasses didn't do much to mask the brightness. She was nearly blinded by it and didn't notice Elliot saunter up next to her, looking up at the tower as well.

"Let me guess, you can't wait to get up there and fall with every ounce of grace you have." Elliot looked over at her and winked.

Jessie smiled and looked back up. Elliot was right. She was pretty damn excited about it.

"Doesn't sound like a bad way to spend the day."

"Meanwhile, when they do the close-up shots, I'll be clinging to the tower for dear life trying not to throw up."

Jessie nudged her shoulder playfully. "You'll be fine. You don't have to climb as high as I do, and they certainly won't let anything happen to their star."

"Pretty sure Cassie wouldn't mind if something happened to me."

"Well, don't let her be the one to attach your safety cables," Jessie joked.

Elliot laughed, and Jessie tried to not let it affect her. She failed. Her stomach flipped, and she knew she should walk away right now. She couldn't take her eyes off the girl and her wardrobe. Her eyes wandered down to the ripped navy v-neck. This time, Jessie noticed the holes in

Elliot's shirt revealed her black, lacy bra underneath, and she found herself wanting to see the rest of it.

"Jessie, can I ask you something?"

She internally screamed at herself to leave, but the way Elliot looked at her combined with how her body felt whenever she was in her presence rendered her paralyzed.

"Sure."

She knew what the question would be and had no idea how to answer it.

"Yesterday in my trailer...when we—"

"Hey princess! I've been looking all over for you." They were interrupted by one of the actors Jessie was introduced to yesterday. She couldn't seem to remember his name.

"Oh, hi." Elliot seemed thrown by his sudden presence. "Jessie, have you met Drew?"

Jessie eyed him and looked back at Elliot. "Briefly."

"I wanted to see if you'd run lines with me." Drew paid no attention to Jessie.

"Our scene isn't until this afternoon."

"I know, but I want to make sure I have the lines completely down before the scene. Besides, they're filming the stunt work right now."

He led her away before Elliot had a chance to argue.

Jessie shook her head. "Fucking actors."

Kat stormed up next to her and slammed her bag down beside her.

"Fucking actors!"

Jessie looked at her quizzically. "Problem, Kat?"

"I'm gonna kill that Cassie chick. She cut in front of me at the breakfast line and then told me I could stand to skip a few meals. What is her deal, anyway?"

"Just some bitter actress who thinks the world owes her something."

Kat scoffed. "Yeah, it owes her a punch in the tit." She sighed and looked up at the tower. "Come on. Let's run this."

20 minutes later, Jessie and Kat were near the top of the tower directly on their marks. The crew was busy making a few adjustments at the request of the director. They hung out up there until the cameras rolled again, at which point, Kat was supposed to kick Jessie off the tower.

"I think my clone has a crush on you," teased Kat.

Jessie sat on some metal scaffolding with her feet dangling. She stiffened at the remark, feeling the tips of her ears turn red.

"What do you mean?"

Kat nodded her head toward the area below the tower where Elliot stood next to Hayley, looking up at them.

"What's going on with you two?"

Jessie shook her head. "Nothing. She's just...we talk. She's nice."

"Oh, I know. She's a sweetheart. Probably the coolest actress I've ever worked with. She's really down to earth, which is pretty rare for someone of her stature."

"Yeah, she seems like it."

"You gonna go for it?"

Jessie rolled her eyes. "You know my rules, Kat."

"How can someone so adventurous be so damn boring?"

Jessie was about to come back with a witty retort when they called "places." They had to prepare for her jump. She knew Elliot was still watching her, and she'd be lying if she said she didn't secretly love that fact. She was in so much trouble.

Once action was called, she pulled herself up to each new level of the tower as Kat followed her. As rehearsed, Kat grabbed a hold of her foot and yanked her down. Jessie allowed herself to fall and then grab onto part of the metal scaffolding, pretending to struggle as she hung from it. She watched as Kat appeared above her, then crawled down to Jessie's level. She grabbed onto her collar and stuck her foot out to push Jessie off the edge. Jessie let go and felt herself free-fall down to the stunt jump. It was awesome and exhilarating and peaceful. She landed perfectly onto the inflatable stunt jump, and the director immediately called "cut." She knew she nailed it and that another take wasn't needed. This is why she was the best at what she did.

*

Jessie's remaining scenes for the day were simple. They only consisted of some parkour work and a few hand-to-hand combat scenes, but by the end of the day she was exhausted. Normally it wouldn't be this difficult, but the heat proved to be a challenging factor. After she wrapped for the day, her car was waiting to take her back to the hotel for the evening, but she asked her driver to stick around for a bit. She decided to be foolish and stay behind to watch a few of Elliot's scenes.

She took a seat and stayed out of Elliot's view—not wanting to be a distraction—and watched the scene unfold between her and Drew's character. She couldn't really hear the dialogue, but their body language said it all. She knew what kind of scene this was. Even though the middle of a dry desert after a long chase scene wasn't exactly romantic, it didn't stop the characters from sharing a kiss. Jessie actually flinched when Drew leaned in and kissed Elliot. She was surprised at how much the kissing scene bothered her and had no idea why she decided to stay when the director asked for another take. Maybe she needed a reminder that whatever this thing was with Elliot was a very bad idea.

Perhaps she also wanted to stay to make sure Elliot was okay. She didn't seem to react well when Drew interrupted their conversation earlier, and she certainly didn't seem to enjoy their on-screen kiss. Drew, however, looked more than happy to do as many takes as possible, and that bothered Jessie more than she liked.

*

Once all the scenes wrapped for the day, Jessie ran to her trailer to get her bag. She wanted to jump in her car and be gone before Elliot saw her. She knew that wasn't going to happen when she saw the blonde waiting for her outside her trailer.

"I'm surprised you're still here. Weren't you dismissed a couple hours ago?"

"What can I say? I just wanted to feel more of that hot desert air in my hair."

Elliot handed her a slip of paper.

"Here."

Jessie read it. Room 1218.

"What's this?"

Elliot licked her lips and grinned. "My room number."

Jessie felt herself go numb. "Wha—your room number? Like...hotel room?"

Elliot laughed. "Calm down. I'm having a party in my room tonight. This place is so boring, and there's really not much to do. We have a late call time tomorrow, so we're gonna have some fun tonight. You should come. I'd really love to see you there."

Elliot walked away without another word, and Jessie, once again, found her eyes following the blonde's perfect ass as she hopped into her waiting car.

Jessie stared at the numbers etched into the piece of paper. Room 1218. Maybe she was working too hard. Maybe she could use a little partying in her life. She did reckless things every single day, but they were done with precision and with multiple safeguards in place. So was it really reckless? Was it really brave if she knew how safe her job was? Maybe it was time to jump without wings or fall without a net. What could go wrong?

Jessie shook the thoughts from her mind and reminded herself. *A lot. A lot could go wrong.*

Chapter 4

Jessie was in her pajamas, toweling off her hair after a refreshing shower when she heard a knock at her door. She was expecting room service since she'd ordered some food, but was met with a very eager blonde dressed in a tube top and purple leggings. The look on the girl's face went from excited to disappointed to downright disgusted when she saw how Jessie was dressed.

"Jess, can't you drop the hermit act just once and come to this damn party? It's literally two floors above us." Kat charged into the room uninvited.

"I was just going to call it an early night." Jessie continued drying her hair as Kat started digging through the suitcase on the chair. "What are you doing?"

"Finding you a party outfit."

"I'm afraid you won't find anything fit for a party in there. I packed pretty casual."

"Why would you do that?"

"Because I wasn't expecting to go clubbing in the desert."

"Well, thankfully this isn't a club. It's a hotel room. We can do casual. Ooh! I can make this work." She pulled out a shirt and some pants and threw them at Jessie. "Now go get changed."

Jessie stood there completely unamused.

"No."

Kat laughed.

"Jess, babe. I know it's been a while since we hung out, but think back. Way back to the last time we worked together. When I convinced you to go out drinking all night, and we showed up hungover on set the next day while still brilliantly pulling off our stunts. Think back to that night we stole the stunt car and took it for a joyride out to Malibu and snuck onto the private beach. And let's not forget the strip club incident."

"We swore we would never, ever mention that again," Jessie protested.

"Fine. You're right. My point is, were any of those things your idea?"

"No."

"And did you initially tell me no when I first suggested them?"

Jessie looked at her suspiciously. "Yes."

"And who ended up convincing you to do all those things in the long run?"

Jessie stared at her, completely nonplussed, before finally relenting.

"I'll go get dressed."

"Do your hair and makeup, too!" Kat shouted at her as she closed the bathroom door.

When Jessie emerged from the bathroom fully dressed with her hair and makeup done, Kat let out a whistle. The outfit she chose for her was obviously a success—dark blue skinny jeans and a loose-fitting black scoop neck, short sleeve shirt. It was a little short, so if she stretched, the shirt rode up, conveniently showing off her toned stomach. She looked down at her faded black Converse shoes.

"Are the shoes okay? I have boots, but—"

"The shoes are great. Elliot will cream herself."

Jessie rolled her eyes. "That's not why I'm going! And can you not be so crude?"

"Fine, but you'll definitely have your pick of any girl there. Maybe even that firecracker you're doubling for."

"I see your little crush on Hayley hasn't dissipated."

"Hey, I can't help it if she's hot. Besides, if it doesn't work out with her, there's always that Ashton guy. Yummy."

Jessie tried her best not to chastise her colleague too much. "You know what I'm going to say, Kat."

"Yeah, yeah. I shouldn't get involved with people I work with. Especially actors." Kat ignored her as she put some finishing touches on Jessie's outfit by folding the shirt sleeves up to her shoulder. "You've got to show off your arms and those badass tattoos you have."

She stepped back for a moment to take a look at her, then moved to collect Jessie's hair and lay it over her shoulder.

"Fuck. It's unfair how gorgeous you are."

Jessie scoffed. "It's unfair how annoying you are. Let's go so that we can get you so drunk you won't notice me leave the party after five minutes."

*

Jessie was surprised at how many people were actually there. She didn't know what she expected. Maybe a small get-together, but not this. It seemed as though every actor, crew member, and extra was invited. It was a lot of people to cram into a hotel room, but from what Jessie understood, it was one of the biggest suites in the hotel. Nothing was too good for the star of the film.

They pushed their way through a crowd of people she barely recognized. She was pretty sure one of them was the boom mic operator.

"Jessie!"

Hayley ran up and threw her arms around her, nearly knocking her over. The obvious smell of alcohol fell off her breath.

"Jessie! You're here!"

"Hayley! You're drunk!"

The actress laughed. "Yup! You should be too! Come on, let's get you a drink!" She pulled her toward the bar and mixed her a gin and tonic before Jessie could even protest. She proudly shoved it in her hand and clinked her own glass to hers.

"Cheers!"

Jessie feigned a smile and saluted her with the glass before taking a drink.

Swill. Pure swill. It was awful, but she smiled through it. She was definitely not a gin drinker. She decided to sip slowly as she pulled Kat over to her.

"By the way, Hayley, you remember Kat, don't you?" She figured she'd throw her friend a bone. Just because it was her rule not to date co-workers didn't mean Kat had to do the same.

Hayley, being the friendly girl she was, pulled Kat into a hug.

"Of course! It's Elliot 2.0! Only more awesome because you do the things she and I are contractually not allowed to do."

"Well, I'm very happy to take on that burden for you ladies." Kat laid it on thick.

Hayley was distracted when she spotted a tall, muscular man and called him over.

"Oh! Do you guys know Ashton? He's in the movie, too!" Once Ashton made his way over, Hayley draped herself all over him. "Isn't he cute?"

He smiled at them as Hayley started kissing his neck. Soon they were both preoccupied with each other's lips, and Jessie turned to Kat and shrugged.

"Sorry, I tried."

Kat shook her head and took a shot of tequila.

"Oh well. Onward and upward!" She took one more shot, slapped Jessie on the back, and left her alone to do God knows what.

Jessie felt a little awkward standing there by herself, but she took this opportunity to put her drink down and pour herself some scotch. She took a sip of it and savored the taste, trying to rid herself of the gin residue. She sipped slowly. She needed to maintain control of herself tonight.

The music blared and with her drink in hand, she explored a little. Most people were in the main area of the room while some were on the balcony. She noticed double doors off to the left and opened them. It led to the bedroom, but it was dark and empty, most likely off limits since it's where Elliot slept. She heard a roar of cheers and turned around. She headed back toward the main part of the living area and noticed a group of people taking shots at the table. Right in the middle of the group was Elliot. Elliot with her husky voice and addicting laugh. Elliot with her alluring eyes and kissable lips. Elliot, who Jessie couldn't stop thinking about. Elliot, who was suddenly looking directly at her. She couldn't figure out how she was able to fall from any height or jump through fire, but just one single look from a certain blonde girl rendered her speechless, sucking all the air out of her lungs.

Whatever it was, Jessie knew she was pretty much screwed. She couldn't take her eyes off the girl and was pretty sure a lot of it had to do with what she was wearing. Elliot wore short denim shorts with knee-high boots and a black and red checkered flannel shirt. It was unbuttoned to reveal a white v-neck shirt underneath. To top it off, a snapback adorned her head, printed with the title of the movie they were filming. *Best of Enemies*. This was probably the sexiest she'd ever seen her. Just as Elliot, not as some character or a Hollywood sexpot. She wanted to see more of it.

She watched as Elliot bit her lower lip and God, that flirtatious smile nearly knocked Jessie on her ass. She moved to sit down on the couch, but Elliot practically tackled her before she had the chance.

"Jessie! You came!" She wrapped her arms around her and whispered, "I was hoping you'd come."

The double entendre wasn't lost on her. She tried to compose herself and gave a playful shrug.

"Who am I to pass up cheap booze in a crowded hotel room?"

Elliot grabbed the drink from Jessie's hand and sniffed it. Her contorted face told Jessie she wasn't impressed.

"This won't do." She took Jessie's drink away and shoved her own up to Jessie's mouth. "Here!"

It was pinkish-red and certainly not something she'd drink on her own accord, but she took a sip and tried not to show her distaste. It was sweet. Too sweet and tart. It was too fruity for her liking, but given the way Elliot looked at her so hopefully, she had to take another sip. It wasn't so bad the second time around. Soon she found herself wondering if the taste of it still lingered on Elliot's lips. If that was the case, she could definitely see herself enjoying it.

Jessie handed it back to her. "How many of these have you had?"

"This is my first, plus the shot I just took." She leaned in. "I'm not a big drinker, but I suppose I have a reputation to uphold. Eventually, I'll find an empty beer bottle and just carry it around. No one will know the difference."

"So you're not drunk?"

"I have a fun buzz going. That's all I need."

Jessie handed the drink back to her and reached out to take back her scotch.

"Nope. No scotch for you. I'll make you another drink!" She pulled her over to the bar and dumped out the scotch in the sink.

Jessie tried her best not to cry out in protest of all that beautiful liquid gone to waste. She watched as Elliot mixed together several fruity mixers, added some rum and a splash of club soda, and then proudly handed the concoction to Jessie. She took it with a smile.

"By the way…" Elliot leaned into her. "You look really good tonight."

"Oh, uh...well, I wasn't expecting to go to a party. It's kind of all I had."

"You look hot." She reached out to touch the intricate tattoo adorning Jessie's right arm. "Then again, you always do."

Jessie swallowed hard and tried not to let the intoxicating scent of Elliot's perfume affect her judgment.

"Elliot..." she said as more of a plea than a warning.

"Just take the compliment, Jessie. It'll make things less awkward."

Elliot backed away and jumped up to sit on the counter. She turned her hat backward, then leaned forward with her hands gripping the edge of the counter. Jessie immediately took notice of how Elliot's cleavage came into perfect view. The remainder of her chill completely evaporated, along with her dignity and stoicism, as she stared unabashedly at Elliot's assets.

Jessie wasn't the only one hypnotized. Drew appeared out of nowhere and sidled up next to Elliot.

"Hey, princess. Wanna dance?"

Elliot sat up straight and folded her arms over her chest, closing off the view of her generous cleavage.

"Not right now, Drew. Maybe later?"

Drew looked from Elliot to Jessie and his disappointment was obvious.

"Okay, sure." He poured a drink and disappeared into the crowd.

Elliot shared a knowing look with Jessie and quirked her brow. Even though the room was loud, a silence sat heavily between them for several minutes. Before either of them could say anything, Morgan came storming up and grabbed a beer from the mini fridge next to Elliot.

"Okay, Chase, who invited that ass hat?"

"What?"

Morgan nodded toward the balcony and both Elliot and Jessie followed her gaze. Cassie stood talking to Drew with a very unpleasant look on her face. Apparently he moved fast.

Morgan huffed. "I was about to ask Drew to dance, and that bitch came up and told me to fetch her a drink, and then shoved her way into our conversation. Like...does she know what I'm capable of doing?"

Elliot jumped off the counter and put her arm around her friend. "Sorry, Morgan. It was an open invitation. I couldn't exclude just one person."

"She just better hope an explosive doesn't accidentally go off in her face."

At that moment, Kat managed to find her way back to Jessie.

"There you are!" She threw her arms around Jessie and put her head on her shoulder. "I thought I lost you."

"Well, you found me. How much have you drank?"

"Enough for you to slip out without me knowing." Kat winked at her. "But I see you're still here having fun. Ugh! Why the hell is that cunt bag here?"

Jessie chuckled despite the cringe-worthy use of her least favorite word. "I'm assuming you're referring to Cassie, and I'll repeat what Elliot said. She couldn't exclude just one person."

At that, Morgan perked up.

"You hate her too? Kat, I think you and I should start spending more time together." She put her arm through Kat's and pulled her away. "Later, Chase! I'm off with my new bestie!"

Elliot smiled at the newly formed friendship, then looked back at Jessie.

"Kinda loud in here. Do you want to go somewhere quieter?"

Jessie had a feeling she knew where Elliot was referring to, and she knew it was a very, very bad idea.

"Sure."

God damn it, Jessie.

*

The bedroom was definitely quieter. Elliot closed and locked the door before turning around and leaning against it. Whether Elliot knew it or not, the way she stood and looked at her was the sexiest thing Jessie had ever seen. Something told her Elliot knew exactly what she was doing.

Jessie kept her distance. She stood her ground halfway across the room and tried to look anywhere but Elliot's chest, which was now conveniently on display again.

"Jessie."

"This is a nice suite. My room's pretty plain. Not that I'm complaining, but...this is fancy."

"Jessie..."

"I can't believe we only have a few days left out here. It'll be nice to get back to the soundstage. And back to LA where the heat doesn't melt your face off. Or your brain."

She was reaching. Reaching for anything to fill the silence. Anything to keep Elliot from luring her over there. She wasn't going to give in. Not a chance in hell.

"Jessie, come here."

"Okay." She walked toward her.

God damn it, Jessie.

Once Jessie was in reach of her, Elliot pulled her closer by the hem of her shirt until they were inches apart. Elliot licked her lips and had a look on her face that Jessie couldn't quite place. It was a cross between trepidation and confidence with a hint of wonder.

"Do you like me?" Elliot's whispered voice filled the silence between them.

Jessie's lips quivered, and she searched her eyes. She couldn't seem to make her voice work.

"That's okay. You don't have to answer that." She leaned her forehead against Jessie's and took her hand, intertwining their fingers. "Your hands are soft."

Jessie found herself being pulled into her even more. She leaned her other hand against the door, her lips too close to Elliot's. When she realized she was getting too close, she tried backing away, but Elliot pulled her back.

"Jessie, we're just talking."

"We're holding hands."

Elliot tightened her grip on Jessie's hand and pulled her against her body.

"Am I wrong for wanting to do that? Or for wanting to do more than that?"

The suggestiveness in her voice left Jessie shaking. She supposed it wasn't really that wrong. Neither was the way she coveted Elliot's lips at the moment.

She pulled away before giving in to her desires, but Elliot didn't want to give in so easily. She grew bold and stepped away from the door, backing Jessie up a bit. Her cleavage was once again in Jessie's direct line of vision. Elliot seemed to invite her to look, so she did.

"You've been staring at them all night."

Jessie smirked. "Kinda hard not to."

"Kinda hard not staring at you too." She grabbed Jessie by the shirt again and pulled her closer. "You know, you can't kiss me like you did the other day and not expect me to want to do it again."

Jessie shook her head. "I shouldn't have done that. I'm so sorry."

"I'm not." She looked at Jessie earnestly. "I don't want to force you, but I do want to know what it'll take to get you to kiss me again."

"It can't happen."

"What if I..." She pulled her closer and snaked her hands up under her shirt, splaying them across her lower back.

Jessie's breath hitched at the feeling of soft, warm hands on her.

"Or I can..." She moved her hands down to grab her ass and pushed her hips into Jessie's.

The heat of Elliot's skin seeped into her psyche, short-circuiting everything inside of her. She cleared her throat and looked at Elliot.

"Tha—that is definitely working."

Elliot wore a smug, victorious smile before taking a step back. Jessie immediately missed the warmth.

"Or...I can just do this." She took off her hat and put it on Jessie, slowly leaning in and lingering just far enough for Jessie to meet her the rest of the way if she wanted to.

And yes, she definitely wanted to.

She pushed Elliot against the wall and pressed her lips against hers, hungrily taking what she'd been denying herself all night.

The noises Elliot made only made Jessie attack her even more. Her hands roamed all over Elliot's body before moving up to her chest. She let out a deep moan as her hands cupped the other girl's perfect breasts, feeling the weight of them under her fingers. It elicited a strangled cry from the actress.

She started slowly sucking Elliot's tongue into her mouth, massaging it with her own. Elliot whined and grabbed the back of Jessie's neck, trying to gain even more access into her mouth. Jessie was addicted to the feeling of Elliot's breasts in her hands, dying to see what other parts of her felt like. Reluctantly, but excitedly, she kept working Elliot's breast with her left hand while her right hand slid down her torso to the button of her jean shorts. Elliot had been making it clear all night that she wouldn't object to it. She undid the button and unzipped her shorts, lingering at the hem of her underwear. Elliot's breathing became erratic, and Jessie could feel a light layer of sweat forming at her forehead. The hat Elliot placed on her head didn't do much to help the situation.

She moved her lips to Elliot's neck, nipping and licking her way down. Her hand stayed at the hem of Elliot's underwear, but Elliot placed her own hand on top of Jessie's and pushed it way down. Jessie's fingers twitched with anticipation.

The sound of glass shattering pulled them both out of their bubble. They heard a couple of screams. A few people yelled "uh oh" and some swear words. A voice that was unmistakably Morgan's yelled out for Elliot.

"Chase! Where are you? You better get out here!"

Elliot leaned her head against the door and sighed in frustration.

"It sounds like things are getting out of control. I can't have them trashing the room."

Jessie's breath was short and heavy, trying to even out. "I guess you're kind of the 'mom friend' of the group?"

"Yeah, I guess you could say that." She went to open the door. "I'll be right back. I have to get them in line."

Jessie nodded.

"I'm serious. I'll be right back. We'll continue this. You stay put." She grabbed her hat from Jessie's head and put it back on her own. She kissed her one last time before walking out and closing the door behind her.

Jessie stood trying to get a grip on the entire situation. That was twice she lost control around Elliot, twice she'd broken her cardinal rule, and twice the girl had gotten her so worked up she couldn't see straight. Or do anything straight, really. She knew what she had to do. She had to end it before it went any further. She knew that it was a dick move, but Elliot would understand. She had to. She opened the door and scanned the area, making sure it was clear before she snuck out and went back to her room.

*

All she wanted was to go for one drink and then come back to her room to eat, watch TV, and fall asleep in peace. Unfortunately, none of those things happened. By the time she got back, her food had been delivered, but it was cold. She wasn't hungry anyway. There was nothing on TV that could possibly take her mind off of Elliot. And sleep? That wouldn't happen. After what happened in Elliot's suite, Jessie's body was completely on fire. She tossed and turned, refusing to give herself any kind of relief. Plus, there was the nagging guilt she felt for leaving Elliot's room without saying goodbye.

Finally, around one am, Jessie gave up on sleep. She contemplated heading down to the fitness room to work out, but knew only one thing could help get her mind off of this. She threw on the clothes she was wearing earlier, grabbed her room key, and headed down to the lobby.

The hotel bar was still open, but completely empty except for the lone bartender who looked like he was about to fall asleep. When Jessie took a seat at the bar, he perked up, finally having something to do now.

"Scotch neat, please. Middle shelf is fine."

He nodded and poured her drink, putting a little extra in. He must have sensed her sorrow, and she reminded herself to leave a big tip. She stared at the drink in front of her, swirling it around a bit before taking a sip and indulging in the way it warmed her entire body. Not unlike the way Elliot did just hours ago.

"So this is where you decided to take the party? I suppose it's a little more mellow than mine was."

Jessie jumped at the voice and looked over to see Elliot take a seat next to her at the bar. She grabbed Jessie's drink and sniffed it, making the same unpleasant face she made earlier.

"I'm assuming it tastes better than it smells?" She looked at Jessie. "May I?"

Jessie nodded, and Elliot took a sip of scotch. She swirled it around in her mouth a bit, really tasting it, before swallowing and wincing.

"Nope. It tastes like it smells. You really are a daredevil if you willingly put this in your body and enjoy it."

"It's an acquired taste. One that I acquired years ago."

"To each his own." Elliot got the bartender's attention. "Shirley Temple, please."

Jessie chuckled. "Rough night?"

"I eventually kicked everyone out. Things started getting a little crazy, and I didn't need the tabloids running a story about how I drunkenly trash hotel rooms."

"So the party's over?"

"Afraid so."

The bartender placed the drink in front of Elliot, who immediately picked up one of the cherries and sucked on it. Jessie turned her attention back to her drink, knowing that if she kept watching Elliot she might end up pulling her into the nearest bathroom to have her way with her.

"Sorry I bailed," offered Jessie as she sipped her scotch.

"No you're not, but it's okay. I figured it'd be best to just sleep it off, but I couldn't sleep, so I wandered around the hotel for a bit. I thought I'd go dip my feet in the pool, but it's closed, so I decided to drown my sorrows in a very responsible, non-alcoholic drink at the bar. Imagine my surprise seeing you here."

"I have a rule, Elliot. A very strict one," Jessie blurted out. No sense beating around the bush.

"Something about not hooking up with actors?"

"Co-workers in general, but yes—actors in particular."

Elliot nodded in understanding. "I'm sorry I tried to make you break your rule."

Jessie shrugged. "It's okay. For what it's worth, I really wanted to."

"That doesn't really make me feel better." She stirred her drink and took a swig. "So how did you come by this rule?"

"I made the mistake of hooking up with an actress on the first movie I ever worked on. She wasn't famous or anything. In fact, I don't even think she's working anymore. She had a small role and flirted wildly with me. I was new in town and kind of lonely and recovering from a bad breakup, so I gave in. Turns out she was just using me to make her boyfriend jealous. It made things very awkward because we still had another two weeks of filming left. I didn't want to get a reputation of sleeping with my co-workers, so I resolved to never allow it to happen again."

Elliot chewed on a piece of ice and nodded solemnly. "That makes sense. Sorry you had to go through that."

"I was young and stupid."

"Nice to see you haven't changed one bit," teased Elliot.

Jessie shoved her arm. "Very funny. I'm much older and wiser now, thank you."

Elliot giggled and grabbed another cherry from her drink. "So what was this bad breakup you went through?"

Jessie stiffened and adjusted her position on the stool. She forced herself to look at Elliot. She'd stared at her drink for way too long.

"Not much to tell. I was with my ex, Maggie, for three years back in Boulder. I was tending bar, and she was working as a waitress while we tried to save up enough to pay off our student loans and get a small place of our own. We were happy, or so I thought. She broke up with me out of nowhere and didn't really give me a reason. I found out two weeks later she moved out of Boulder to somewhere out east with one of my best friends from high school. We were all really close and hung out together all the time. I just didn't realize that the two of them were closer than I thought."

Elliot shook her head. "That's so shitty. I'm sorry."

"It hurt. I'm not gonna lie, it took me a while to get over it. That's one of the reasons I moved out to Los Angeles."

"So is thrill-seeking your way of coping with the heartache?"

"That's very astute. You should've been a psychologist. I suppose that's what it was about at first. But now...I can't see myself doing anything else. I love it. I'm good at it. And honestly, if Maggie hadn't broken my heart, I'd probably still be in Colorado up to my ass in student loan debt."

"Silver lining."

"Exactly."

"What about you? Any heartaches you've overcome?"

Elliot signaled the bartender for another Shirley Temple. "Nothing too tragic. I haven't really been with anyone long enough to experience that kind of difficult breakup. But that's not to say I haven't had my share of heartbreak. Just a different kind."

"How so?" Jessie found herself captivated by the way the girl spoke.

"I love my life. I really do. I have no reason to complain, but it gets a little lonely. As a rule, I tend to not do relationships. I've tried, but it's hard to maintain one when I keep the schedule I keep. Plus, it doesn't help when I date someone who gets insanely jealous whenever I have to kiss someone on screen."

"I'm sure it's not easy for them to see that." Jessie thought back to the way she felt watching Elliot kiss Drew on camera. It wasn't fun.

"And I understand that, but this guy outright forbade me from ever kissing on-screen again."

"Okay, that guy sounds like a dick."

"Yeah, I broke it off right then and there. I wasn't really into him anyway, if I'm being completely honest. But let's not forget about all the hot, young actors the tabloids have me dating. Some of them I've never even met. It's crazy what people will believe sometimes. As far as the people I do date…a lot of the time it's hard to tell if they're interested in dating the real me or the famous me."

"I'm sorry."

Elliot laughed to herself. "Listen to me, poor little rich girl bitching about how hard life is for her. Honestly, I really don't have much to complain about. I'm grateful for what I have. I know how lucky I am. I just wish my career would allow me to be more...open with certain things."

"You mean the fact that you're very much into girls?"

"That's exactly what I mean. I've been with a few girls over the years, and I've been very lucky that no one's found out about it."

"Would it be so bad if people found out?"

Elliot looked at her with a sense of worry. "Yeah. That's what everyone tells me, anyway. Especially with this movie coming out. Gotta maintain a certain image. Sexy Hollywood bombshell and all that shit."

"Yeah, that makes sense. Well, if you ever need to talk to someone about it."

"Thanks. Hayley and Morgan are the only ones who know. And now you."

"Well, you can trust me."

Elliot flashed her a smile. "I believe you."

Jessie held her gaze for a moment before changing the subject.

"It's impressive the way you handle your fame, though. I've only barely witnessed it with those people crowding you in the lobby, but you seem to handle it really well."

"Yeah, I don't mind the fame part. It's nice being recognized. Sometimes it can get a little scary, like if there's an overzealous fan or something. But for the most part, it's pretty cool."

"I couldn't do it. Walk down the street with everyone staring, watching my every move, thinking they know me by what they read in a magazine."

"You work in the entertainment industry and you don't want to be famous?"

"What can I say? I'm a rare breed. I like my life the way it is. Simple. Uncomplicated. Private."

"Sometimes I wouldn't mind having that. It sounds nice."

Jessie drank the last of her scotch and wiped her mouth. "So how do you cope with all this?"

"I have certain outlets that still make me feel human. I volunteer a lot for different charities."

"Really?" Jessie was surprised and felt guilty for that. She initially wrote Elliot off as just another shallow actress, but was slowly beginning to realize she was wrong.

"Yeah. Actually, I've been working on this project I'm really excited about. It's taken a lot of planning, and it's still in the beginning stages, but it's so important to me. I'm starting a foundation that focuses on helping abused and battered women."

"Elliot, that's amazing."

"I'm working with this foundation to break ground on a center for women who can come in and speak to counselors, lawyers, and doctors pro bono. We'll offer free babysitting if they need to go to work or to job interviews. We'll help them relocate and find a new place to live. We'll help them file restraining orders against whoever's abusing or threatening them. And we're going to offer free self-defense classes."

Jessie couldn't keep from smiling. "That's such a great idea. What a noble cause. And you know what? When it opens, I'd be happy to teach some self-defense classes."

Elliot leaned forward excitedly. "Really?"

"Yeah, I'd love to. I'm highly skilled in Krav Maga, which I think would be the best thing to teach them."

"That'd be great!" She pulled her in for a hug. "I'll keep you posted on the progress."

Jessie loved the smile on Elliot's face, and she loved the fact that she put it there. She held onto her embrace for a second too long before they separated, in awe that Elliot never seemed to stop surprising her.

After a few moments of silence, Elliot dropped a $50 bill onto the bar and stood up.

"I should probably try to get some sleep."

"Yeah, me too."

Elliot lingered for a bit, as though in contemplation.

"Jessie?"

"Hmm?"

"Do you think you'll ever find someone worth breaking your rule for?"

"Elliot..."

"I was just curious."

"You said yourself that as a rule you don't really do relationships, and I'm not looking for a one-night stand."

"It doesn't have to be a one-night stand. We're here for another few days. It can be a two-night stand."

Jessie laughed. "You're really sweet, you know that? I didn't expect that from you, but you are. Goodnight, Elliot."

"Goodnight, Jessie. And for the record, I might be willing to break my rule. You know...for the right person." She lowered her eyes shyly and turned to head back toward the elevator.

Jessie was left to contemplate her words. Would it really be such a bad thing to break her rule for someone as exceptional as Elliot?

*

Moments later, Jessie found herself pacing outside of room 1218. She didn't know how she ended up here, but she knew there was nowhere else she'd rather be at the moment. Once she finally swallowed her nerves, she knocked on the door. It took a moment before Elliot answered the door in her sleep shorts and loose fitting t-shirt. Jessie almost forgot how to speak until she realized Elliot was waiting for her to say something.

She hadn't thought this through. Really, what was there to say? She knew why she was here. Elliot knew why she was here. But she hadn't invited her in yet. She was obviously waiting for something. Jessie smiled and gave a slight shrug.

"I guess some rules are meant to be broken."

Elliot smiled, grabbed Jessie by the collar of her shirt, and pulled her into the room, closing and locking the door behind them.

Chapter 5

Once Elliot locked the door of the suite, she pulled Jessie into the bedroom and closed the door. She pushed her up against it and flashed a mischievous smile before driving her body forward flush against her. She felt Jessie's body tense immediately, so she pulled her in for a kiss to try and loosen her up. Once she pulled away, Jessie looked somewhat dazed, and Elliot couldn't hide her smile.

"Jessie?"

"Hmm?"

"Do I make you nervous?"

Jessie's eyes focused on her as she spoke quietly. "I don't get nervous."

Elliot brushed a few strands of hair out of her face and kissed her again. This time, it was a bit softer and sweeter.

"Oh yeah, that's right. You're not scared of anything."

Elliot felt Jessie's strong arms spin her around so that her back was against the wall. Jessie's lips kissed her neck. She grabbed Jessie's waist and pulled her closer, loving the prickling against her skin as Jessie grazed her teeth along her neck. Jessie pulled back and looked at her with an intensity Elliot had never seen before.

"I didn't say I wasn't scared. I said I don't get nervous."

Elliot was taken aback by her honesty. Usually, she was always the one too honest, saying exactly what was on her mind. She had to fight every urge not to blurt out the fact that she was actually kind of nervous. But something about the way Jessie looked at her was calming. The weight of her stare grounded her. Slowly, her nerves disappeared, and she began to feel a bit more daring. She gave a few experimental grinds against Jessie, then leaned forward and nipped at her earlobe.

"Okay then. Show me what you got."

Jessie let out a sexy groan and grabbed Elliot by the shirt, attacking her lips as she pushed her back across the room. Elliot was overwhelmed by the girl's strength. She was so turned on, she barely winced when she backed into the vanity on the other side of the room. While continuing to kiss her, Jessie lifted her up onto the vanity, knocking some hair and makeup products off in the process.

Jessie pulled away and looked down at the mess.

"Shit. Sorry."

"Don't worry about it," Elliot panted.

She pulled her back into a searing kiss. She didn't have time to worry about the mess; her body was on fire. Jessie's hands felt incredible as her nimble fingers went up under her shirt and caressed her back as her other hand kept a good grip on Elliot's hip. Their tongues were wet and hot against each other, unearthing and discovering every part of each other's mouths. She wrapped her legs around Jessie's waist, pulling her in closer and trying to get a little friction between her legs.

Jessie traced her fingers over Elliot's back and moved her mouth down along Elliot's jaw. As much as she enjoyed this, Elliot needed more.

"Please," Elliot's breathy voice filled the room. "I need your hands on me."

She grabbed Jessie's hand that explored her back and moved it down to the hem of her shorts. Jessie paused for a moment, making sure Elliot was okay with it. Elliot gave her a barely perceptible nod, and Jessie moved her hand past the hem of her shorts.

She teased her, taking her time, exploring her, gently tracing her fingers everywhere except where Elliot needed. Normally, Elliot would appreciate this kind of attention, but right now wasn't the time. She'd been insanely turned on since the party and couldn't get this woman off her mind. She needed her. It wasn't even a matter of desire or want. It was an absolute necessity to have this woman in every way she could.

Panting, she grabbed Jessie's wrist and moved her hand while thrusting her hips forward. She needed her right now. There wasn't even time to remove their clothing.

"Jessie, I promise there will be plenty of time for exploring later. We can take all the time we want, but right now, I need your fingers inside me."

Jessie's mouth fell open, and she nodded intently, fully giving Elliot what she needed.

"Fuck, I knew you'd be good with your fingers," growled Elliot. "Something about the way you handled that prop gun."

Jessie groaned against her neck and skillfully continued what she was doing while biting Elliot's neck harder and setting a breakneck pace. Elliot's body came alive, buzzing and tingling from every nerve ending. She only allowed herself to worry briefly when she heard the vanity squeak, hoping it wouldn't break. She braced herself on the vanity as more items were knocked to the ground, including a hair dryer and a perfume bottle. Jessie stopped immediately and looked down at the mess.

"Shit."

Elliot wanted to scream out her frustration. She was so close, and Jessie stopped. She leaned up and grabbed her cheeks.

"Jessie, focus. Forget the stuff on the floor. Please!"

Jessie nodded. "Right. Sorry."

She continued, and within moments Elliot gripped Jessie's shirt, clinging to her as she tried to catch her breath.

*

Jessie held onto her as she came down from her high. Elliot pulled back and looked at her through hazy eyes. Her face was red and sweaty, and her lips formed the perfect little smirk, telling Jessie that she was satisfied but also aching for more.

She watched as Elliot leaned back on the vanity, shaken loose from all the strenuous activity performed on it, and looked down expectantly at Jessie's pants. Jessie took the hint and unzipped her pants, taking them off more smoothly than she thought she would under Elliot's heavy, sex-induced gaze. She looked back up at Elliot, who took in the sight of Jessie's legs before quirking an eyebrow at her shirt. Jessie shed that too.

It was amazing what this girl could get her to do with one simple look.

Elliot jumped off the vanity and wrapped her arms around Jessie's waist, pulling her in for a much needed kiss. It was desperate—all teeth and tongue—as Elliot pushed Jessie backward towards the bed. Jessie was both frustrated and fascinated. For someone who prided herself on having control over every aspect of her life, she certainly gave it up rather quickly to a woman she barely even knew. So why did it feel so right?

Elliot gave a little nudge to her sternum and pushed her back onto the bed before straddling her. It was obvious Elliot was on a mission, and Jessie had no choice but to help her achieve it. Elliot took off her shirt and tossed it aside, giving Jessie an eyeful before continuing to undress.

"Are you ready for me, Jessie?"

Jessie swallowed hard and nodded furiously. She was definitely ready.

*

Elliot was quite pleased with her ability to reduce Jessie to a needy mess. It was a far cry from the stoic, fearless stunt woman she'd come to know, and it was a side of her she really liked seeing. She held onto Jessie as her body shook and writhed beneath her, feeling the sweat against her skin. She watched as Jessie's wall officially came crashing down. The wall she worked so hard to build up over the years was slowly being picked apart by Elliot Chase. In this moment, Jessie's stoicism and hardened exterior fully faded away. Suddenly, it wasn't the "aloof, badass stuntwoman" Elliot was making love to. It was simply Jessie, and she was beautiful. All Elliot could see was the vulnerable, sweet, scared, and trusting Jessie Knight she'd come to know in the last few days, and suddenly, it all made sense. Elliot tried so hard to break through to her. She came at her full force with a sledgehammer, when apparently all she needed was the touch of her fingers to tear down her wall. She couldn't believe it was this simple.

With one final curl of Elliot's finger, Jessie began to shudder uncontrollably, moaning and unraveling underneath her.

Moments later, Jessie let out a sigh of contentment, stroking Elliot's back as she rested on top of her. It was a beautiful moment—peaceful—and Elliot never wanted it to end.

However, it was short-lived. Elliot didn't expect the badass side of Jessie to take over again so suddenly, but Jessie sat up, abs flexed and eyes hungry. She had Elliot on her back in mere seconds and slowly ghosted her lips across her chest and down her stomach. Elliot gasped and clamped her eyes shut when Jessie reached her destination.

Jessie's tongue was everything Elliot dreamed it'd be. She wondered how the hell she'd gone this long without ever having sex with Jessie Knight. Now that she was experiencing it, she never wanted to go a day without it.

By this point, Elliot could barely string together a coherent sentence. She began gripping the sheets, but Jessie's hands moved their way up over Elliot's, coaxing her to let go. Once she was calm enough to, Jessie intertwined their fingers, holding her hands tightly as she continued.

Elliot was caught completely off guard. She wasn't prepared for this. Most of her sexual partners were more concerned with getting off than the intimacy of the act. Feeling Jessie's hands hold her own while her tongue reached new places within her brought out a whole new set of feelings she didn't know she harbored. She couldn't think about that now, not when everything felt so damn good. She felt her stomach begin to coil. Elliot looked down to see Jessie's eyes on her. Jessie gave her hands one more squeeze, assuring her she was there with her and that everything was okay. Then, Elliot let go. She didn't hold back. There was no point. Jessie had to know what she was doing to her.

Once her body began to calm, Jessie crawled back up, bringing their still-joined hands up over her head and kissing her sweetly.

Elliot hummed in response, unable to speak at the moment. Jessie caressed her cheek softly and kissed her intermittently as Elliot's breathing began to even out. She knew that they were far from done.

*

Hours later it was still dark outside, but the hint of light through the crack of the window curtain proved dawn was approaching. Jessie was on her stomach, feeling Elliot's fingertips dance along her skin, tracing along the different tattoos on her back. It was late, far too late for her to be up, but she was wide awake. Besides, the sun was still at least an hour from rising, and there was a beautiful naked girl in bed next to her.

"Jessie?"

She turned to face her, resting her head on her arms. "Hmm?"

"I'm thinking this should be more than a one-night stand."

"Of course. Didn't we agree it'd be two nights?"

Elliot pushed her playfully. "I'm serious. What do you think?"

Jessie paused briefly, trying not to read too much into the fluttering in her stomach. "What happens when we get back to LA?"

"We still have some filming to do at the studio, so we'll see each other. After that, who knows? We'll figure something out."

Jessie turned on her side to fully face her, causing Elliot's fingers to fall and graze the side of Jessie's torso.

"Figure something out?"

"I'd like to see you again."

Jessie smiled. "You mean you'd like to fuck me again."

"Well, yeah, because you are insanely good in bed. But would you maybe want to pursue something more?"

This went against everything Jessie believed in, everything she trained herself not to want. And yet, she couldn't stop herself.

"What, like a date?"

"Yeah, a date."

"But you're not…you know…out."

Elliot shrugged. "We can keep it covert for a while. Contrary to what some people believe, the world doesn't have to know about the inner workings of my romantic life."

Jessie was torn. Her brain screamed at her to end it now, to get out before it was too late. But she'd been ignoring it all night, and she wasn't about to start listening to it now. She crawled over toward Elliot and kissed her.

"I think I can clear my schedule for a date with you."

*

Elliot lost track of how many rounds they'd gone so far. It didn't matter. All she knew was that she loved the feeling of Jessie lying on top of her, head resting on her chest, and her fingers gently playing with her hair. She could hear the brunette sigh deeply, seemingly preparing herself for whatever she was about to say.

"Elliot?"

"Yeah?"

"I'm trying really hard not to fall for you."

Elliot felt a tug at her heart.

"Why?"

"Because…" Jessie took another deep breath. "I know how it'll end."

"You don't know anything. I really like you. I think that's been very clear from the moment we met."

"We both know what this is."

Elliot had to try to control her emotions. Everything was heightened, which was common after a night of insanely hot sex. She steeled herself and continued running her fingers through Jessie's hair.

"Is that so? What is this, then?"

"Elliot..."

"No, Jessie. You don't get to do that. You're ending this before it even has a chance to start. I won't let you."

Jessie was silent.

"What are you afraid of?"

"It's nothing."

"Oh, it's definitely something. Hey." She tugged at her hair, trying to get Jessie to look at her. "It's okay to feel things."

Jessie tried to hide her smile.

"I know."

Elliot rolled her eyes and giggled. "I can't believe the biggest badass in Hollywood is afraid of a little blonde actress."

Jessie sat up and straddled Elliot.

"I'm not afraid of you."

Elliot leaned up on her elbows. "Prove it. Stop plotting our demise before we even have a chance to be anything."

Jessie leaned down and kissed her. "You know, you're really cute when you're demanding."

"Oh, I can be very persuasive sometimes."

*

Jessie was sitting up with her back against the headboard as Elliot kneeled facing her, exploring her entire body. She loved being able to put her hands and mouth on Jessie anywhere she pleased. She couldn't get enough of her. This was evident as it was now sunrise, and they still hadn't managed to find sleep. Instead, they kept finding new ways to enjoy each other.

After another mind-blowing round, they still didn't want to pull apart. They were too tired for another, so they resorted to making out, which seemed like a welcomed compromise. Elliot moaned into the kiss. She was practically delirious at this point. She lost count of how many orgasms they'd shared between the two of them, and she knew her lips were definitely swollen. God knows they left countless marks on each other, but she didn't care. That was a problem for tomorrow's Elliot to worry about. Present Elliot was just fine with the way things turned out tonight.

She fell asleep pressed against the skin of the beautiful girl next to her and slept harder than she had in a long time.

*

When Elliot opened her eyes and lifted her head, it was hard to distinguish what time it was with what little light came through the closed drapes. She lowered her head back onto the pillow and felt her nose being tickled by an errant curly hair belonging to the naked girl in bed next to her. She smiled, finding herself somewhat relieved that Jessie hadn't snuck out some point after they fell asleep. Her back faced Elliot. She wanted so badly to plant kisses up and down it, but knew that'd be cruel considering the long night they had, so she decided to let her sleep. She nuzzled into the back of her neck, pulling her close. The brunette only stirred briefly before falling back to sleep. Soon enough, Elliot found herself restless, needing to know what time it was and to make sure they hadn't missed their call time.

She scooted away from Jessie and carefully got out of bed, trying not to disturb her. She grabbed her purse hanging on the chair and pulled out her phone, shocked to see she had 32 missed calls and 25 text messages. She forgot she'd left her phone on silent. Panic sank in for a moment before realizing they were still three hours away from their call time; that couldn't possibly be the reason for all the missed calls.

She noticed most of the calls were from her agent and publicist. A few were from Morgan and Hayley and a couple were from her mom. There were also a couple random numbers she didn't recognize. The panicked feeling set in again because she knew something must be wrong. Did something happen to the set? Was the movie shelved? How could that even be possible when they had a huge budget?

She looked through a couple of texts, most of which were different versions of "where are you" and "call me."

A text from Hayley caught her eye.

I can't reach you. Been knocking on your door, but no answer. You need to call me. Or Morgan. Asap.

She realized there was no way she could've heard anyone knocking on the front door with the bedroom door closed. Plus, she and Jessie were passed out pretty hard all morning. Suddenly, another text from Hayley came through that said *I'm sorry* followed by a link.

She looked back at Jessie, not wanting to wake her, and went into the bathroom and closed the door. She half expected the link to be leaked pictures from the party last night, but she didn't remember doing anything too crazy that would warrant this many missed calls and texts. She sighed and braced herself before clicking on the link, but nothing could prepare her for what showed up on the screen.

Chapter 6

Elliot emerged from the bathroom in a daze. She could barely register anything around her. She had enough sense to grab her shorts and t-shirt on the floor and threw them on. She gripped the phone in her hand as a few more texts came pouring in, and Jessie began to stir. Elliot sat down at the edge of the bed, staring at her phone as more and more alerts popped up. Her stomach dropped, the blood drained from her face, and she felt like she was going to pass out.

She registered the sound of Jessie yawning behind her, then felt the bed move as Jessie crawled over, draped her arms around her, and lazily planted kisses along her back.

"Mmm...good morning." She began kissing the back of her neck. "You are far too dressed right now. We still have a couple hours until we need to be on set."

Elliot felt a shudder and shrugged away from Jessie's embrace, unable to turn and look at her. She kept staring at her phone, willing it to stop ringing.

"Was it you?" Elliot asked through gritted teeth.

"Was what me?" Jessie didn't seem to take the hint and kept kissing her, humming in pleasure.

"The video."

"Mmm, what video?"

Elliot stood up, causing Jessie to nearly lose her balance. "This isn't a fucking joke, Jessie. Tell me the truth. Was it you?"

Jessie sat back down and pulled the sheet up to cover herself.

"What's wrong? What video are you talking about?"

"Have you checked your phone?"

"My phone is in my room."

A heavy silence hung in the air between them. Elliot still couldn't bring herself to look her in the eye. She tried to force the words out of her mouth without bile building up behind them.

"There's a sex tape on the internet. Of us. From last night." Once the words officially left her mouth, everything became all too real, and she felt sick to her stomach. She finally forced herself to look at Jessie, who stared at her incredulously, but all Elliot could see was betrayal.

She felt her stomach churn thinking of the ramifications of everything. Her reputation. Her career. Her family. Nothing would ever be the same.

"I'm going to be sick."

She ran to the bathroom, fell to her knees, and heaved up everything inside of her.

*

Jessie didn't have time to react to Elliot's words before she disappeared into the bathroom. The moment she heard her throwing up, Jessie jumped out of bed and followed her, leaving behind the sheet that was keeping her decent. She ran into the bathroom and witnessed Elliot on the ground, hovering over the toilet. She knelt down next to her and started rubbing her back. The tile was cold on her knees, and she couldn't help but feel vulnerable being completely naked. She was trying to make sense of what just happened, but right now her priority was making sure Elliot was okay.

She kept rubbing Elliot's back until she pulled away, flushed the toilet, and sat on the floor with her, their backs against the wall. Jessie remained on her knees a few feet away from Elliot, watching her carefully. Her face was pale, and her hair was a mess as she wiped her mouth with the back of her hand.

Jessie stood up, grabbed a washcloth, and ran some cold water over it. She knelt in front of Elliot and pressed it against her forehead. She noticed Elliot start to panic, so Jessie pulled her in to hold her. Elliot allowed her to for a moment before jerking away and getting up.

Jessie stood up too, the dripping washcloth still in her hand. Elliot grabbed her phone from the counter, clicked on the link that was sent to her, and tossed the phone to Jessie. The video on the screen revealed a familiar looking hotel room with two very familiar looking girls having sex. It showed them against the vanity, and then it cut to them on the bed with Elliot on top of her. It cut to different parts of the night they shared. She flashed back to those very intimate moments when they were hand in hand, eyes locked, and Jessie suddenly understood why Elliot felt so sick. Finally, the video faded to black. The whole thing was about two minutes long and obviously edited. Nothing else from their night together was shown, but the quality was decent and their faces were clear. There was no way they could deny it was either one of them in the video.

She put the phone down on the sink and searched for something to say. What could she say in a moment like this? She felt chills run up her entire body and suddenly felt very cold. She wished she wasn't naked at the moment. She looked up at Elliot, whose eyes were focused on the floor.

"Elliot...I..."

"I think you should leave."

"Elliot..."

"Go."

She felt like she'd been punched in the gut. Repeatedly.

"Let's figure this out."

"There's nothing to figure out." Her voice was cold and void of any type of emotion. "You wanted the entire world to know you fucked Elliot Chase. Congratulations. They know."

The words cut her. She charged up to Elliot and grabbed her arms. Not forcefully, but enough to get her to look at her.

"Elliot! I didn't—"

"You were alone in my room. I left you there to check on the party."

"And then I left right after you. Why would I set up a camera and then leave on the off chance I'd run into you at the bar later?" She was desperate, shaking, naked, and trying to get Elliot to believe her. Or at the very least, look at her. She knew she should cover up, but what was the point, really? She had nothing left to hide from Elliot. Or the rest of the world for that matter.

The devastated look on Elliot's face was breaking her.

"Elliot, I swear. I had nothing to do with this. I would never do that to you." Perhaps it was the fear in her voice or the honesty of her words, but Elliot finally looked up. Her eyes were weepy, but otherwise showed no emotion.

She pushed off against the wall and walked past Jessie.

"Still, you should go. I have phone calls to make."

She followed her out to the room and caught the clothes Elliot threw to her. She dressed quickly, her eyes remaining on Elliot, who sat on the bed deep in thought.

"Jessie, I need you to go now." She looked up at her, pleading. "Please."

Jessie nodded, her heart breaking. But she'd have to keep that to herself; Elliot was falling apart, and one of them had to keep it together.

"You believe me, right?" Her voice sounded so small, so different, and her breath was heavy, waiting for a response.

Elliot shook her head. "I...yeah." She nodded. "Yeah. I think so. I just...I need to make some calls."

Jessie nodded and turned to go, but stopped, interrupted by a thought. She turned back and ran to the dresser that had a bunch of junk on top of it: piles of clothes, a laptop, Elliot's purse, some books, magazines and scripts, and a few other things. Jessie rummaged through everything.

"What are you doing?"

Jessie examined the laptop. It was closed and turned off; that couldn't have been what filmed them.

"It looked like this is where the camera was set up, based on the angle of the video."

Elliot jumped up and started going through everything. They stopped when Jessie found a phone sitting perfectly on its side between stacks of scripts. It was well hidden, but the phone's camera had the perfect view of the entire room. She picked it up and examined it. It took all of her energy not to throw it against the wall in anger.

"Shit!"

Elliot grabbed the phone and examined it. It was on camera mode, but no longer running. The phone read "Device Storage Full."

They looked through the phone to see if anything else was on it, but there wasn't. No proof of who owned it. No photos, no numbers. Just one very long video and a quickly dying battery.

"Whoever planted this must've had it uploaded and sent directly to them. Then they edited and released it. Fuck."

Jessie started pacing.

Elliot looked at the time. "I have to call my publicist. Right now."

"Want me to hang onto this? I'll call the police, file a report."

"I'll take it. I have lawyers. My team will handle this."

Jessie handed her the phone and grabbed her other hand.

"I'm so sorry, Elliot. I'm sorry this happened, but it's going to be okay." That was a lie. They both knew it wouldn't. "I just...it wasn't me. I promise you."

"I know," she answered in a whispered voice. "I know, but...it still happened, and it can't be undone. I need you to go now."

Jessie reluctantly backed away and headed toward the door. "I'm here when you need me. I'll see you on set."

They both immediately cringed at the thought of having to face their peers on set in a couple of hours.

*

Elliot sat for a moment after Jessie left. She texted Morgan and Hayley. She knew Morgan was already on set but asked Hayley to meet her in 20 minutes. While waiting, she called her publicist.

"Elliot, how are you holding up, love?"

"Be honest with me, Liz. How bad is it?"

The silence on the other end wasn't reassuring.

Liz sighed. "It's not great. Can you tell me what happened?"

"I don't know. Someone planted a phone in my room and filmed us. I don't know who did it."

"Was it Jessie?"

Elliot felt her chest tighten. "Shit, they've already identified her?"

"Yeah. News travels fast."

"Damn it. No. No, I really don't think it was her."

"Are you sure?"

Elliot didn't want to think about it anymore. If Jessie was behind it, she couldn't handle the thought of being betrayed like that. If it wasn't her, then she felt guilty for even thinking it was her in the first place.

"I don't know. I don't think she'd do this. How did you find out about it? Did someone call you?"

"I got a call at seven am from TMZ asking me to confirm that it's you in the video. I had no idea what he was talking about. I asked him to send me the link. I guess someone sent it out to every online news outlet and gossip site, but no one seems to know where it came from. We have people trying to track down the IP address, but even if we find out, there's no guarantee we'll know who's behind it."

Elliot began pacing back and forth. "So what do we do?"

"You go to work. You show up on the set, keep your head down, and do your job. Let me do mine. Keep your phone on you, and I'll call you with any updates."

"Liz…" Elliot's voice was cracked, "is my career over?"

"No. I don't want you thinking that. But Elliot, I need to know…do you want me to confirm your sexuality with the press? I've been getting constant calls for comments."

Elliot looked up at the ceiling and took a deep breath. "I think it's pretty damn obvious and goes without saying at this point. We can't deny that it's me in the video either. The picture is way too clear. All I ask is that you leave Jessie's name out of this."

"People already know who she is."

Elliot closed her eyes. This was exactly what Jessie didn't want.

"I know. Just don't confirm it's her. Not until I talk to her. Make sure they know that neither of us knew we were being filmed and that legal action will be taken."

*

Back in her room, Jessie immediately checked her phone and noticed several missed calls and texts. Calls from Peyton, Kat, her mom. *God, her mom. And her dad. How could she face her family after this?*

She noticed she had multiple friend requests on Facebook and thousands of new follower requests on Instagram. Thankfully, all her social media profiles were set to private, but it made her feel nauseated just knowing that her name was out there, that she was identified as the other girl in the XXX video with Elliot. She clicked on a few different stories online. When she got to the TMZ article, her heart stopped.

There was her name in big, bold letters: *Stunt Woman, Jessie Knight, Caught in Lesbian Tryst with Elliot Chase*.

Under the headline was a link to the "not safe for work" video and a photo of her that was obviously lifted from her Facebook profile.

She shut off her phone and lay down on her bed, staring up at the ceiling. She couldn't deal with this right now. She had to get ready for the day. She had to focus on her work.

*

Jessie garnered a few looks in the hotel lobby as she waited for her car. She put on her headphones and tried to drown everyone out. She looked around but didn't see Elliot anywhere. She was probably escorted out the back door so as not to attract a crowd. Jessie noticed some paparazzi outside and figured it was only a matter of time before more showed up. It was no secret where the cast was staying for the shoot, but there weren't any paparazzi in sight until this morning.

When her driver showed up, she ran and jumped into the car in an attempt to evade the photographers, but knew they'd managed to snap a few photos of her.

The long drive to the set left her a lot of time to contemplate everything. She knew she should be concerned about her reputation, but she was more worried about Elliot. Elliot didn't deserve this. Then again, neither did she. This is what happens when you're weak and break the rules.

Once she got to the set, Kat immediately ran up to her and pulled her into her trailer.

"Jesus, Knight, are you okay?"

Jessie shook her head. "It's bad. It's so bad. And now I think Elliot hates me."

"Hey, she doesn't hate you. She's probably just scared. I mean, you've both been violated in the worst possible way."

Jessie sat down and put her head in her hands.

"Look, I know this isn't the best time, but we film in half an hour, and I need to know if you're in this. Are you with me? I need you focused. It's a big stunt today."

Jessie nodded. "I'm with you. I can do this."

She was pretty sure she could. She could compartmentalize and then fall apart later.

Kat leaned against the counter. "So what happened? I mean, I'm assuming you guys didn't film yourselves."

"No! God, no. We're not that stupid. I don't know what happened. Someone planted a phone and the camera was on. I found it this morning."

"Where is it?"

"Elliot has it."

"Elliot?"

"Yeah."

"Why would you leave it with her?"

"She said she'd make sure her lawyer gets it."

"You don't think..."

Jessie looked up at her. "What?"

Kat hesitated for a moment. "Some actresses try to become more famous by releasing a sex tape."

Jessie stood up. "Don't even suggest it. Elliot would never, ever do that."

Kat held up her hands in defense. "Hey, I'm just playing devil's advocate. I don't really think she would either. I'm just trying to go through every possible scenario."

"Well, cross that one off the list. She's talking to her team, and I'm assuming they're going to file a police report. That's all I know for right now."

Kat shook her head. "I'm so sorry. I shouldn't have made you go to that party."

"It's not your fault. I had an amazing night with Elliot. Now it's just tainted. I just hope she's okay. Have you seen her?"

"Not yet. I'm sure she'll be here soon. Come on. We need to do some practice runs."

As they walked from the trailers to the set, she noticed a few looks and glances thrown her way along with some whispers. She kept looking forward as they headed towards the motorcycles.

Once again, she was dressed in black leather. The heat was unbearable, but the sweat dripping down her face had more to do with the situation she was in than it did with the heat.

*

Hayley rode with Elliot to the set. For the most part, they sat in silence. Hayley met Elliot in her room, and Elliot fell into her arms sobbing after getting off the phone with Liz. All Hayley could do was try to assure her that it would pass and that everything would eventually go back to normal, but Elliot knew normal wasn't a thing that existed for her anymore.

She'd always tried to live a decent, honest life. She was kind to people, friendly and forthcoming. She volunteered her time to help those less fortunate. She tried to use her fame and fortune for good. She knew to always be thankful for what she had, and she was always so careful to keep out of trouble, out of the gossip headlines. She even made it a point to have a no-nudity clause written into all her film contracts. Now, not only had the world seen her completely nude, but they'd also witnessed her in the most vulnerable moment of her life. Granted, it was only two minutes long, and she supposed it could be worse if footage from the entire night had been released, but still...it was two minutes too long. There was no telling when and if more footage would be released.

After changing in her trailer, Hayley escorted her to the set. Elliot's stomach churned as a hushed silence came over everyone. She knew what they all were thinking. They had to have seen or heard about the video by now, but no one dared glance in her direction. She looked at Hayley questioningly.

"Morgan threatened to gut and hang anyone who even looked at you the wrong way or said something to you that wasn't work-related. James made some threats too."

If Elliot was capable of smiling right now, she would have. Instead, she just continued walking with Hayley by her side. She was thankful that her friends had her back.

"And we've got a special form of punishment lined up for Jessie if we find out she's the one behind this."

Elliot shook her head. "I don't think she did it. I don't know for sure, but she seemed just as shocked and upset as I was. Tell Morgan to call off her threat to Jessie for now."

"Fine. I swear to God, when we find out who's behind this, they will pay."

"I hope so."

Elliot stopped when she noticed Jessie in the distance sitting on the motorcycle and talking to Kat. She was dressed in the same black leather outfit as Hayley. Suddenly, her mind brought her back to last night. She always looked so damn sexy, whether dressed head to toe in leather or completely naked.

Her thoughts prompted her to remember what last night's nakedness led to, and she felt herself turning red from embarrassment. She didn't want to be here. She didn't want all these prying eyes staring at her and picturing her naked with Jessie. It wasn't fair. No one was supposed to see that. Something so incredible had turned into the worst moment of her life, and she found herself wanting to hate Jessie. She hated her for being so attractive. She hated her for giving in to Elliot's incessant flirting. If she'd been stronger and stuck to her convictions, they wouldn't be in this situation. If she wasn't so damn sexy and sweet, Elliot never would've pursued her the way she did. It was all Jessie's fault. How dare she make her feel things she'd never felt before? She hated that something so beautiful had turned into something that made her want to wretch.

Still, she couldn't keep her eyes off of Jessie.

She watched as the other girl wiped the sweat from her brow and discussed something with Kat. Morgan came up and showed them the detonator, no doubt explaining what the explosion in the scene would entail.

*

Jessie could feel Morgan's glare bore into her as she explained the logistics and timing of the pyrotechnics in the scene. Once Jessie and Kat fully understood everything, Morgan turned her focus solely on Jessie.

"I'm a professional, so I'll make sure this whole thing goes off perfectly. Elliot seems to think you're innocent, so I fully have your back with this stunt, but if I find out you had anything at all to do with—"

"Morgan, can you check my squibs for me?" Kat came to Jessie's rescue just in time.

Jessie breathed a sigh of relief when Morgan left to help out Kat. She was nervous. She didn't get nervous, and yet, here she was with a queasy stomach and a racing heart. She had to pull it together. This stunt was a bit complicated, more so than the rest of the ones she'd done so far on this film, but she practiced it with Kat three times now and had rehearsed it with the stunt coordinator a couple weeks ago. She knew it inside and out. All she had to do was drive down the road with Kat on her tail, pull up to the ramp, jump through the explosion the pyrotechnics team set off, and land on the other side unscathed, driving for another half mile for the long shot. She knew the timing, knew her marks, knew when and how the explosion would occur, and exactly when and how the jump would happen. She was ready.

She heard a few crew members whisper something and look over to where the tents were set up. Jessie glanced over and saw Elliot walking next to Hayley as James approached them and gave her a hug.

Jessie looked on and took notice of Elliot's broken posture and blank look. She wanted to forget about the stunt, drive over to her, put her on the back of the bike, and drive off into the sunset to a place where no one knew their names, and the internet didn't exist.

Her fantasy was interrupted by the assistant jib operator talking to the key grip. "I'd pay any amount of money to see the rest of that video. God, how hot would it have been to be in the middle of that dyke sandwich. I knew that girl was freaky."

Jessie completely lost her cool, jumped off the motorcycle, and charged at him, knocking his scrawny frame to the ground.

"If you say one word about her again, I'll kick your ass!"

It took Kat, the key grip, and the A.D. to pull Jessie off of the unsuspecting guy. He stood up, coughing and dusting himself off.

"Fucking crazy bitch!" He looked at the A.D. "Are you going to let her attack me like that?"

Nate immediately got on the radio. "Security, we're going to need you to escort Mike Bradford off the set. He's officially banned."

Mike looked at him incredulously. "Are you fucking kidding me? She just jumped on me."

Nate shrugged. "That's not the way I saw it."

Kat smiled. "Not the way I saw it either."

Morgan shot daggers at him. "Pretty sure your story won't hold up, Mikey."

Jessie gave them all an appreciative look.

Mike cowered as he saw security approach. "Fuck you guys."

Jessie looked over and saw Elliot in the distance watching the scuffle that just took place. They locked eyes for a moment until Elliot somberly turned away. Jessie swallowed, put on her helmet, and got onto the bike.

"Let's do this so I can get out of here."

Once the director looked everything over, he called for silence on the set. The clapboard slammed down, speed was called, followed by action, and Jessie took off with Kat right behind her.

She got the bike up to 75 miles per hour like the stunt called for. She tried to shake off what just happened. She tried to get rid of the vision of that weasel-faced Mike watching the video and ogling over Elliot. She tried to forget the fact that the entire world had seen them nude and witnessed them in the most intense moment of passion she'd ever experienced. She had to clear her mind of all that because this stunt was the most important thing at the moment.

Suddenly, she realized she drove too far and missed her cue. She tried to recover at the last second and aimed for the ramp, but the angle was all wrong. The explosion went off, and she flew right into it when she was supposed to be on the other side by the time it detonated. She felt the powerful heat run up and down her body. She was fully protected from the flames with her outfit and the helmet, but it was too hot to keep gripping the handles on the bike, so she pulled her hands off. All hell broke loose. The bike lost its balance and flipped over with Jessie still on it. She stayed on the bike for a couple of flips, before being thrown from it. The bike went one way, flipping with its engine still roaring, and Jessie went the other, tumbling over and over onto the asphalt.

She'd prepared for moments like this and was able to tuck her head and roll into the momentum, but she was getting dizzy. Her body started to hurt, and she just wanted to stop rolling. Finally, after what felt like an eternity, her body slowed to a halt. She landed on her back, but couldn't bring herself to move. She grunted in pain, and her left hand felt like it was on fire. Her heavy breathing fogged up the windshield on her helmet, and she could hear sirens in the distance. The on-set ambulance must've seen the crash and was on its way over.

It was utter chaos, but everything seemed to move in slow motion for Jessie. The sirens grew louder as she heard voices all around her. She moved her head to see the bike on its side, the engine sputtering. It was on fire, and someone put it out with an extinguisher. She heard Kat calling for the medic.

Her head was pounding and the only sound she could make out was a constant low groan. No words seemed to form just yet. She could see a shadowy figure kneeling over her, and it took a moment to realize it was Morgan. Her voice echoed.

"Jessie...Jessie...look at me." She glanced over at the ambulance. "We need a medic right fucking now! Get over here!"

The medics jumped out of the ambulance and went to check on Jessie.

Morgan tried to keep her conscious by talking to her.

"I swear, Knight, you better survive this. It'll make a seriously badass story, so you have to be okay. Dude, you were literally on fire and then put it out when you flipped over like 50 times. I'm telling you, if you can survive this, you can survive anything."

Jessie could only comprehend some of what she was saying, but she got the last part. Something told her Morgan wasn't just referring to surviving the crash.

She still couldn't speak likely due to the serious state of shock she was in. The medics put her on the stretcher when she closed her eyes. She opened them again and noticed a shock of blonde hair standing over her. Her eyes closed once more, then opened again. The blonde looked down at her with fear and worry in her eyes.

"Can you take the helmet off of her?" She heard the familiar voice ask.

She closed her eyes again as the medics carefully removed her helmet. The hot desert air hit her face, and when her eyes opened again, her hand stung. She realized Elliot was holding it, not knowing the fire had burned through her glove. She refused to flinch though. She needed Elliot to keep holding it no matter how much it hurt.

All she wanted to do was sleep, but that would mean she could no longer see the beautiful girl at her side. She was so tired, so she closed her eyes for just a moment, thankful that she could still hear the girl's voice and feel her hand on her own.

"Be careful. Is she going to be okay? How is she? God, Jessie, are you okay? Please be okay."

She was in a state of sleepy consciousness but could hear and feel everything around her. She felt herself being loaded into the ambulance, the blonde's presence still with her the entire time. She heard someone yell at Elliot in the distance.

"Elliot, you can't go. You need to stay here."

She heard Elliot reply.

"Like hell I do. I'm going with her."

Then everything went black.

Chapter 7

Jessie's eyes shot open, slowly adjusting to the darkness of the room. She could hear the whirring and beeping of monitors. She held up her arm and found an IV needle attached to it. She was dressed in a hospital gown, free of the binding leather she wore earlier. She took stock of her body, starting by wiggling her toes. She was relieved that she could see them moving under the blanket. Next, she moved her head from side to side. This was good. It meant she wasn't paralyzed, which very well could've happened after that gruesome accident. She tried to examine as much of her skin as she could, only noticing a few cuts and bruises and some road rash, particularly on her knees. Nothing hurt too badly except for her head and her left hand, which was bandaged. She wasn't sure if it was cut or burned, but she did remember letting go of the handlebars because her hand felt like it was on fire.

She tried to adjust her position in the bed when she noticed locks of blonde hair splayed out on the bed next to her legs. Elliot sat in a chair, hunched over at the waist with her head resting on her arms. That couldn't have been a comfortable position, but she was sound asleep. Instinctively, she reached out to touch her, but pulled back, not wanting to wake her up. She felt a wave of relief knowing that Elliot was there by her side. There were still so many unresolved issues between them, but that would have to wait. All that mattered right now was that Elliot was here, and Jessie was okay.

She took a moment to think back and remember exactly what had happened. She knew she messed up. She was distracted. Botching the stunt was 100 percent her fault. She was one second behind in the timing and several feet off her mark. Honestly, she didn't know how she wasn't more banged up than this.

Elliot suddenly jolted awake and looked around the room, searching for something familiar. She found it when she saw Jessie's face. A small smile formed on her lips.

"Hey." Her voice was weak but hopeful.

Jessie smiled back. "Hey you."

"How long have you been awake?" Elliot sat up and stretched a bit. "You should've woke me up."

"Just a few minutes. You looked so peaceful. What time is it?"

Elliot glanced over at the clock on the wall. "It's almost midnight. You've been in and out of sleep most of the evening. How do you feel?"

"It feels like I have a bad hangover. Like the mother of all hangovers."

"And yet you still manage to look ridiculously sexy. Especially in that hospital gown."

Jessie actually felt herself blushing. Why was this girl so damn disarming?

"Are you in pain?"

"Not much. Just a little."

"Good." Elliot stood up and shook her head. "You asshole."

Jessie felt her stomach drop and her chest tighten. She started panicking, thinking Elliot was about to blame her for everything that had happened.

"You scared the shit out of me! Promise me that from now on, if you're not prepared to do a stunt, you won't do it! Simple as that."

Jessie tried to hide her relief while simultaneously stifling a giggle. Elliot was kind of cute when she was concerned and bossy.

"I'm sorry."

"Promise me."

"I promise."

"You promise what?"

"I promise I'll never do another stunt if I feel unprepared or distracted."

That seemed to calm Elliot down a bit. She sat back down and heaved a deep sigh.

"I should've requested that we get the day off. They would've understood given the extenuating circumstances. I should've known you weren't mentally in shape to do that stunt."

Jessie reached out to rub the top of Elliot's hand.

"I'm a grown woman. I could've said no."

"You're also stubborn as shit. I should've known better. I was selfish. Thinking too much about myself and what this whole sex tape means for me and *my* career. I didn't even consider the fact that you were struggling and distracted by the whole situation too."

Jessie leaned her head back on the pillow. "I guess we found out the hard way."

She noticed Elliot give a little nod as she examined her injured hand.

"Elliot, I really am so sorry that this is happening to you."

"To us," corrected Elliot.

"Right. To us."

Elliot thought for a moment. "I heard what happened with Mike. You know, you can't just beat up every person who makes an offensive remark about me."

Jessie's eyes focused downward as she nodded solemnly.

"But thank you. It's kind of sweet that you were defending my honor."

Jessie felt a subject change was best.

"Have they said when I can get out of here? I still have a stunt to do."

"Calm down there, cowboy. The doctor has to clear you first, but you should be out by tomorrow morning or afternoon. They wouldn't tell me the specifics, but they did say it's a miracle you made it out unscathed. You've got a few contusions, a pretty serious burn on your left hand, some cuts, and I'm guessing a severely bruised ego."

Jessie closed her eyes, her lids too heavy to keep open.

"Very funny. My ego is very much intact. How many people can say they flew through a firebomb, flipped their motorcycle, was thrown from it, *and* walked away? Besides, from what I hear, chicks dig scars."

She heard the faint sound of Elliot's laughter before being pulled back into another deep slumber.

*

Elliot stayed awake for the rest of the night, but didn't mind. She comforted Jessie whenever she woke up and then coaxed her back to sleep. The girl needed rest when all she could talk about was getting back on the motorcycle and getting the shot right. She assured her the crew was more concerned with her well-being than the fact that they didn't get the shot. Production decided to tack on one more day of shooting. Jessie would have all day tomorrow to recover, and if the doctors cleared her, she'd be able to run the stunt again the following day.

Elliot found herself trying to meditate in the darkened room whenever Jessie was asleep. She listened to the sound of Jessie's breathing, her heartbeat on the monitor, and allowed the sounds to become a part of her. She needed to clear her mind and decompress. Today had been the most stressful day she'd ever experienced. In the last 24 hours, she was sure she'd gone through literally every emotion a person could. This room only consisted of her and Jessie, and for a few brief moments she allowed herself to feel at peace, to forget all about what led them here.

Then she remembered.

Her life was a mess. News of the sex tape was everywhere, and it was only gaining momentum. Not only that, but Jessie's on-set accident was all over the news. Some people suggested that the accident was staged in order to shift focus from the star's filmed "sexcapades." It was ridiculous and insulting.

Elliot was thankful that the hospital staff was respectful. They stationed a security guard outside the door and one outside the main entrance to the hospital in order to keep out anyone trying to catch a glimpse of Elliot or Jessie. She arranged with the director to work well into the night tomorrow in order to make up for the scenes she missed filming today. She hadn't left Jessie's side and refused to do so until Jessie was cleared to leave, resting back at the hotel.

*

The studio arranged everyone to be moved to a different hotel for the final few days of shooting. They were still investigating what happened at the last hotel and didn't want to take any chances that a staff member had planted the camera. When Jessie was released, she was driven to the new hotel where all her stuff waited in her new room. Elliot rode with her back to the hotel and made sure she was resting comfortably before going to her new room to crash. She'd been up most of the night and all morning. They canceled the day's shoot due to the accident and the fact that everyone had to switch hotels. Besides, it was pretty clear everyone needed a break. The heat was out of control, and the crew was overworked; everyone welcomed the respite.

It also gave Jessie another day to recuperate before attempting the stunt again, which Elliot was thankful for.

Elliot had been in touch with her publicist all day, who was hard at work fielding calls and putting together a statement that they both approved. It essentially spoke of a private moment among two consenting adults being illegally and unknowingly filmed and shared publicly. It was a sign of disrespect and an invasion of privacy. They were working on tracking down the culprit and planned on bringing them to justice.

Elliot was satisfied with the statement. The phone was now in possession of her lawyers, who were also working on an injunction to get the video taken down from the internet. She knew by now it'd probably been downloaded a million times, but she tried not to think about that.

In the meantime, she stayed off the internet, and only answered calls and texts from Liz, Hayley, and

Morgan. And Jessie, of course, but she was probably sound asleep by now.

She still put off calling her mom, who had now left 17 messages. She didn't know what to say to her. Though her messages of support and concern were comforting, she just needed to get some rest before speaking to her. She was too exhausted and delirious to think about anything else.

Elliot fell into her bed, still fully clothed from the day before. She thought briefly about Jessie and wondered how she was doing. She thought about going back down to her room and checking on her before falling asleep.

Hours later, she awoke to a pitch black hotel room. It was two am, and she'd somehow managed to sleep for almost 10 hours straight. She was groggy and dazed and fumbled around for a light switch.

She stood for a moment, trying to wake herself up. In desperate need of a shower, she went into the bathroom, turned on the water, and waited for it to get warm.

She started to take off her shirt, but stopped, unable to remove it. She stood frozen in the middle of the bathroom while the steam from the water materialized around her and fogged up the mirror. She looked around, slowly examining each white wall of the bathroom and every shelf and drawer on the sink. She opened the bathroom door and peeked her head out, then closed it again. She needed to shower. She needed to wash away the filth and grime from the last 36 hours. She felt dirty, in desperate need to wash away her sins. What she'd done with Jessie didn't feel sinful, but in the eyes of her once adoring public she was a whore. She managed to read a few choice words about her online before banning herself from the internet; they were not kind.

She needed to cleanse herself, but couldn't bring herself to remove her clothes. What if there were cameras somewhere in the bathroom. What if they were everywhere? She couldn't see them, but that didn't mean they weren't there.

The steam filled the room to the point where she could barely see in front of her. Her chest tightened, and she couldn't seem to catch her breath. She shut off the water and ran out into her room to grab her phone. She sat on the floor with her back against the bed and called the one person who might understand what was happening.

"Hey. Did I wake you?"

"Not really. I've just been watching TV. I'm feeling a lot better." Jessie's voice was stronger than it had been earlier. She sounded almost back to normal.

"I'm sorry, I just didn't know who else to call." Her voice broke. It had to have been obvious to Jessie that she was crying.

"Elliot? What's wrong?"

"I...I can't...I need to shower. I need to...I don't want them to see me."

"Who?"

"Everyone!" The tears fell freely now.

"What room are you in? I'm coming over."

"No. I can't be here. I can't be in this room anymore."

"Okay. It's okay. Just breathe. Come to my room then. We'll figure this out together."

Elliot nodded, trying to reign in her tears. "Okay. I just need some time. I'll be there in 20 minutes."

"Take all the time you need. I'll be here."

*

A half-hour later, Elliot was at Jessie's door. She had to fight every urge not to fall right into Jessie's arms when the door opened. She nodded hello and walked through the door, defeated. Jessie put an arm around her and guided her into the room. Elliot stopped and looked around. It took her a minute to realize what Jessie had done. The entire room was covered in white satin sheets. There were sheets covering the window and every wall, sheets draped over the dresser, the desk, the television, and entertainment center. Everything was covered in white. Pure and untainted, a fortress blocking out everything. There was no chance in hell any camera could penetrate it.

Elliot turned to Jessie and wrapped her arms around her, pulling her close and burying her face in her neck.

"Thank you."

"You're welcome."

"How did you do this?"

"I asked housekeeping to bring me some extra sheets." She took Elliot by the hand and brought her to the bathroom. "Come on. Let's get you cleaned up."

She pushed the bathroom door open and led Elliot inside. Elliot was overwhelmed to find a sheet covering the mirror in the bathroom as well. She was near tears again when she turned to see the bathtub filled to the brim with bubbles and hot water. Tea lights adorned the sides of the tub. She turned to say something to Jessie, but words seemed to fail her.

Jessie shrugged and smiled. "I had housekeeping bring up a few other things, too. Come on. Let's get you undressed." She turned Elliot around so that her back was to her and grabbed the hem of her shirt. "Is this okay?"

Elliot nodded, and Jessie pulled the shirt over her head, then moved to take off her bra. "Is this okay?"

Elliot nodded once more and the bra was gone. Jessie wrapped her arms around her protectively, allowing Elliot to get used to her newly exposed skin and held her for few moments.

She moved her hands down around Elliot's waist to the button of her jeans.

"Is this okay?"

Elliot's breath hitched, and she paused for a moment.

Jessie kissed her shoulder. "It's okay. You're safe."

Elliot nodded, and Jessie unzipped her pants, removing them along with her underwear until Elliot was completely naked. She guided her to the tub and helped her in, rubbing her shoulder and trying to get her to sit back into the tub.

"Take your time. Relax. I'll be right outside if you need me. It's just me and you here. No one else."

Elliot nodded once again, and Jessie headed out the door.

"Thank you," Elliot's voice trembled as she shut the door behind her.

*

The next day, Elliot felt refreshed. Much of it had to do with how amazing Jessie was last night. She wanted to stay the night with her, but they both agreed it was best to sleep in their own rooms.

Elliot realized she hated being on set without Jessie. It was a weird, uncomfortable feeling and not just because everyone looked at her with either pity, lust, or judgment;

she'd just gotten used to the other girl's presence. She knew Jessie had to rest up for tomorrow. It was the last day of filming, and they needed to nail that stunt. There was only one more night at the hotel after that before they all headed back to Los Angeles.

The day moved fairly fast as they had a lot of lost time to make up for. Elliot filmed most of her scenes with James, Ashton, and Drew. For the most part, everyone was very professional, but there was definitely tension in the air. It seemed no one really knew how to act around Elliot. Hell, even Elliot didn't know how to act. She put on the bravest face she could muster and trudged on. She was pretty sure her performance in each scene was subpar, but no one said anything. She definitely wasn't looking forward to seeing the final product.

She sat in the makeup chair getting touch-ups as they set up for the next scene and heard Drew's voice in the distance. He said her name a couple times. He was obviously talking to someone, and it was clear he didn't know Elliot was nearby. She turned to see him talking to Ashton and James and barely made out what he was saying.

"I mean, damn. No wonder she rejected me. I had no idea she was a card-carrying dyke."

Elliot felt all the air leave her lungs, but stayed where she was. She watched as James's fists clenched.

Drew continued. "But did you see the video? God, that girl has got a seriously hot ass."

Ashton reacted before James did, grabbing Drew by the shirt and pushing him up against an expensive piece of camera equipment.

"It was you, wasn't it? You piece of shit!" Ashton charged after him.

"Whoa!" Drew cowered, trying to keep away from both Ashton and a visibly upset James. "It wasn't me! I swear!"

"Bullshit! You obviously have a thing for her. What, were you jealous? Is that why you did it?"

"No! I didn't...it wasn't me! I wouldn't do that to someone!"

"Oh, but you don't mind watching it over and over again, making lewd comments about it? She's your co-worker. She works her ass off. Harder than anyone here, and you have the audacity to talk about her like that?" Ashton was in his face as James continued to fume. Elliot could tell he was trying to control his anger.

"I'm sorry. You're right. That was really disrespectful of me. I shouldn't have said anything, but I swear I had nothing to do with it."

Elliot was torn. She wanted to put a stop to this, but she also kind of loved watching James and Ashton put the fear of God into Drew. She didn't really think Drew would do something like this. Granted, he was a bit of a douche, but he wasn't cruel. And frankly, he wasn't smart enough to pull off something like that.

Security came and diffused the situation. Drew didn't say another word to anyone except on camera when it was necessary.

Elliot opted to stay out of it, but reminded herself to hug James and Ashton and thank them for having her back.

She had no idea how, but she managed to get through the rest of her scenes. Even the ones she had with Drew. She could barely look at him, but forced her way through them nonetheless. Elliot was done for the day, waiting for Hayley to film her last scene. She waited for her in the tents and watched on the monitor. There were a few people left behind in the tents, waiting to be excused for the day. Elliot tried to ignore their stares as she sat waiting. She felt exposed, completely naked in front of everyone in the tents who, by now, had to have watched the video. Even people who she knew respected her must've watched it, though they'd never admit it. It was like a bad accident. How could they look away?

She just needed to get through the next two days. Then she could go back to Los Angeles...where she'd face a slew of questions, whispers, and even more prying eyes.

*

When Elliot got back to the hotel, she went straight to Jessie's room to check on her. She was healing quite nicely and already back to working out. She was in the middle of a set of pushups when Elliot returned.

It was rather impressive. After an accident like that, Elliot would be afraid to even leave the house. Jessie was a special kind of person, and Elliot admired her persistence. She wanted to ask her how she was holding up with the whole sex tape situation, but had no idea how to even start that discussion. Jessie seemed somewhat impervious to it all, but Elliot knew she had to have been bothered. Perhaps the reality of it all hadn't set in yet since Jessie had been dealing with the accident and hadn't really been in contact with anyone outside of the film.

Elliot figured it was best to bring it up at another time. Jessie needed to focus and prepare for the stunt tomorrow.

They talked for a bit. Jessie assured her she was ready and more than capable of pulling off the stunt perfectly. She'd leave no room for error, and Elliot believed her.

*

It turned out Jessie was *not* ready. The next day when the shot was set up, Morgan confirmed she was ready to go. Kat was ready. The cameras were ready. The set was quiet, but Jessie just stood there, eyeing the motorcycle and willing herself to get on. She couldn't move. Kat came up to her and put a hand on her shoulder.

"Jess, come on. You can do this. You're ready. We ran it five times this morning."

That was true. She'd been on the bike multiple times already today to rehearse. So why was she freaking out now? She looked over at the tents and saw Elliot standing there watching. She then looked down at her injured hand. The bandages were gone, and it was healing nicely. It didn't hurt anymore, but for some reason, she started nervously rubbing it with her other hand.

Kat continued to try to coax her onto the bike, but Jessie backed away and walked over to Morgan.

"Hey," she said quietly to Morgan. "Can you...I just need...I need some time. A few minutes. Please. Can you do something?"

Morgan nodded sympathetically and got on the radio.

"Nate sorry for the delay. There's a problem with the pyrotechnics. I need another 15 minutes to fix the issue."

A voice came over the radio. "Copy that. Everyone stand by. Morgan, confirm when ready."

Jessie thanked her silently and took off jogging towards the trailers, not stopping until she reached hers, and went inside. She grabbed her phone and texted Elliot.

I need you.

As if on cue, the trailer door opened, and Elliot came in.

"Jess, are you okay?"

"I can't do this. I can't. I was lucky last time. Really lucky. If I crash again...I just can't."

Elliot wrapped her arms around her and squeezed, trying to help regulate her breathing.

"I've never freaked out like this. Something's wrong. You told me to admit if I wasn't prepared for a stunt. Well, I'm not prepared. I can't do it."

"Shhh. It's okay. Just focus on your breathing. Here, sit down." She guided her to a chair, sat her down, and knelt down in front of her. "Hey, look at me."

Jessie took a few deep breaths and met Elliot's eyes.

"You can do this. I saw you execute the practice runs perfectly."

"That was practice. The explosion didn't even go off."

"Since when do you care whether or not there's an explosion? An explosion is nothing to you. You never bat an eyelash any time Morgan detonates something, and just the noise alone is enough to startle the shit out of me. You're not afraid of the explosion. You're not afraid of the stunt. You're afraid of your own fear."

Jessie scoffed through her panic. "That doesn't even make sense."

"Sure it does. You're afraid of the fact that you're afraid, and you don't know what that means for you. If something goes wrong again this time, it'll only add to your fear, and you don't know how to face that because you've never had to before. You have yet to face something that really terrifies you. Well, this is it. So you can face it head on, or you can run. Either way, I won't judge you. I will tell you this though. I wouldn't even suggest you do the stunt if I thought there was the slightest chance you'd get hurt. I think you should do it. I believe in you. You don't know how to fail."

"I failed spectacularly the other day."

Elliot shook her head. "That day was a shit storm, and today it's still a shit storm. But we can't let this destroy everything we've worked so hard for. You can't let fear dictate your life."

Jessie was silent, almost stunned at how much sense Elliot's words were making.

"Come on." Elliot stood and grabbed her hand to pull her up. "Do the stunt so we can finish filming and get the hell out of this desert."

"And you're sure I can do it?"

Elliot placed a soft, sweet kiss to her lips.

"I'm sure."

Elliot led her out of the trailer. They didn't bother exiting at different times. There was no point in trying to keep their relationship a secret. Or whatever this was. Could it even be called a relationship at this point?

Either way, Jessie thanked her and walked back to where everyone waited. She was confident, strident, and didn't remotely hesitate before hopping on the bike, putting on her helmet, and signaling that she was ready.

She nailed the stunt perfectly. In one take.

*

The day was winding down, and Elliot had to wait around to see if they needed her for any re-shoots. Even though the sun was setting, crew members, actors, and extras were all gathered in the tent to get out of the heat. Some were staring at her and whispering, but Elliot tried tuning them out. Thankfully, most of them left her alone and didn't even look in her direction.

She glanced to her left and noticed Cassie staring at her wickedly, giggling and murmuring something to the girl next to her—another actress on the film who had a smaller role like Cassie's. Elliot turned away and tried to ignore them.

Jessie had just finished her last stunt, which was a simple hand-to-hand combat scene with Kat, then met up with Elliot in the tent with a cold bottle of water.

Elliot greeted her with a smile and took the bottle from her.

"How did it go?"

"Piece of cake."

"Mmm...cake. I'm hungry."

"We're almost done here, I think. We can get some food after. Thank God tonight's our last night here."

"So close to freedom." Elliot's smile soon faded when she realized what her "freedom" entailed. Nonstop scrutiny while trying to do some damage control. Not to mention the constant thought that no matter where she goes or what she does, people have seen her completely naked and in very compromising sexual positions.

She didn't want to think about it anymore. She was tired of constantly feeling like she was going to throw up. She just had to wait out the storm.

Suddenly, the TV monitors in the tent started flashing and went blank. Everyone looked around to see what was happening.

The screens turned back on, and Elliot had a sinking feeling in her stomach when a video started playing. She turned to look at Jessie, who was completely ashen. Her own voice began to come from the monitors.

"God, that feels amazing."

She felt herself hyperventilating as she watched herself get pushed against the vanity by Jessie.

Morgan jumped up and ran outside, mumbling something about cutting off the generator.

Jessie's face looked completely bloodless as she stared at one of the screens.

Elliot's own words echoed in her ear once again.

"Are you ready for me, Jessie?" The scene changed to show Elliot hovering over Jessie on the bed.

Someone was playing the entire two-minute edit. She looked around, panicking, trying to figure out who was behind it. At some point, Hayley stormed in demanding to know what was going on and who was doing this. A few people laughed, watching the screen while others turned away and refused to watch out of respect for Elliot. Others were just as shocked and speechless as Jessie.

The scene changed again. The last thirty seconds of the video played, showing Jessie over Elliot, kissing her while saying, "You're so beautiful."

Jessie ran out of the tent, the embarrassment too much for her to handle. The monitors in the tent all turned off suddenly, along with the lights and air conditioning. Morgan must have shut off the generators. Elliot immediately chased after Jessie, leaving Hayley to interrogate everyone and insist that the person responsible confess.

She found Jessie a few yards out of the tent with her hands on her knees like she was bracing to throw up. Elliot put her arm around her and started walking towards the trailers without a word. Morgan and Hayley soon caught up with them and told them that they were wrapped and free to go. There were a few other things that needed to be done before the crew started striking the set, but they were able to go back to the hotel.

Morgan swore to them that they'd be avenged. Elliot didn't have it in her to respond.

*

That night, they split up after Elliot dropped Jessie off to her room and then went back to her own room to pack. Neither girl said much to the other on the way back to the hotel. The entire ordeal was a never-ending nightmare.

Jessie sat on her bed staring at nothing when she heard her phone go off. It was a text from Elliot.

I finally talked to my mom. It was the most awkward conversation I've ever had in my life. But she was supportive. She's flying into LA and taking me to lunch next week.

Jessie texted her back.

I've been putting off talking to anyone. I told my friend Peyton I'd call her when I'm back in LA.

Her heart sank when she read Elliot's response.

I hate this. I hate whoever filmed us. I hate whoever put the video up on the monitors. I hate that you've been dragged into this. I'm sick of feeling paranoid all the time. I'm sick of the paparazzi being camped out front, waiting to get a shot of the porn star. I'm sick of everyone staring and whispering. I don't know how much more of this I can take and it's only been three days.

Jessie tried to think of a comforting reply, but there were no words that could possibly make Elliot feel better. She sent her a quick text telling her to meet her at the back entrance of the hotel in ten minutes. Then, she called Kat.

Five minutes later, Kat showed up at her door dangling a key in front of her.

"You owe me."

"I know."

"Seriously, Jessie. You owe me. This was not easy to get."

"I know."

"I heard what happened in the tent. That's so shitty. I'm really sorry."

Jessie nodded solemnly. "Thanks."

*

Five minutes later, Elliot opened the door to the back entrance, looking around first to make sure no one was around. When she pushed the door open and stepped out, she was greeted by one of the sexiest sights she'd ever seen: Jessie in a leather jacket and tight jeans sitting on a motorcycle. She had her hand extended to Elliot.

"Come on, beautiful. Hop on."

"What...where did you get this?"

"I borrowed it from the film. Shh. Don't tell anyone."

"Jessie, you could get fired for this."

"At this point, I suppose anything is possible. But it should be fine as long as I bring it back here by noon tomorrow."

Elliot flashed her a grin.

"Where are we going?"

"We need to get the hell out of here. It's 65 miles to Vegas. Feel like going for a ride?"

She handed her a spare helmet. Elliot didn't hesitate to put it on and mount the bike behind Jessie.

"Let's go."

*

Elliot loved this. She loved being on the motorcycle speeding away into the night with her arms wrapped around Jessie's waist. The faster they drove, the freer she felt. She gripped Jessie tighter, pushing her chest up against her back. This was just what she needed—to be lost with Jessie on a deserted road in the middle of nowhere. She got lost in the feeling, lost in the speed and movement, lost in the way Jessie felt in her arms. Her whole body vibrated and came to life.

They'd been driving for at least half an hour when Jessie pulled over to the side of the road, shut off the engine, and got off the bike to take her helmet off. It was dark out, but Elliot didn't miss the way Jessie's hair cascaded down her shoulders in the moonlight. Elliot stayed where she was seated on the bike, but took off her helmet too.

"Everything okay?"

"Yeah, I just needed to stretch my legs and get some water." Jessie reached into her bag and pulled out a bottle of water. She took a drink and then offered it to Elliot, which she gladly accepted. The cool water felt soothing to her parched throat.

Jessie took a few steps back and forth, stretching her legs as Elliot looked on. God, she was unbelievably sexy. This certainly was not the time to be having those thoughts—especially after everything that had happened—but Elliot's attraction to Jessie was never in question and it obviously wasn't going away anytime soon. She knew from the other night that whatever they had could never be just a one-time thing, especially after how good she made her feel.

Jessie took another swig of water and tucked the water back into her bag.

Elliot leaned back on the bike.

"So what are we going to do in Vegas?"

Jessie grinned at her. "Whatever the hell we want. We have to get the bike back in..." She looked at her watch. "15 hours. We can drink, gamble, see a show...though it might be too late for that one. We can—"

"Get a hotel room?"

Jessie tried to fight the smile forming on her face and turned stoic.

"Elliot, we don't have to. I just want to get our minds off of everything, and people in Vegas don't care about anyone but themselves. No one there will care what we've done. They care about good buffets and winning at craps. Really, we can do anything. We don't need a hotel. We won't even be there a full day."

Elliot cocked her head and looked at her earnestly. "Why are you so sweet?"

"I don't know how to be any other way around you."

Elliot felt her heart clench. "Jesus, Jess. Get over here."

Straddling the bike, Elliot kept her balance and pulled Jessie to her by the collar of her leather jacket.

"Kiss me."

Jessie licked her lips and nodded. She looked around to make sure they were in the clear. Elliot would've laughed at her trepidation if she didn't relate to it so much.

"I think we're alone."

She watched as Jessie's plump lower lip trembled before Elliot's lips covered it, sliding her tongue along the soft, smooth expanse. An adorable sound caught in the back of Jessie's throat as Elliot's tongue delved into her mouth. She moved her hand to the back of Jessie's neck and pulled her even closer. Jessie almost lost her footing and planted her hands onto the seat for support.

Elliot leaned back against the seat with Jessie's lips chasing hers the entire way. Jessie's lips took control of the kiss, and Elliot was more than happy to relinquish it.

"Jess?"

"Yeah?"

"Take me to a hotel."

Jessie nodded, panting. "Yeah. Okay."

She jumped back on the bike, started it up, and drove the rest of the way to Las Vegas. They couldn't get there fast enough.

Chapter 8

By the time they reached Las Vegas, it was nearing midnight. They took their chances that one of the MGM SKYLOFTS was available for the night and were in luck. Jessie checked them into the hotel under the names Anna Graham and Barb Dwyer, which were just two of the many aliases Elliot liked to use at hotels. They both agreed it was best for Elliot to hang back and not draw too much attention to herself, so she waited by the elevators. She may have gone a bit overboard wearing the hat and five dollar aviator sunglasses she bought at the gas station when they drove into town. They weren't exactly needed at this time of night, but no one seemed to really notice her.

After checking in, Jessie met her at the elevators with the key. They entered the elevator in silence, each taking up their own corner as the door closed, and took the long ride to the top floor where their three bedroom penthouse suite waited for them.

Elliot tried to position herself as far as she could in the corner, out of the security camera's line of sight.

Jessie watched as Elliot's eyes focused on the ground. Jessie tried to keep her cool by leaning against the wall, but what Elliot couldn't see was her hands behind her, gripping the railing with sweaty palms and anxiously awaiting the top floor.

"We'll be safe, right? No one knows we're here. It...it can't possibly happen again, can it?" Elliot asked, unable to look up from the ground.

They both knew she was being paranoid, but Jessie was aware that Elliot needed some reassurance.

"No. Not a chance. It's just us here. No one knows where we are."

Elliot nodded, and they waited in silence until they reached their floor. When the elevator doors opened, they stepped out and found their assigned suite. Jessie fumbled a bit trying to get the keycard in the door. She was flustered, Elliot's words still running rampant in her head. She tried to ignore the mocking laughter behind her.

"You're not as coordinated as I thought you were."

Jessie finally got the door open and smugly gestured for Elliot to go in ahead of her. Once they were in, and the door was closed and dead-bolted with the "Do Not Disturb" sign in place, Jessie flipped on the lights, stopping to take in their surroundings.

"Wow. This is huge."

Elliot shrugged as she tossed her sunglasses and hat on the table.

"It'll do."

Jessie had to remind herself that Elliot had probably stayed in nicer places than this, but this was a first for Jessie. She figured she was allowed to be impressed.

They walked through the foyer side-by-side, passing the kitchen and the first bedroom on the left. They veered right into the first living room, and Jessie immediately took notice of the pool table in the middle of the room. She walked over and ran her fingers along the green felt.

"This is easily the nicest hotel room I've ever been in."

Elliot was a few steps behind her, noticeably silent with a disconcerted look on her face.

"Elliot? Are you okay?"

She seemed to snap out of her stupor. "Yeah. It's just...hotel rooms."

Jessie moved into her, closing the gap between them, and placed her hands on Elliot's arms, trying to comfort her.

"Hey, we're okay. Nothing can touch us here."

It took a moment before Elliot could meet her eyes and when she did, Jessie's heart broke for her.

"I can't think about it. Please, don't let me think about it." Elliot's watery eyes begged her. Her lips were aching to be kissed, and Jessie couldn't stand to see the girl so tortured. She'd been through hell. They both had. Tonight, they were going to forget.

Jessie pulled her in for a bruising kiss, her tongue immediately finding Elliot's, and immersed herself in her taste. Elliot's hot breath against her left her feeling weak and warm. Suddenly, there was nothing more that Jessie wanted to do than throw Elliot down and take her. They'd finish the tour of the suite later. They had all night for that. Right now, Elliot needed her, and as scary as it was for her to admit, she needed Elliot as well.

With her lips still attached to Elliot's, she shrugged off her jacket and let it fall to the floor before pulling Elliot's jacket off too. She ran her fingers through Elliot's hair, moving her hands down to her torso and spun her around to push her up against the pool table. Her desire was too strong, and there was no time to find another surface; this would have to do.

Elliot pawed at Jessie's shirt, silently asking for it to be removed. Jessie granted her request. She pulled her lips away from Elliot and took a step back, her breath heaving, head dizzy and skin flushed. She allowed Elliot to watch her as she removed her shirt, then reached back and unhooked her bra, tossing both to the floor. Next came her boots and socks, and finally her pants, which she pulled down along with her underwear. She stood completely nude before Elliot. After Elliot's eyes studied the expanse of her body, they landed back on Jessie's.

Jessie swallowed hard and felt her body shudder slightly. She looked down at her own body, then back up at Elliot, her eyes trying desperately to convey what she was feeling.

"You're safe, Elliot. I'm right here with you."

Elliot nervously licked her lips and nodded in understanding. Jessie knew that was her invitation to approach. She started slowly pulling Elliot's shirt over her head while the blonde kicked off her shoes and socks. Jessie's hands then moved to unbutton Elliot's jeans, and she pulled them down. She traveled with them, getting down on her knees to continue removing them. Once they were discarded, she hooked her fingers into the band of Elliot's underwear. She tried vehemently to move slowly, despite the fact that she could sense Elliot's arousal. It was intoxicating, but Jessie had to control herself. She needed to wait for Elliot.

She looked up at her with all the compassion in the world. Elliot looking down at her was the most vulnerable she'd ever seen her, and it was the most vulnerable she, herself, had ever been. After a barely perceptible nod from Elliot, she placed a kiss on each thigh and pulled down her underwear, grazing her fingers along the smooth skin of her legs.

She stood back up and placed gentle kisses along Elliot's shoulder, reaching around to unclasp her bra. She felt her breath palpitate with excitement as she peeled the garment away from Elliot's chest. She allowed herself exactly two seconds to admire Elliot's breasts before forcing her eyes back up. Enough people had seen Elliot naked in the past few days. Then it dawned on Jessie. Enough people had seen *her* naked in the past few days too. She blanched at the thought of all those unwanted, perverted eyes watching them and stepped back for a moment, trying to keep her thoughts in check.

"Hey." Elliot leaned forward, pulled her back, and wrapped her arms around her. "You're shaking. Come here. Your shoulders are trembling. I promise it's okay. I'm here with you too. Just you and me, remember?"

Jessie swallowed the lump in her throat and nodded gratefully at her words. She realized she needed to forget about everything just as much as Elliot did. After that, her body took over, giving her worried mind a rest. She practically lunged at Elliot and kissed her, grabbing her ass and lifting her up onto the pool table. Without instruction, Elliot scooted her way fully onto the table. Jessie crawled up on top of her, completely intent on making Elliot forget about reality for a while.

*

"I can't feel my legs!" exclaimed Elliot, coming down from her bliss as she stretched out along the felt on the pool table.

They stayed there for a while, panting and praising each other until Jessie finally managed to move over to Elliot and cuddle her.

"This table isn't very comfortable, is it?"

"Hey, it did its job."

"We're definitely going to have to pay for this felt."

Elliot laughed into her shoulder. "So, what would you say to a bath?"

"You and me, wet and naked together? Let me think on it."

*

Elliot leaned against the tub and absorbed the weight of Jessie's back against her chest, her wet, dark hair tickling her chin as it rested on Jessie's shoulder. She rested her arms on Jessie's stomach. The bubbles had started to disappear, and both girls were more than clean enough by this point, but neither moved from their position.

Elliot planted lazy kisses along her wet shoulder. "Mmm...I don't want to get out."

"Who says we have to?"

"It can't be healthy to be in a tub for this long." Elliot moved her hands up and started massaging the other girl's shoulders.

Jessie relaxed into it. "Well, you're not making it easy for me to get out."

"I can't help it if my hands can't keep off of you."

Jessie hummed in response and took a deep breath. "Elliot?"

"Hmm?"

"What's going to happen when we get back to LA?"

Elliot was taken aback for a moment, not wanting this feeling of ignorant bliss to end.

"There is no LA. Not while we're here, anyway."

"Sorry. I don't mean the whole...controversy. I just mean for us. Things have changed."

Jessie's arms trembled, and Elliot couldn't tell if she was cold from the tepid water or if she was nervous. She moved her hands up and down Jessie's arms, trying to comfort her.

"What do you mean?"

"I mean...are you still going to want that date?"

Elliot had to bite her lip and bury her face in Jessie's back. This girl was fucking adorable. Elliot knew she'd be the dumbest person alive if she declined a date with her. True, things were a bit more complicated now. They'd probably have to be really careful about being seen in public for a while, but right now, with Jessie in her arms—shaking and feeling so small—she didn't care about the consequences.

"Yes, of course I still want to go on that date with you." She wrapped her arms around Jessie's, pulled her back down, and felt her heave a sigh of relief. "I'm not going to lie, Jessie, it's going to be rough for a while. Really rough. And honestly, I'm scared of the moment you decide it's too much for you and want to call this off. I don't blame you, but it still scares me."

Jessie reached her hand back and massaged the back of Elliot's neck.

"Weren't you the one who just gave me a profound lecture on not letting fear dictate your life?"

"Oh, so you're gonna throw that back in my face? Typical woman."

Jessie giggled and Elliot felt like she could burst from happiness just from that sound. This was a shitty situation they were in, but Jessie still managed to make her feel normal. She'd only known this girl a week, but it felt like a year. Perhaps it was everything they'd been through. It was enough to bond two people for life. What was scary was the fact that the shit hadn't even really hit the fan yet. They had no idea what they were in for once they were out of the secluded desert, back to reality in a town unrelenting in its need to know every move Elliot made. But she couldn't let herself think about that. Jessie had literally fucked away all thoughts of the sex tape, and she refused to undo all her hard work.

She nuzzled into her neck and breathed her in for a moment. How was it possible for a person to smell so damn incredible? It was so calm and soothing, she let out a yawn.

Jessie took it as a cue and pushed off of her, pulling herself up out of the tub.

"Come on. Let's go relax in bed." She grabbed the white, fluffy robes hanging on the door and handed one to Elliot as she got out.

*

Once they were dry, they shed their robes and crawled into the California king bed in the master bedroom. Jessie insisted on being the big spoon and cuddling Elliot since Elliot held her so sweetly in the tub. They put the TV on in the background, but paid no attention to it, knowing very soon the sun would come up and their night of make-believing everything was okay would be over.

Jessie was exhausted, but she couldn't sleep. She knew Elliot was still awake too due to her weight shifting every once in a while, so she held her tighter. Elliot gave her arm a squeeze to let her know she was still with her.

She turned around to face Jessie and wrapped her arms around her neck. "I don't want to leave this place."

Jessie closed her eyes and inhaled the scent of Elliot's hair. "I don't either."

"So let's stay. Forever. We'll live here. We have everything we'd ever want. We'd never have to leave."

"I like the way you think."

"So, we can stay?" Elliot asked hopefully.

"Yeah, we can stay." Jessie reached for a little white lie. After all, they were still make-believing that nothing existed outside this room.

*

The next morning, they woke up tangled in the sheets together. Eventually, they drove back to their hotel to gather their belongings and head back to Los Angeles, forgetting all about their thoughts of staying hidden away forever.

Chapter 9

They'd been back in Los Angeles for a couple days and agreed to get settled before seeing each other again. Elliot had to take meeting after meeting with her team in order to do some damage control while Jessie had numerous calls to make. They texted back and forth. A couple times, Elliot informed her that her publicist and lawyer requested Jessie put out a statement, but Elliot assured her that she was in no way obligated to do so. Jessie said she needed to think about it, but knew that it wasn't likely. The less she had to think about the whole situation, the better. She just wanted to lay low, keep away from the paparazzi, do her job, and maybe see Elliot at some point if that was possible. She didn't ask Elliot when they'd see each other again. She figured if Elliot didn't bring it up, then they'd at least see each other on set at the studio next week.

Jessie was at home, folding the rest of her clean laundry when she heard a knock on the door. She didn't have to ask who it was. She knew.

When she opened the door, a hurricane blew past her.

"What the hell happened?" Peyton charged into the apartment, her face full of concern and confusion.

Jessie took a deep breath. She wasn't ready for this.

"They're still investigating."

"My God, Jess. That was…explicit. Like really, really bad."

"Jesus, Peyton! You watched it?"

Peyton's silence spoke volumes.

"Oh come on! Seriously?"

"Not the whole thing!" Peyton defended. "I just wanted to see if it was legit and if it was really you. This isn't the kind of thing you'd normally get yourself caught up in, and I didn't believe it at first."

Jessie plopped down on the couch and massaged her temples. She wasn't prepared to find out her best friend actually watched the sex tape she was in.

Peyton sat down next to her.

"I mean…at least you looked good in it."

Jessie buried her head in her hands. She knew that was Peyton's feeble attempt at a joke, but now was not the time.

"There's no silver lining to this, so stop trying to find one." She couldn't bring herself to look at her friend. "I've managed to avoid this thing for over a week. How bad is it?"

Peyton leaned back against the couch cushion. "I've gotten calls from a lot of people back in Boulder. I basically told them all to mind their own damn business. Except for your parents. I couldn't tell them that. I think you should call them."

She let out a long-winded groan. That was the last thing Jessie wanted to do. She'd planned to call them as soon as she got back to LA, but couldn't. She didn't want to know if they saw it. She couldn't live with the information. As long as she didn't talk to them, for all she knew, they hadn't seen it. The only person she'd had any contact with besides Elliot and Kat was Peyton, and that was only because Peyton wouldn't stop calling her until she agreed to let her come over.

"Jessie, there's one more thing."

Jessie braced herself for the worst.

"What?"

"Maggie emailed me asking about it."

Well, that was certainly the last thing she expected to hear. After Maggie left her, she became a ghost. Jessie had no idea where she went or what happened to her. And no one else seemed to know, or they just didn't bother to tell her. She looked at Peyton incredulously.

"Are you kidding me? She walked out on me and went radio silent for years, and now she emails you out of the blue asking about the sex tape?"

"If it helps, it seemed like she was jealous."

"How could you tell? It was through email."

"Just the way she worded the questions."

"What did you tell her?"

"Nothing. I didn't respond. It's not my place to tell her anything. If she contacts you for whatever reason, I think you should tell her to go fuck herself because you're too busy courting Elliot Chase to talk to her."

There it was again. Peyton's failed attempt at humor. Jessie at least mustered a smile for her.

"I doubt she'll contact me. Just don't respond. I'm sure that's the last you'll hear from her."

Peyton leaned forward and rested her elbows on her knees.

"How are you holding up?"

"I'm okay."

"Jessie, it's me. I've known you for 20 years. Cut the shit. How are you holding up?"

Jessie had to look away. Peyton knew her better than anyone, but she still couldn't look her in the eye when she was feeling vulnerable.

"I'm humiliated, okay? I will never be known as anything else but the girl in the Elliot Chase sex tape. The airport was insane when I landed. There were cameras and flashes everywhere. I was blinded. I wasn't even on Elliot's flight. She landed three hours before me. It was mainly the crew and other doubles on my flight, which means the paparazzi was waiting specifically for me. All those cameras made me feel even more naked and exposed than when the video was released. They know my name, they know my face. It won't be long before they know where I live. God, they watched me do things with her that I would never talk about to anyone because it's nobody's business. And now it's all out there for the world to see. It's just so fucked up, but I can't freak out. If I freak out, then Elliot will freak out even more. She's got enough shit to deal with right now."

"You're allowed to freak out. You're allowed to be angry. Get upset. Fucking yell."

"What's the point? It won't change anything."

"Yeah, but you can't keep it all inside. Especially not for Elliot's sake. She's a big girl. You're hurting just as much as she is."

Jessie suddenly felt the urge to call Elliot, but knew she should wait until Elliot called her. Instead, she decided it was time to face the inevitable.

"Peyton?"

"Yeah?"

"Will you stay with me while I call my parents?"

Peyton offered a supportive smile. "Of course. I'll go get the whiskey."

*

Later that day, Elliot was in her own personal hell. She was called in for an emergency meeting with her publicist, manager, and agent. She'd already met with them twice since getting back to LA to discuss damage control. There wasn't a whole lot of movement in the case since the police were still investigating. They hadn't gained much ground on finding out who was behind the whole thing, and it really upset Elliot that whoever was at fault might actually get away with it.

Her lawyer told her they were trying to get an injunction to keep the video from being broadcast online, but these kinds of requests took time, and they'd have to go through the proper channels to get it done. Elliot didn't like to be in limbo. She hated waiting. She'd already lost weight, sleep, and her dignity over this situation, and things were only getting worse.

Their previous two meetings were to discuss how to position Elliot for her next few projects. She was set to film a new movie called *Feast or Famine* after her current film *Best of Enemies* wrapped, and she was in negotiations to star in a reboot of *Bonnie and Clyde*. She was the director's number one choice and given everything going on with the sex tape, they wanted to make sure the director still wanted her for the role.

She still didn't quite know why she was here, but she paced back and forth as her manager, Ava, and her agent, Kyle, tried to keep her calm.

"How am I supposed to remain calm when you guys won't even tell me why you called me here?"

Liz took a deep breath and stood up from her desk.

"Elliot, have a seat."

"I prefer to stand."

Liz sat back down and looked at her phone. Elliot could tell she was avoiding the subject.

"Will someone please tell me what's going on?"

"We got a call from the studio. They're wavering on their casting choice for *Bonnie and Clyde*."

Elliot stopped pacing.

"What?"

"The director still wants you, but the studio is balking." Liz looked at Kyle, who wouldn't meet her eyes. "She's meeting us here shortly."

Elliot looked at her suspiciously.

"Why?"

Liz looked at Ava for some help, but she was about as useless as Kyle, pretending to text away on her phone.

Liz gestured for Elliot to finally sit down. She complied.

"They didn't get into specifics, but they did state it had something to do with you being a liability."

"The tape." She started to understand and could feel her blood pumping with rage. Elliot stood up again and started pacing. She didn't know why, but her thoughts immediately went to Jessie. For some reason that helped calm her. She kind of wished she was with her right now instead of actually having to face all this bullshit head-on like a grown up. She wanted to be back in Vegas in their little bubble.

"They're thinking of recasting you." Liz took a beat as if this next part was going to hurt. "With Cassie Ryan."

"Tell me you're joking. Cassie? Are you kidding me?"

"It's not definite, but I do know that Lucy Tate has been salivating over this."

"Who?"

"Cassie's agent. Apparently she's been in constant contact with the studio offering up Cassie as a replacement for you and telling them your reputation is damaged. She's basically running a smear campaign."

"And they're seriously considering replacing me?"

"I have sources telling me she tried to get you kicked off of *Feast or Famine* too, but that deal has been in place for months."

"Elliot, I'm sure everything is fine." Kyle finally grew a pair and spoke up, trying to assuage his client.

"How do you know that?"

"I...don't know. But it's Lucy Tate. She's just some hack agent with B-level clients and, from what I've heard, a crazy bitch."

"A crazy bitch who will own all your asses if you don't take me seriously."

They all jumped at the interruption and turned to find Lucy Tate lingering in the doorway. With her too-short skirt and too-high heels, she sauntered in and sat down across from Liz, rudely tossing an envelope on her desk. She stuck out her hand.

"It's nice to formally meet you. I'm Lucy Tate."

Liz glared at her and then opened the envelope, ignoring her outstretched hand.

"Charmed." She dumped out the object in the envelope and looked up at her quizzically. "What's this?"

"A flash drive."

"What's on it?" Elliot couldn't help but chime in, needing to know exactly what was going on. She felt Ava place a hand on her shoulder and pull her over to one of the chairs on the side of the office along the wall.

"Your sex tape, darling."

"What!?" Elliot stood up and charged at Lucy. Ava managed to grab ahold of her before she did anything regretful.

"I think it would be best that Ms. Chase drop out of *Feast or Famine* and *Bonnie and Clyde*, allowing Cassie Ryan to accept the lead in both films."

Kyle stood up and leaned on the desk right in Lucy's eye line.

Elliot was livid and moved to stand up again, but Ava held her back. She wondered where Ava kept all her strength hidden. The woman was no bigger than she was.

"This is bullshit!" If she couldn't move, she'd at least be heard.

Lucy rolled her eyes. "Could you kindly tell your client to refrain from speaking to me like that? It's really very unbecoming."

Elliot opened her mouth to spew out a few choice words, but before she could, Liz stood up.

"Get the hell out of my office."

"I don't think you understand what I'm getting at," Lucy replied calmly. "It's in your client's best interest to do as I ask. This isn't the edited version of the tape. I have in my possession the entirety of Ms. Chase's raunchy little amateur porno. All six hours of it. It'd be a shame to see more footage released. Unless, of course, she bows out of those films."

Elliot jumped up and snatched the flash drive from her hand.

"How did you get this?" She was ready to throw punches.

Lucy simply laughed. "By all means, keep that one. I have several copies. You can have it as a little keepsake of your torrid affair with that dyke stunt double."

"Don't talk about her like that! In fact, don't talk about her at all." Elliot got in her face.

Lucy had no reaction. "Ms. Chase, I suggest you calm down before you really piss me off."

Elliot's jaw tightened and her teeth clenched. "It was you. You set it up. You're the one who filmed us."

Lucy feigned ignorance and placed her hand over her chest. "Why, Ms. Chase, I did no such thing. I wasn't even there."

"But your client was," accused Liz.

It all clicked into place for Elliot. "She's right. Cassie was there. She happened to be at that party, and I know there were plenty of opportunities for her to sneak into that room and set up the phone." Her mind flashed back to the party, trying to remember every time she saw Cassie that night. "You put her up to this! You told her to plant the camera, didn't you?"

"I really don't like being falsely accused of things."

"How else would you have the whole video?"

"Someone sent it to me anonymously, and I just happen to be using it to my advantage." She took a challenging step towards Elliot. "Drop out of the films, or I'll release five more minutes of footage for every day you don't. You have exactly 24 hours before the first five minutes gets released. I'll await your call." She looked Elliot up and down. "I've seen it, hun. Trust me, you don't want that to get out. There are far dirtier things you did that night than what was on the two minute supercut."

With that, Lucy walked out, leaving the four of them somewhat speechless and very livid.

139

Liz gave Elliot a sympathetic look. "We'll get to the bottom of this. She's not going to get away with it. In the meantime, you're not quitting anything."

"Maybe I should."

"You can't be serious. Let's think about this for a minute."

"There's nothing to think about. I can't have any more of that tape released."

"Let's just talk this through before you do anything rash."

"This isn't a rash decision. I'm not letting that monster release a single second of the footage. Jessie doesn't deserve that."

Liz leaned back and cocked her head. "Jessie? What does she have to do with it? Elliot, this is your life. Your career."

"It's hers, too. She's just as affected by this as I am, and I'm not going to drag her into this even more than she already is."

"Hear me out, Elliot. I know you want to protect Jessie, but you have to think about this logically. That's what you pay us for. We take the burden so you don't have to. Please just trust me on this. I have a call scheduled with the legal team today, and they can tell us what the next step is. I'll have them relay to the police to check out Lucy or Cassie as possible suspects. It could be that someone *did* anonymously send her the raw file. This will take time. You have to be patient."

Elliot sat there pouting like a child. She hated that Liz was making sense right now.

"Okay. You're right. But if this isn't solved in 24 hours, I'm opting out of the films."

"All I ask is that you give us time to figure this out, okay?"

Elliot nodded.

"I know this sucks, and you don't deserve it. That Jessie girl certainly doesn't either, but you can't jeopardize your career and allow yourself to be bullied by this woman."

Elliot could feel herself starting to tear up again. Why did she have to pursue Jessie so hard? Why was she stupid enough to throw a party in her hotel room? Why did she invite Cassie when everyone was clear about their disdain for the girl? Why did one single night of passion turn into her worst nightmare? And why was it that the only thing she could think about right now was the girl she spent that night with?

"You should go home. Get some rest. Try not to think about this. I'll call you with any updates. We'll regroup tomorrow morning with a plan."

"I have to be on set at noon for a costume fitting," Elliot reminded her.

"We'll have something figured out by then. Elliot, I know you're going to fight me on this, but I think it's best that you stay away from Jessie."

"What?!"

"Just for the next few weeks or so."

"Liz—"

"I'm serious, Elliot. The last thing Lucy needs is more fuel for the fire, and the paparazzi are watching you like a hawk. If you want this to die down, you can't see her."

"I can't agree to that plan."

"You have to. She'll understand. Ava and Kyle agree. We talked about it before you came over. It's for the best."

Elliot closed her eyes and let out a silent sigh. Her team was the best in the business, and this kind of thing is exactly what she paid them for. She'd have to be the dumbest person alive not to listen to them.

"Okay. I won't see Jessie for a while. Except on set. I can't control that."

"But you don't have to talk to her on set."

"You're right. Okay. I won't see her, and I won't socialize with her on set."

Elliot was going to be smart about this. She had to. Her career was at stake, and she didn't want Jessie to suffer any consequences from her decisions.

*

Elliot couldn't relax. She felt sick to her stomach, pulling her car over two separate times because she almost threw up. Both times were a false alarm, but her stomach was still queasy. She kept the windows down for the rest of the drive.

When she reached her destination, she sat in her car and kept telling herself she was doing the right thing. She repeated those words. She was so tired and just wanted to sleep, so she got out of the car and told herself that she wasn't going to see Jessie. She'd text her and let her know what was going on and that was it. Jessie would understand. She knew she would. She just had to wait until everything blew over.

She paced back and forth outside of Jessie's apartment building, trying to calm herself down and convince herself that Liz was right. She tried reminding herself that her team knew what was best for her. Jessie was under enough pressure. She didn't need the added stress of Lucy's threat against Elliot, and she didn't want Jessie dragged even further into this. She stopped pacing and stood for a moment, looking back and forth between her car and Jessie's apartment, trying to decide between listening to her head or her heart.

She didn't even remember knocking, but when the door opened and she saw Jessie on the other side of it, Elliot instantly forgot everything she and Liz talked about. Jessie greeted her with those big green eyes, obviously surprised to see her. Elliot didn't hesitate to throw herself into Jessie's arms, and the other girl was all too happy to wrap them around her.

So much for being smart about this.

Chapter 10

Jessie awoke on her couch the next morning in the exact same position she fell asleep in: on her back with Elliot nestled into her neck. She took a few moments to indulge in the feeling of Elliot on top of her, their breathing in sync. Last night was rather emotional. Elliot cried for an hour straight, and Jessie couldn't get anything out of her except sobs and hiccups. She held her until she was ready to talk. Once her crying subsided, she told Jessie about her meeting with Lucy and how she had one day to decide what to do before more footage got released.

Jessie was pissed, but showed no reaction. She simply let Elliot continue with her story, offering words of encouragement, and then held her for the rest of the night until they fell asleep on the couch.

Jessie ran her fingers along the small of Elliot's back for a few moments before sliding out from under her, doing her best not to wake her. Once she was up, she watched as Elliot turned and clung to one of the couch cushions. Jessie grabbed a blanket from her closet and placed it over her. She wrote a note, telling her she'd be back soon, and left it on the coffee table next to Elliot's phone.

Once she stepped outside, she made a phone call and hopped in her car.

*

After a half hour drive, Jessie pulled up in front of a small office building in Van Nuys. It wasn't much to look at, and it wasn't the nicest part of town either. When she walked in, she noticed there was no receptionist. The carpet was stained, and the air conditioning didn't seem to work, which was never a good thing in the valley during the summer.

She walked past the reception desk and peeked into the tiny office off to the left.

"Hello?"

She was greeted by a snarling woman with the worst case of resting bitch face she'd ever seen.

"Can I help you?" The woman sat at her desk fiddling with the oscillating fan next to her.

"Lucy Tate?" Jessie stepped into the office with her spine straight, shoulders back, and chest puffed out.

"Yeah?" She finally cast a glance over to Jessie. It only took a moment for it to hit her. "Oh, it's you."

"It's me."

She stood up and looked Jessie up and down.

"Let me guess, you're wearing a wire?"

Jessie scoffed and shook her head.

"Recording this conversation on your phone?"

Again, she shook her head.

"Somehow, I don't believe you."

Jessie pulled her phone out of her pocket and put in on the desk to show her that it wasn't recording. Lucy looked at her expectantly, so Jessie took it a step further. She took off her white t-shirt, revealing her sports bra to prove that she was not, in fact, wearing a wire. She actually welcomed the air hitting her stomach. It was stifling in here.

She threw the shirt next to the phone and quirked an eyebrow at Lucy.

"Need me to take off my pants, too?"

"No, thank you. I've seen you naked enough to last me several lifetimes."

Jessie refused to let that comment get under her skin as she put her shirt back on.

"You wanna pat me down?"

"Let me guess. You've come to defend your girlfriend's honor?"

"Well, hers and my own. As you just reminded me, I was in that video too."

"My fight is with Elliot and that bitch of a publicist she has. Not you. It's unfortunate that you got caught up in all this, but I suppose every war has its casualties." Lucy sat back down and put her feet up on her desk.

It was too stuffy in here, and Jessie could barely stand to look at the woman's face for much longer, so she decided to lay everything out.

"You can't possibly be stupid enough to blackmail Elliot. That implicates you in several illegal activities."

Lucy merely shrugged. "High risk, high reward. Something tells me your girlfriend will comply. If she goes to the police, all the footage gets released at once."

"And if she does go to the police, you're willing to go to jail for this?"

"I won't go to jail. There's no proof that I had anything to do with that video. It was merely sent to me anonymously."

"But you're extorting Elliot. I'm pretty sure that's against the law."

Lucy smirked. "It's more of a trade. I'm offering her a deal. It's basically a mutual agreement between two actresses: one helping the other out by throwing a few roles her way. The tape thing was merely a threat on my part."

"A threat you plan on carrying out."

"If Elliot doesn't agree to the deal, yes."

"What do you want?"

"Honey, what I want, you can't give me. Now I have a Pilates class to get to, so I'm going to need you to run along." She waved her hand towards the door.

Jessie didn't say a word. She grabbed her phone from the desk and walked out of the office. Once she got to the reception area, however, she ducked under the desk and waited for Lucy to leave. Five minutes later, Lucy left and locked the door behind her.

Once Jessie heard her car start, she crawled out from under the desk and sent off a quick text. She waited by the front door for a few minutes before hearing a knock. She opened the door to let Morgan in, closing and locking it behind her.

"Quick. We have maybe an hour before she gets back."

"On it." Morgan wasted no time in charging into Lucy's office and looking around for any kind of evidence that could implicate her. The first thing she went for was the computer on her desk, which she easily hacked into.

Jessie searched around the rest of the office for any kind of clue that could help them before looking over at Morgan.

"Any luck?"

Morgan shook her head. "There's nothing on here. Just a bunch of client files, clippings, business-related emails. That's it." She pounded the desk in frustration. "Damn it."

"Just keep checking." Jessie continued looking around until she came across a large metal safe tucked away in the corner behind some filing cabinets. "Hey, come look at this."

Morgan helped her move the cabinets aside and knelt down to look at the safe.

"Can you crack it?" Jessie looked at her hopefully.

Morgan rolled her eyes. "You really think that on top of being a master in pyrotechnics, a computer prodigy, and having a winning personality, I can also crack safes?"

Jessie looked at her expectantly, and Morgan smiled.

"Well, I can give it a shot."

Jessie kept an eye on the door and checked her phone to see if Elliot had woken up and texted her. She paced a bit and wondered if this was a stupid idea. Not only could she and Morgan get into a huge amount of trouble if they were caught, but perhaps it would be best to let the police handle it even though they really didn't seem to be doing much.

"How much longer?" She walked back over to Morgan.

"I've never done this before. Give me a minute. Look around for something that could be the code."

Jessie went through Lucy's desk drawers. They were a mess, full of loose pieces of paper and old food wrappers. She found a piece of scrap paper with a bunch of random numbers on it.

"Try 21, 39, 52, 25, 19."

"Okay, that's too many numbers. Also, I'm pretty sure you just read off a phone number."

Jessie took a closer look at the numbers. They were written so close together, she didn't realize it was a phone number.

"Okay, scratch that. Keep trying and I'll keep looking."

She emptied out the top drawer and rummaged through everything in it.

"Today would be good, Jessie."

"I'm looking. This place is a mess."

At the bottom of the drawer was a post-it note with what looked like a number combination. She grabbed it and handed it to Morgan.

"If this isn't it, we have to go."

"Done." Morgan popped the safe open and pulled out the contents. There was a laptop.

Jessie's jaw nearly dropped. "Damn, you're good."

"You do realize I didn't actually crack the safe, right?"

"Still, you opened it with such precision. Now let's see what's on this thing."

It only took Morgan a matter of minutes to get into the computer.

"Holy shit."

"What?"

Morgan laughed. "This woman is an idiot."

"Why? What's on there? Did you find it?"

"Yeah, the file's on here, but I need to check a few things. Hang tight and keep looking out for her." Morgan immediately got on the phone. "Teddy? I need you to do some research for me, and I need it done in a matter of minutes. I'm sending some information, and I'll do what I can on my end here."

Jessie wished she could help, but knew she'd most likely get in the way. Morgan knew what she was doing, and she wanted Lucy to burn just as badly as they had, so she continued pacing in the office waiting room, looking out the window for Lucy's car.

After about 20 minutes, she started to get antsy and went back into Lucy's office.

"Morgan, she's probably going to be back soon. Can we hurry this along?"

Morgan finished up her phone call and uploaded the computer files onto her flash drive.

"Just about done. It turns out she was dumb enough to have a cloud account under her own name. I found it in her email trash. The file was uploaded from a cell phone, but my friend couldn't find any credit card records for it. Whoever had the phone didn't turn off the GPS though, and that information came with it when it uploaded. One guess where this video was sent from. And get this, it was an instant upload timestamped right after the video was filmed. There's literally no way she wasn't involved in this whether she planned it or knew who did."

Jessie stared at her in awe. "That unbelievable asshole."

"Now here comes the tricky part. I have the original file here on her laptop. I can destroy it and put an end to all of this, but then that's proof that we were in here trespassing and essentially stealing. I called Liz and told her to have the police get a search warrant right away and to have them search the safe, but there's a good chance they won't make it by five pm. She might very well release more footage."

"But if she finds out we were here, we'd be accused of tampering with evidence, and the whole case could be tossed, right?"

Morgan nodded. "That could very well happen too."

"What do you think Elliot would want to do?"

Before Morgan could answer, they heard a car pull up, and the engine shut off. Morgan shut the laptop and put it back in the safe.

"Too late now. Help me move the cabinets back."

Once they got everything situated back to the way it was, they ran into the reception area and dove under the desk. Morgan winced when Jessie's knee accidentally landed on her hand. Jessie threw her hand over Morgan's mouth to keep her from swearing, which seemed like something Morgan wouldn't even think twice about. In retaliation, Morgan elbowed Jessie in the ribs, then clamped her hand over Jessie's mouth before she could vocally react. They stayed crouched underneath the desk, holding each other's mouths shut. The main door opened and closed, and they watched as Lucy walked into her office and shut the door. They managed to sneak out without her realizing.

*

"Elliot." Jessie knelt down next to the couch and ran her fingers over Elliot's temple, trying to gently wake her. It seemed she'd been asleep this whole time. "Elliot, wake up."

"Hmm?" Elliot turned over and looked at Jessie with a confused look on her face.

"I thought you'd be awake by now."

"Did you go somewhere?"

Jessie smoothed out her blonde hair and kissed her lips. "Yeah, I went out for a bit. Looks like you needed the rest."

"What time is it? I have to be at the studio for my fitting."

"You still have a couple hours, but I'm going to need you to get up. I have something I want to show you."

Elliot reluctantly got up. After washing her face and brushing her teeth, she hopped in Jessie's car as the brunette drove them to their destination.

After a few minutes of silence, most likely from Elliot still trying to wake up, Jessie took her hand and rested it on her thigh.

"So…Morgan and I paid a visit to Lucy today."

"What?" Elliot didn't sound happy. Jessie was afraid of this, but knew she had to tell her.

"I just wanted to see if I could talk some sense into her."

"Jessie, you shouldn't have done that."

"I know. I'm sorry, but she has no right to blackmail you like this." She squeezed her hand tighter, hoping Elliot wouldn't let go. "Anyway, we found some evidence that Morgan's going to make sure gets to the police. They're obtaining a search warrant. It might take a little time, but I think it's safe to say she won't be blackmailing you for much longer."

"Did she threaten you at all?"

"No, but she definitely managed to piss me off."

Elliot gave her hand a squeeze, and Jessie felt a little better.

"I think you definitely shouldn't give in to what this woman wants. Let the police handle it."

"But what if she ends up releasing more footage?"

"Then we'll have to deal with that, but we've dealt with it before. Also, I think maybe I should release a statement."

"You said you didn't want to."

"I know. I still don't like the fact that I have to, but it's time I stop hiding from this. I can't keep avoiding it."

Elliot was quiet for a bit, processing everything.

"Liz suggested I go on the *Today* show for an interview. Talk about how it was an invasion of privacy and be open and honest about the whole thing. Cut Lucy off at the pass. The interview is set for tomorrow morning."

"Will you have to fly to New York?"

"No, they said they'd do it via satellite."

"Are you going to talk about me?"

"Not if you don't want me to. I'll do whatever you feel comfortable with. I told you where my team stands on the situation with us. Liz, Ava, and Kyle think you and I should cool it for a while."

Jessie could feel her body stiffen at the suggestion.

"And what do *you* think?"

Elliot smiled at her and kissed her hand. "I'm here with you, aren't I? I think they can go fuck themselves."

Jessie smiled back. She certainly liked that answer.

"So you're okay if more footage gets released? Because if I don't give in to her demands by 5 pm—"

"I won't be bullied, Elliot. I sure as hell won't let you be bullied either."

Elliot looked down at her lap, trying to hide the blush on her face. She leaned her head against Jessie's shoulder and with her other hand, ran her fingers over their intertwined hands.

"Jessie?"

"Hmm?"

"Why are we driving to the valley?"

"You'll see. Morgan asked that we meet her and Hayley for a little cheering up."

Jessie parked her car about a block away from where she was earlier. She and Elliot ran across the street to where Morgan and Hayley stood. They walked until they were across the street from Lucy's office, hidden by a few bushes. Morgan handed Jessie a cup of Starbucks coffee, and Hayley handed Elliot the Starbucks iced green tea she liked.

"You guys wanna tell me why we're hiding across the street from a dumpy building in Van Nuys?"

Hayley checked her watch. "If James did what I asked, she should be exiting the building in just a few minutes."

Suddenly, the door to the office opened, and Lucy stepped out. Elliot immediately had a physical reaction to seeing the woman, and Jessie wrapped her arm around Elliot's waist, trying to keep her calm.

Morgan held up her cell phone and recorded as Lucy got into her Mazda 3. They heard very loud cursing, watching as she banged her hands against the steering wheel and got out of the car.

"Piece of shit car," Lucy mumbled as she popped the hood. The look on her face was priceless. "What the hell! Who did this? Who the hell did this!" She looked around, and the girls hid deeper behind the bushes. They watched as Lucy angrily threw her phone on the ground and cursed up a storm. She picked up the phone and tried calling someone, but it wouldn't work. "Fucking phone!"

Morgan started laughing uncontrollably.

"Kinda hard for her to drive a car without an engine."

Hayley laughed along with her, and Elliot looked shocked.

"Wait. Morgan, you removed her engine?"

"I can neither confirm nor deny that."

"What did you do with it?"

"It may or may not have been sent to a chop shop."

"Oh my God, Morgan!"

Jessie was relieved. It was the first genuine laugh to come from Elliot since sobbing last night. Though this didn't even begin to make up for the shit Lucy put her through, it was still pretty damn funny.

Morgan kept filming, stating that she'd never get tired of watching Lucy lose her shit.

Elliot looked over at Jessie. "You knew about this?"

Jessie shrugged. "I didn't take part in it, but I didn't exactly tell them not to do it."

"It was Hayley's idea to get James to call her and set up a fake meeting, saying he wanted to be repped by her," added Morgan.

"You guys are evil geniuses," stated Elliot as she happily watched Lucy continue to lose her shit.

"We got your back, Chase. Always." Morgan and Hayley tapped their coffee cups together and each took a drink as a defeated Lucy went back into her office.

*

On the way back from her fitting, Elliot called Liz to discuss strategy. Liz informed her the police were securing a warrant to search Lucy's office and not to worry. Elliot told her that she wouldn't comply with Lucy and would wait to see what happens, at least for now. Liz agreed that was the best course of action, especially since

Elliot would be interviewed by the *Today* show in the morning.

Elliot turned her Bluetooth speaker up as she drove from the studio back to Jessie's place.

"Now, I don't want you to be nervous, Elliot. They're sending me in advance the questions they plan to ask. You and I will go over them tomorrow before the interview. The most important thing is to talk about being the victim of a cruel person's sick, twisted game and how you hope whoever was behind it gets apprehended and punished accordingly."

"Okay. I also plan on telling them I have no regrets about that night. That we were both consenting adults who had a mutual attraction to one another."

"Good. Yes, that's good. If they ask, and if you're comfortable, you can take the opportunity to come out." There was a pause before Liz asked, "Where are you heading now?"

"Jessie's."

"Elliot…"

"Liz, I'm not going to argue with you about this, so instead I'm just going to hang up. I'll see you tomorrow bright and early."

*

Once she got back, Elliot had some hot tea waiting for her, and she and Jessie curled up on the couch. With the TV off, Jessie's computer out of sight, her phone on silent, the curtains closed, and the door locked, it was just the two of them.

They sat and drank their tea as Elliot told her she spoke to her lawyer, who reaffirmed that she shouldn't do a thing, to just wait it out. Her team prepped her on what might happen if Lucy carried out her plan. They warned her that things would probably get worse before they got better, but told her she needed to stay strong.

Jessie put her tea down and placed a soft, sweet kiss on Elliot's cheek, lingering for a moment before moving her lips up to Elliot's ear.

"We will make it through this."

Elliot could feel Jessie's words warming her insides. She looked at the time. Five o'clock was nine minutes away. It was obvious Jessie could tell what she was thinking. She grabbed Elliot's mug and placed it on the coffee table before getting off the couch and kneeling in front of her. She took both of Elliot's hands into her own.

"Hey, look at me."

Elliot looked down at those sparkling green eyes and felt a sudden surge of hope.

"I know I haven't known you for very long, but seeing the way you've handled everything…it just shows how strong you really are. This very well could've just been a one night stand, but I'm glad it wasn't. Because I really like you, Elliot. I know you probably feel conflicted about being with me because it reminds you of the worst thing that's ever happened to you. Honestly, it's the worst thing that's ever happened to me too. But if it hadn't happened maybe we wouldn't have gotten this close in such a short amount of time. I'm going to focus on that—the positive side of this. Even though I'm angry and embarrassed and want to beat the shit out of that woman, I'm just going to focus on you. Maybe you can try to focus on something positive too."

Elliot wasn't expecting that. She really had no idea how Jessie was always able to calm her down, either with her words, her actions, or with just a simple look. She leaned forward and pulled her hands away from Jessie's only to place them on her cheeks. She leaned down and kissed her, trying not to let her tears from Jessie's words ruin this moment.

"I think I can do that." She pulled Jessie up to her level, straddling her on the couch, and kissed her passionately. Elliot took her hands once more as the kiss deepened. Soon her hands detached, and she wrapped her arms around Jessie's waist, pulling her closer. Jessie kept one hand on the back of the couch for balance, and the other combed through Elliot's hair before settling on the back of her neck. Their mouths breathed hotly against each other as Elliot's lips devoured Jessie's, her tongue tasting the sweetness of her mouth.

Jessie pulled back for a brief moment and gazed down at her, running her fingers through Elliot's hair. As good as that felt, her lips felt better, so Elliot pulled her back in for another kiss, this time canting her hips upward and trying to get some sort of friction. Jessie's moan in response was pure poetry. Her hands moved up from Jessie's waist to the hem of her shirt, and she pulled it off without any hesitation.

Jessie licked her lips and looked down at her with complete adoration.

"You want to?" Jessie's voice was barely above a whisper. The adorable way she posed the question made Elliot fall for her even more.

Elliot nodded in response. "Yeah, if you want to."

Jessie smiled. "I want to."

She removed her bra before Elliot had a chance to process and stared at her in awe.

"Wow. You are really, really pretty."

Jessie laughed. "Is that so?"

Elliot nodded.

"How can you even tell when you're only looking at my chest? My face is up here."

Elliot looked up and tucked a strand of hair behind Jessie's ear.

"See? I was right. Really, really pretty." Elliot kissed her way down her chest. Jessie lurched forward and moved her hips against Elliot's. Trying not to be too distracted by Jessie's sensual movements, Elliot took her time exploring Jessie's chest, running her tongue along the sensitive flesh. Jessie unzipped her jeans. She got up for a second to slide them off and straddled Elliot once more.

"Elliot?"

"Hmm?"

"Can I take your shirt off?"

"God, yes."

Elliot was wearing a plaid button-down shirt. Jessie unbuttoned it slowly while kissing a trail along her neck and collarbone. Once unbuttoned, she pulled off the shirt, revealing Elliot's shoulders, and then immediately rid Elliot of her bra. Elliot loved the awestruck look Jessie got whenever she came face to face with her breasts. It made her feel like the sexiest woman alive. Jessie's hands reached out to touch them as her smile grew wider.

"Can I see all of you?"

Elliot nodded and went to take off her pants and underwear. Jessie lifted up to give her some room while taking off her own underwear at the same time. Instead of straddling her again, she crawled down and got on her knees in front of Elliot. She kissed the inside of her thighs, and Elliot could feel her skin twitch from the way it tickled her. It felt incredible. Jessie tugged lightly against the back of Elliot's legs, and she scooted forward, giving Jessie the access she wanted. She trembled with anticipation as Jessie continued to kiss her way up the inside of Elliot's thigh.

She couldn't take her eyes off the girl, and the moment Jessie looked up and they locked eyes was also the moment her tongue made contact with her. Elliot let out a choked cry and bit her lip, trying to concentrate on making this last a little longer.

She couldn't speak. All she could do was feel what Jessie was doing to her and watch as her eyes, locked on Elliot's, danced with delight. She could hear Jessie's excited moans every time she hit a spot that made Elliot's body jerk uncontrollably. In a matter of seconds, with Jessie's tongue immersed in her in the most skillful way, Elliot felt a powerful orgasm rip through her entire body. Her hips lifted up, and she cried out Jessie's name.

It wasn't until she came out of her blissed-out state that she realized there were tears in her eyes. Jessie was still kneeling in front of her, her head resting in Elliot's lap, massaging her thighs and waiting for Elliot to come back to her. Elliot lifted Jessie's chin with her finger and leaned down to kiss her. She leaned further into the kiss, not wanting to lose the feeling of Jessie's lips against hers. Jessie moved back as Elliot chased her lips. She got off the couch and gently laid Jessie down on the floor. She positioned herself between Jessie's legs while still kissing her.

She felt Jessie's lips veer slightly to the corners of her mouth, then her cheeks, and Elliot realized she was catching her tears with her mouth, refusing to let any of them fall. The gesture made Elliot want to cry even more, but she managed to keep her emotions in check.

"You okay?"

The way Jessie looked up at her made her feel like she'd never been more okay in her entire life. She nodded and offered her a reassuring smile. She moved her hand down between their bodies, her fingers aching to bring pleasure to the girl beneath her. She watched as Jessie's eyes went wide. Her mouth hung open slightly, and her lips quivered as Elliot's fingers made contact with the slickness between her legs. Elliot searched her eyes, not wanting to miss a single reaction.

Jessie's breath shook. Elliot would never forget the look of awe on her face when she moved her fingers down and plunged two of them inside her. The strangled moan from Jessie's throat matched the pleading look she gave her. Elliot moved her fingers in and out, building a steady pace, and curled them with every other thrust. She loved how wet and warm Jessie was. She loved knowing that she was the one who turned her on like this.

Jessie's hands came up to cup her face as they focused solely on each other. Then they traveled down to her hips where she held on as Elliot made love to her in the sweetest, most beautiful and intense way she'd ever experienced.

Elliot kissed her and coaxed her down, brushing the stray hair off her sweaty forehead. They breathed deeply, staring back at one another until Elliot rested her head upon Jessie's chest. They stayed there, breathless and blissful, forgetting all about the threats they faced, not even realizing the 24 hours were up some time ago. In this moment, it didn't seem to matter.

Chapter 11

The next morning, Jessie woke up alone to the sound of her alarm blaring. She expected this. Elliot warned her she'd leave before sunrise to prepare for her *Today* show interview, but Jessie still felt a slight tug at her heart, not feeling Elliot in bed next to her. She reached out anyway, grabbing the pillow Elliot slept on in an effort to feel at least the smallest remnant of her presence.

She was met with a folded up note left on top of the pillow. Groggily, she opened it and turned on the lamp on her nightstand. She couldn't hide her smile as she read Elliot's words.

Jessie,

I really loved waking up next to you, but I hate the thought that you weren't able to wake up next to me. Maybe next time we can make up for that. I hope you have a great morning. Try to watch the interview if you get a chance.

By the way, how about that date? I'd love to take you out tomorrow. (You can't see, but I'm actually blushing while writing this, so be gentle with your answer.)

Elliot

Jessie beamed after re-reading the note a couple times. Before she had a chance to get too excited about the prospect of her date with Elliot, she remembered Lucy's threat and immediately grabbed her phone. After a quick

Google search, she felt a wave of relief when nothing had been reported of new leaked footage, but it still didn't stop her insides from feeling a bit uneasy.

She tried to get her mind off of it, thinking about her date with Elliot. She wanted to text her "yes" but would rather respond in person. Or at least over the phone.

Feeling quite satisfied with this turn of events, she threw on her workout clothes, got ready to go to the gym, and made some breakfast before sitting on her couch and turning on the TV in time to watch Elliot's interview.

After two minutes of commercials, Jessie turned up the volume as she watched one of the hosts introduce Elliot, announcing she was being interviewed via satellite from Los Angeles. When the camera showed Elliot, she was seated on a tan couch looking incredible in leggings, a blue patterned tunic, and high black boots. Her hair was pulled up conservatively. It definitely wasn't what Jessie was used to seeing her wear, but she knew Liz had instructed Elliot to wear something more conventional due to the nature of the interview. She still looked absolutely stunning.

Forgetting all about her food, she watched nervously as the host asked Elliot questions about the action film she was shooting and the upcoming films she had in the works. It wasn't long before the interview took the turn she was expecting, and the host delved right into the main reason Elliot was being interviewed.

Jessie turned up the volume even more while her leg shook uncontrollably. Coffee was probably not the best idea this morning.

"Now, Elliot, I know this is a rather difficult subject for you, but we do have some questions about the events that led to a very public sex tape of you being leaked."

Elliot nodded solemnly. "Of course."

"You put out a statement essentially saying 'it was a private moment among two consenting adults that was illegally and unknowingly filmed and shared publicly, that it was a gross invasion of privacy.'"

Elliot nodded. "That's correct, and I still stand by that statement."

"I'd have to agree with you. It was a terrible invasion of privacy. Take me back to the moment when you found out that footage of you involved in several intimate acts with another woman was released to the public."

Jessie cringed at the question and could see the grimace Elliot was trying to fight. She knew they were going for a dramatic effect, but did he really have to be so descriptive about it?

"It was surreal," began Elliot. "At first, I didn't really believe it, but after getting multiple texts and phone calls and seeing it all over the internet, there wasn't much room for doubt."

"Is that when you began to panic?"

"No, I'd have to say the panic didn't set in until the shock wore off. And the shock didn't set in until the denial wore off. I will say that I went through almost every negative emotion one can go through. It only got worse as the story spread. The worst part was that I had to be on set that day. It was extremely traumatic. It still is. The most traumatic experience of my life."

Elliot tried to keep her eyes on the camera, but Jessie caught her looking down a few times as she re-lived everything that happened. She suddenly felt the urge to be there next to her, holding her hand.

"We've heard reports that law enforcement has found out who the responsible party is and are close to making an arrest. Would you care to comment on that?"

"I can't really discuss specifics due to the impending case, so I'd like to respectfully move onto the next question."

"Fair enough."

Jessie watched as the interviewer went through his note cards.

"Can you tell us a little about the woman in the tape with you?"

Elliot shook her head. "All I can say is that she's a very sweet girl who didn't deserve to get caught up in all this. I would appreciate it if everyone respected her privacy."

"Well, I wouldn't be doing my job if I didn't ask if you two are dating. Is there something going on with you two?"

Jessie stiffened upon hearing the playfulness in his voice, but it wasn't the question that had her so frazzled. It was the impending answer. Elliot thought for a moment before answering.

"Well, that all depends on her."

Jessie almost snorted with laughter at her response, remembering Elliot's note this morning. She shook her head and grabbed her phone. It was a snap decision, and it wasn't how she wanted to do this, but Elliot made it pretty clear she was waiting for an answer.

Jessie grabbed her phone and sent off her one-word text while Elliot continued. "I think now you can understand why I'd like to keep my private life private, especially with everything I've been through."

"Of course," he agreed. "You know I had to ask."

Jessie heard a buzz go off and watched Elliot jump a bit.

"Oh! I completely forgot to leave my phone in my bag." Elliot feigned embarrassment on camera as she checked her phone. "I know this is rude, but it might be important."

Jessie leaned forward, her leg still bouncing up and down. She wanted to say she hated how much Elliot made her nervous, but she kind of loved it. No one else had ever made her feel so vulnerable. She couldn't stop herself from grinning when she saw Elliot's reaction to her text. It was the first genuine smile Elliot had given during the entire interview.

"Oh, look at this." Elliot held up the phone and gave a sly smile. "I have a date tomorrow."

The interviewer laughed. "Is that so? And may I ask with whom?"

Elliot giggled. "I thought we were past that line of questioning."

"Like I said, I'm just doing my job."

"Well, I think this safely answers your previous question."

"I'll take it." He turned to the camera. "You heard the exclusive here, folks." He leaned back in his chair. "So against popular belief, things are pretty serious between you two?"

Elliot took a breath before answering. "I am serious about her, but the situation we've been put in has been very testing. The ultimate test, you could say. We're sort of taking it one day at a time. Not many people have the beginning of their relationship put on blast for the entire world to see. Especially the most intimate part."

The interviewer nodded. "I'm sure it's been quite stressful."

The interview went on for just a few more minutes. Things only turned somber once more when he asked if she had any initial suspicions of who released the tape. Elliot simply answered that her head was too clouded to think of any specific names that morning.

Elliot did a phenomenal job. She was honest, forthcoming when she felt safe enough to answer, and reserved when she needed to be. She even threw in some humor, despite the rough situation.

Jessie turned off the TV and headed out to the gym. She wanted to meet up with Elliot, but she had to work out her anxiety. Besides, she was due back on set in three days. She knew Elliot was in and out of meetings for the rest of today, so she decided to get a decent workout in.

Jessie couldn't wait until their date tomorrow.

*

Getting ready for her date with Elliot was the closest to normal Jessie felt since the sex tape incident. She kind of liked the feeling of excitement before a first date— wondering what to wear and whether or not to bring flowers. Granted, this wasn't a typical first date. They were way past that point by now, but she'd missed this feeling. The one she hadn't allowed herself to feel since Maggie. The beginning of something special with someone special.

Jessie must've changed her outfit five times, which was ridiculous, really. Elliot told her to dress casual, but that could mean a number of things. She ended up settling on a pair of gray three-quarter length jeans, and a white v-neck with a blue blazer over it. She wore her hair down and her makeup minimal.

Now all she had to do was wait. Elliot informed her she'd pick her up at 4:00 p.m.

When her doorbell rang, she practically leapt off the couch, but calmed herself before opening the door. All the chill she reined in was gone when she saw Elliot in her doorway, dressed in a fitted red and blue plaid shirt tucked into tight black jeans. A pair of Ray Ban sunglasses rested on top of her head. She looked perfect, and Jessie was completely taken aback.

Elliot's smile was magnetic, and it took Jessie a moment to realize there was a bouquet of flowers in front of her.

"Oh!" She reached out to grab them. "Thank you. These are..." She looked Elliot up and down. "Beautiful. Come in while I put these in water."

Elliot entered but grabbed Jessie's hand.

"Wait a sec." She pulled her in for a hug. "You look great. How do you look so hot in everything you wear?"

Jessie hugged her back. "I was about to ask you the same thing."

They finally released each other. Jessie prepared the flowers while Elliot leaned against the kitchen counter and watched her with a sly smile.

"Are you ready to go?"

"Are you going to tell me where we're going?"

"Where's the fun in that? I'll just say that we're making a few different stops, but the first one is the most important."

Once in Elliot's car, Jessie spent most of the drive watching her in her sunglasses while absentmindedly singing along with the radio. She reached out to take her hand, which Elliot readily gave her, along with a reassuring squeeze and a smile.

*

If Jessie wasn't falling for Elliot before, she was certainly falling hard now based on their first stop. Jessie smiled as she sat in a chair while a five-year-old boy rested on her lap. The chairs were set up in a circle, and she sat across from Elliot, who was reading from *Harry Potter and the Prisoner of Azkaban*. The other kids seated around the circle watched Elliot, completely enthralled as she read each page with conviction, even impersonating each character's voice. As hard as it was to tear her eyes away from Elliot, she found herself looking around the room at all the kids listening intently to Elliot. Their ages ranged from around 4 to 13, though some looked a little small for their age.

Jessie loved the fact that Elliot brought her here. Elliot told her that Children's Hospital Los Angeles was one of her favorite places to volunteer. Over the past year, she'd gotten to know a lot of the sick kids who were often in and out of the hospital. She tried to make time to come by and read to them whenever she could, which lately wasn't often because of her schedule. This was the first time she'd been back in two months and Jessie was honored that she brought her along. Before story time began, Elliot introduced Jessie to most of the kids. A few of them Elliot hadn't met before, so she had the nurse on duty introduce them to her so that they didn't feel uncomfortable. It took no time at all for the newer residents to warm up to Elliot while the ones she knew from previous visits vied for her attention.

Jessie tried not to stare dreamily at her while she dazzled the kids with her dramatic reading, but it was hard not to. She was magnetic and literally sitting right across from Jessie.

After an hour of reading and a round of applause from the kids and even a couple of the parents, Elliot announced that she'd ordered some gourmet sweets from a local bakery. The nurses brought them in. Elliot eyed Jessie from across the room and winked as she scooped up a young eight-year-old girl with leukemia and gave her a piggyback ride to her room. She mouthed, "I'll be right back."

Jessie laughed as she waved to the little girl who then waved back. She felt a tug on her shirt and looked down. It was the boy she'd been holding on her lap earlier. He held his arms up, obviously wanting a piggyback ride too. She tried to contain her emotions seeing those big, hopeful eyes look up at her. She squatted down and he draped himself over her back before she grabbed a hold of him and stood up.

"Where to, good sir? I'm new here, so you have to give me a tour."

She noticed his little finger pointing to the left, so that's where she went. He pointed left once more and led them into a room with four small beds. He pointed to the bed by the window, and she dropped him off as he crawled under the covers. She tucked him in a bit, grabbed the stuffed Donald Duck on the nightstand, and gave it to him.

"You don't talk much, do you?"

He smiled and shook his head.

"That's okay. It's always the quiet ones that notice more. You're probably super smart, huh?"

His smile grew wider, and he nodded.

"Do you want me to bring you a cupcake?"

She didn't think it was possible, but that smile got even bigger, and she had her answer.

"Great. I'll be back in a few minutes."

When Jessie got back to the recreation room, her heart nearly imploded at the sight of Elliot on the floor with one kid braiding her hair, another painting her nails, and at least five crawling all over her trying to show off for their favorite visitor. Jessie was about to join in the fun when a nurse pulled her aside to talk to her privately.

"Jessie, right?"

"Yes."

"Listen, we love it when Elliot comes to visit. She's so good with the kids, and it's plain to see you are too."

"Thank you." Jessie got the feeling by the look on her face that this wasn't exactly why she wanted to talk to her.

"I'm sorry to say that some of the parents are a little concerned with her being here due to…recent events. Particularly her presence here with you. They feel it's not an appropriate fit for her to come here anymore."

Jessie's jaw tightened, and she clenched her fists. She was about to go off on the nurse, but knew by the way the nurse lowered her head that she disagreed with what the parents were saying.

"Which parents?" whispered Jessie.

The nurse nodded her head over to two sets of parents standing in the doorway keeping a close eye on both Jessie and Elliot. Jessie made her way over to them and gestured for them to follow her out into the hall. The other parents in attendance didn't seem too concerned about their presence, only these four.

She turned to face them, folding her arms and straightening her back.

"From what I understand, you don't feel comfortable having Elliot here reading to the kids." She started off calmly, trying to remain respectful of the fact that their kids were obviously sick.

"We don't feel a children's hospital is an appropriate place for someone who participates in and distributes pornographic videos."

Jessie closed her eyes and steeled herself. She wasn't one to lose her head very often, but she found that lately when it came to Elliot, all bets were off and the claws came out. Still, she had to remind herself that these parents were struggling, hurting from seeing their kids in the hospital like this.

She opened her eyes and let out a deep breath before taking a step closer to them.

"What you said is incredibly offensive to Elliot and to me. I don't know if you're aware of what actually happened, but that film was taken without our knowledge. The people who planted the camera and released the footage were arrested. If the reason you think Elliot shouldn't be here is because of that tape, then you're going to need a much better reason, and something tells me you won't be able to come up with one. Even if you do, I'm not letting you take this away from her. Look how happy she is here, and look how happy those kids are. I don't see anyone else taking time out of their day to be here. If you don't want your children to participate, that's fine. I understand. But informing the nurse that you'd like her to ask Elliot to leave is, to put it delicately, a dick move. I won't let you ruin her day, and I refuse to let this stupid tape affect her future volunteer work here. Are we clear?"

She looked back and forth between each parent and watched as they all slowly nodded in agreement.

"Thank you."

She turned and headed back into the recreation room, taking a spot on the floor next to Elliot. The little girl who braided Elliot's hair asked if she could braid Jessie's.

"Sure, in just a minute. I have a special delivery I need to drop off to a room down the hall. Do you want to come with me?"

The little girl nodded excitedly and took Jessie's hand as they each picked out a cupcake from the boxes of treats on the table. She escorted Jessie down the hall to deliver the cupcake to the little boy who was now fast asleep in his bed, clinging to his stuffed Donald Duck.

"Let's just leave it on this table over here," whispered Jessie. The little girl nodded and carefully placed the cupcake on the table before they quietly stepped out of the room.

*

After leaving the hospital, they made their way to the next stop on their date. Elliot felt like she was on a natural high. Her heart usually felt both light and heavy after visiting the children's hospital. She loved spending time with them but hated that some of them had terminal cases. Today, with Jessie being there, it somehow made it a little bit easier. Jessie was a natural with the kids, and she loved watching them interact with her.

They sat across from each other at Elliot's favorite pizza place that boasted the best slices in Los Angeles. By the look on Jessie's face as she took her first bite she knew Jessie would agree.

"This is so good."

"I told you."

Elliot pulled out one of the loose braids in her hair, trying to get it back to its natural state. The polish on her nails had dried and bits of it stuck to her fingers as well. The kids loved giving her makeovers, but they had a tendency to get a little sloppy. She should really know better than to get a manicure from a 10-year-old.

She stared across the table at Jessie, who was already enjoying her second slice, and chuckled.

"What?"

"Your hair," Elliot pointed.

Jessie's hair had far more braids then Elliot's did. They were woven through her dark mane, and she had to admit, it looked kind of hot.

"I like it," admitted Jessie. "It's stylish."

"I do too."

After their slices, they walked to their next stop hand-in-hand. The sun was almost down by the time they reached their destination. Jessie looked up at the old abandoned building they stood in front of.

"Now what?"

Elliot pointed up. "Now, we climb."

A set of stairs flanked the side of the building, and Elliot led Jessie up each flight. There were five flights in all. Elliot had forgotten about the treacherous climb and was winded by the time they got to the top. She knew Jessie was probably laughing at her on the inside, but thankful she didn't show it outwardly.

Once they were on the roof, Jessie took in her surroundings. Others were there as well, along with rows of reclining chairs, a makeshift bar, and a concession stand.

"What is this place?" asked Jessie.

"Rooftop Film Society. They project movies onto that wall over there, and we can sit and watch, stare up at the stars, or take in the view."

"This is incredible! How did you find out about this place?"

"I know people."

"Yes, I suppose you do," replied Jessie, a bit flirtatiously. "So what movie are they showing?"

"*Indiana Jones and the Last Crusade.*"

The look on Jessie's face told her she made the right call.

"Are you serious? I love that movie!"

"I know. I remember you mentioning your obsession with Indiana Jones, wanting to explore and go on adventures when you were a kid. It was cute."

"Hey, he was cool!"

"I'm not arguing. Come on. Popcorn's on me."

Elliot took Jessie's hand and led her to the snack line. They grabbed some complimentary blankets and found two seats together. Elliot could feel people staring. Normally, Elliot wouldn't mind; it's part of her job. But this was her first official date with Jessie, and she kind of wished she could leave her fame behind for the night.

Unfortunately, that was not in the cards. She noticed a few people taking pictures of the two of them sitting together. Jessie seemed to notice this too and slouched a bit in her seat.

"I'm sorry," whispered Elliot. "If you want to leave, we can."

"No. Are you kidding? It's Indiana Jones! It'll be fine. Well, maybe not fine because I'm sure the tabloids are going to have a field day with this, but I don't care. I'm just happy to be with you. On a date. You've pretty much knocked it out of the park, by the way. This is the best time I've had since getting back to LA."

Elliot smiled and grabbed a handful of popcorn before throwing one of the blankets over them and scooting closer to Jessie. They spent the next half hour talking quietly while waiting for the movie to start. A couple times, they were interrupted by fans of Elliot who asked for a picture with her. She was happy to oblige, never wanting to let down her fans, but tonight, she wanted to give all her attention to the beautiful girl who accepted her date on live television. After snapping a few pictures, she sat back down next to Jessie and held her hand under the blanket. They spent the entire movie like that.

The drive home was quiet because they were both exhausted, but Elliot considered the date a success. Jessie made it pretty clear she agreed. When they pulled up to Jessie's, Elliot got out and opened her car door before walking her up to the apartment.

"You really know how to treat a lady," observed Jessie as they reached her front door.

"You really know how to make a girl fall for you." Elliot had to admit it was a rather bold statement, but they were way past formalities at this point. Except for one thing. "Well, goodnight, Jessie. I had a great time, and I'd love to do it again."

She leaned in and gave her a kiss on the cheek, lingering just long enough for Jessie to move in.

"I think it's safe to say you've got yourself a second date," replied Jessie.

Elliot flashed her a flirtatious grin and turned to leave.

"Great. I'll call you tomorrow."

"Wait! What? You're leaving?"

The shock and desperation in Jessie's voice was enough to make her heart flutter. She turned and gave her a mischievous look.

"It's our first date, Jessie. I have to be respectful."

"Well, disrespect me! Please." Jessie ran after her down the hall, wrapped her arms around her waist, and pulled her in for a kiss. It was soft, sweet, and almost chaste if it weren't for the slight tongue action Jessie threw in.

When they pulled apart, Elliot had to fight off every urge she had to follow Jessie back into her apartment, but she remained strong, if only for the fact that she kind of liked teasing the other girl.

"Good night, Jess. I'll see you soon."

Chapter 12

Elliot snacked on some watermelon flavored sour straws on the couch in her dressing room in full wardrobe and makeup. She tried to avoid smudging her lipstick and the dried blood and dirt on her face. Hayley partook in something a bit healthier, opting for some fruit in the basket on the coffee table. She was in full wardrobe and makeup as well, which included faded dark paint around her eyes as part of her character's disguise.

"So the date went well." Hayley took a bite of her apple.

"It was perfect." Elliot threw her head back and dropped an entire sour straw into her mouth before licking the remnants off her fingers. "The entire time, I didn't even think about—"

"The tape?"

"Yeah."

"Good. Jessie's great, Elliot. I'm glad you've been able to work through this whole thing."

Elliot smiled. "Me too."

Hayley rolled her eyes. "Wow, you really like her."

"Yeah, I think I made that pretty clear on live TV the other day."

"Did Liz shit herself?"

"Surprisingly no. I think she's more concerned about turning the focus to Lucy and Cassie for what they did."

Hayley got up to throw away her apple core.

"Speaking of Cassie, did you hear that they cut her role completely?"

Elliot leaned forward. "They did? They're not recasting her?"

"Nope. They fired her on the spot and said her part wasn't important enough to keep."

"Well, good riddance. I hate that I even tried being nice to that girl."

"That's just who you are, Elliot. Too nice for your own good."

Elliot leaned back onto the couch, grabbed her phone, and noticed a text from Jessie.

Good morning, beautiful.

She found herself smiling like an idiot.

"Jessie's on set today," informed Hayley, who caught Elliot in her little moment of reverie.

"I'm aware."

"Are you guys going on another date?" Hayley fussed with the leather straps on her black jacket.

"I want to."

"Are you going to wait for her to ask you?"

"Maybe."

"Elliot," warned Hayley.

"What?"

"If you like her, ask her out again."

"Believe me, I want to. I just don't want to appear too eager." She got up and tossed the candy wrapper in the trash. "I seem to lack any semblance of self-control when I'm around her. Honestly, the only reason I teased her with a little kiss at the end of our date is because I was on my period. Now that I'm done, I just...fuck. I can't wait to see her again."

Hayley stared at her quizzically.

"Crap."

"What?"

"I owe Morgan 20 bucks. She bet me you'd fall in love with her before filming ended. I bet her it would be after."

"Wait, I'm not in love with her. We're still just barely getting to know each other."

"I don't know, Elliot. Going through something that the two of you went through is enough to bond two people for life. It's kind of hard not to really get to know someone in that kind of situation."

Elliot was dumbfounded.

"I...I'm not in love with her."

Hayley smiled at her.

"Okay, Elliot. You're not in love with her."

Before Elliot could say anything else, a voice came over the intercom calling her and Hayley to the set. Their discussion, and Elliot's adamant denial of her feelings for Jessie, would have to wait.

*

As Elliot walked to the set with Hayley, she took a deep breath to prepare herself. She'd been back on set a couple times since the sex tape was released, but each time, she could still feel the eyes of the crew and other actors on her. Today, however, they were looks of pity more than judgment. Perhaps it was due to the newfound revelation that Lucy set the whole thing up.

Elliot started to wonder if it would always feel this way. She wondered if a shadow would always be cast over her because of this one thing that was out of her control.

She missed the feeling of being happy and carefree on set, ready to work hard and play hard. Now, she couldn't wait for this film to wrap so she could start fresh on a new film with a new crew where, hopefully, the sex tape would be a distant memory. In fact, the only part of this whole situation she was willing to hold onto was Jessie. The girl was a reminder of the worst moment of her life, but she was also her savior in a way. Jessie somehow made it easier to get through.

She and Hayley ran the scene a couple of times before action was called. There was a bit of running involved as Elliot's character chased Hayley's. The soundstage was set up as an abandoned warehouse where Hayley led Elliot, trying to stay hidden from her.

The scene only took about an hour to complete thanks to the director's demand for perfection and efficiency, and then it was time for the stunt doubles to be called to the set. Elliot tried to ignore the quickened pace of her heartbeat when Jessie walked onto the set dressed in all black wearing the same face paint around her eyes as Hayley. Elliot hadn't seen her since their date, and she suddenly wished she'd done more than just kiss her goodnight. Jessie walked by, giving her a sly wink before blocking the stunts with Kat. It was nothing too crazy, but it did involve a lot of fight work, this time with more weapons.

Jessie and Kat familiarized themselves with the prop guns and knives while Elliot stared unabashedly at Jessie. Hayley had long since gone back to her own dressing room with Ashton in tow, leaving Elliot alone to deal with her ever-growing thirst.

*

After almost two hours of filming the stunts—normally a very tedious thing to watch—Elliot was still completely enamored watching Jessie. Every move was done with such precision. She remained patient and diligent when she and Kat got everything right, but Marcus had a complaint about the lighting and the camera angle. If Jessie was frustrated, she never showed it.

Every once in a while between takes, Jessie glanced over at Elliot, who was sitting in a director's chair pretending to be busy on her phone, but really watching everything Jessie did. By the time the crew broke for lunch, Jessie was a sweaty mess, and Elliot wanted to devour all of her.

"Hey," Elliot greeted as she jumped out of the chair.

"Hey!" Jessie dabbed her neck and face with a towel, trying not to smudge her face paint more than it already had from the sweat.

"You did a great job out there."

"I must have. You seemed quite mesmerized."

Elliot put her hands up defensively. "I was just sticking around to make sure they didn't need me for anything."

"Sure. Sounds legit," teased Jessie.

As much as Elliot enjoyed their banter, she had other things on her mind. Things that had been on her mind since their date. Things that had escalated quite rapidly in the last couple hours. She grabbed Jessie's hand and pulled her off toward a dark corner behind the facade wall of the warehouse set where she knew no one would find them.

The crew was pretty much all cleared out, and the studio lights were shut off. The only light around them was the dull illumination of the emergency exit lights.

Elliot kept her grip on Jessie's hand as she heard the last few people file out of the soundstage, and the door close behind them.

"Finally," she whispered as she pulled Jessie into her.

Jessie took the invitation and ran with it, pushing Elliot up against the wooden facade wall.

"Miss me?"

"If I say yes, will you make fun of me?"

"Immensely," answered Jessie before leaning in to kiss her.

Elliot greeted her mouth hungrily, slotting her own lips between Jessie's plump, soft ones. She wrapped her arms around Jessie's waist and pulled her closer. Jessie's hands braced against the wall for support as her body pressed up against Elliot's.

Jessie hummed, softly moaning against her lips before pulling away.

"Maybe we should take this somewhere else. Your dressing room?"

"Maybe we should."

Chapter 13

Jessie woke up the exact same way she'd woken up every morning for the past two weeks: Elliot completely naked in her bed with her arm draped around Jessie's torso. Her blonde hair was wildly unkempt, most likely due to the marathon sex they had last night.

They decided it was better to stay at Jessie's place since the paparazzi had been camped outside Elliot's house ever since they got back to Los Angeles. The press had no clue where Jessie lived, so it was a nice reprieve for both of them.

Jessie closed her eyes and breathed the other girl in like she did every morning. It was a way of not only convincing herself this was real, but also a way of keeping this memory with her for the rest of the day.

She wasn't quite sure when it was that she fell in love with Elliot. Perhaps it was the day she met her, but she knew better than that. It was most likely a gradual thing that happened over time, quite possibly sped up by the two of them being thrown into such a terrible situation and having to claw out of it together. But Jessie was sure of one thing: she was in love with Elliot Chase.

Normally, she'd consider this a rather treacherous predicament. She didn't have the best track record when it came to love, and she definitely broke every rule she had by being with Elliot in the first place. But it was moments like this, Elliot softly snoring next to her, holding onto Jessie as if trying to anchor herself, that made her believe maybe this time things would be different. Maybe this time it would work out. Even if it didn't, it was well worth the memory of waking up next to Elliot like this.

Jessie dreaded having to get up, but she knew Elliot needed to get to the set. Jessie had the last few days off. With the film wrapping up shortly, she was actually only needed for one more day of shooting next week before all the stunt doubles were officially wrapped. All that was left to film were a few pick-up scenes with the actors.

She'd been using her time off wisely, hanging out with Peyton and going to the gym while trying to secure her next job. She usually received a few offers every week without having to hunt for work, but lately, she hadn't heard much. She figured it was most likely due to her publicized contract with the current film, how she wouldn't be free to work until after next week. Still, she always liked to have something lined up so there wouldn't be too long of a gap between jobs. She rarely went more than two weeks without work, but she tried not to let it bother her too much.

She had a vigorous workout planned for this morning and needed to get a start on her day. She reluctantly got out of bed, trying not to wake up Elliot so that she could sleep a little longer, and made them breakfast.

She was nearly done making their smoothies and avocado toast when Elliot appeared in the doorway wearing nothing but Jessie's favorite grey button-up. Only, it wasn't buttoned up, and Jessie nearly dropped her plate.

"Jesus, Elliot."

"Sorry. Did I scare you?"

"No. You just...you look really, really good in that shirt."

Elliot looked down at her body and then back up as she bit her lip.

"How good?"

"So good, I'm debating on skipping the gym and making you very late for work."

"Well," Elliot laughed. "We can't have that." She started buttoning up the shirt.

"Wait, what are you doing?"

"I can't be late for work, and you get grumpy when you miss your workouts. Coffee?" She poured herself a cup and pulled down another mug for Jessie.

"Yes, please." Jessie tried to hide her disappointment, but Elliot was right. It would be very irresponsible to spend the remainder of the day in bed. "Those buttons look like they're about to pop."

"Wouldn't that be a tragedy?"

Jessie raised an eyebrow. "More like a fantasy."

They sat and ate in silence for a few moments before Jessie noticed Elliot smirking at her.

"What?"

Elliot shrugged as she took a bite of her toast. "Nothing. Just...I really love our mornings together. Breakfast with you might be my favorite thing."

"What about dinners with me?"

"They're good too. And let's not forget dessert. That's always fun." Her voice dripped with innuendo. "But this right here...I think I like this best. Have I ever told you how beautiful you are in the mornings?"

Jessie felt her cheeks burn.

"Once or twice."

"Well, that's not going to work. I should tell you every day."

They shared a sweet smile and went back to eating in a comfortable silence, neither one wanting to ruin the moment, when Elliot's phone went off.

She looked at it quizzically.

"Turn on the news real quick."

"Why?"

"I don't know. Liz just texted me to turn on the news. Channel four."

Jessie turned on her TV and found channel four. She turned up the volume when she saw footage of Lucy Tate being led out of her office in handcuffs with a headline that read: *Hollywood agent Lucy Tate and actress Cassie Ryan arrested.*

"Oh my God." Jessie grabbed her phone and ran a search for Lucy's name before finding an Associated Press article. "Listen to this. They've arrested them on multiple charges: blackmail, extortion, tampering with evidence, invasion of privacy."

"Wow. This is...good. This is good news."

Elliot's ambivalence was obvious to Jessie.

"This is great news. Why don't you seem happier? They're getting what they deserve."

Elliot nodded. "I know. I just...I felt like things were finally starting to calm down a little. With the arrest, it's going to drag everything out again. People are just going to keep talking about it. If they plead not guilty, then there's going to be a trial, and it'll be dragged out even more."

"I know. It's going to take a long time for people to forget, but this is a huge step towards this nightmare finally being over."

Elliot gave her a smile and conceded. "You're right. It's closer to being over now. They obviously had enough evidence to charge them. It'll be hard for them to prove they weren't involved. Lucy all but admitted it when she came to Liz's office."

Jessie reached out and took her hand.

"They're going to pay for what they did. We just have to wait it out."

"Can we turn this off? I don't want to see her face."

"Of course."

After a few subject changes to happier topics, they finished breakfast. Elliot left for the studio, but not without a rather steamy goodbye kiss that left Jessie completely floored. She needed a few minutes to recover before getting ready for her workout at the gym.

It was official. She definitely loved this girl.

*

Once Jessie changed into her workout clothes, she grabbed her keys and headed out. She headed down the stairs of her apartment complex toward her car. The moment she rounded the corner, she was immediately confronted by multiple flashes and people yelling her name. There were at least 50 people camped out in front of her apartment building, most of them holding invasive cameras with large lenses attached to them.

"Oh God," she muttered to herself. She could feel herself panic from all the cameras in her face and the unrelenting shouts from the crowd as they tried to get her attention.

She bolted toward her car, trying to shield herself from the crowd of people around her. She heard bits and pieces of what some of them were yelling, but the term she heard most was "sex tape." A few of them also asked for a reaction to the news of Cassie and Lucy's arrests. She suddenly wished for an invisibility cloak or the power to teleport to anywhere but here.

Once she was safely in her car, her body went on auto-pilot. She slowly pulled out of the parking spot as the prying lenses kept snapping photos of her. When she was a few blocks from her apartment, she pulled over and tried to regroup, thankful that she managed not to run anyone over in her haste to get out of there.

She closed her eyes and gripped the steering wheel, trying to catch her breath. She felt her entire body tense up while looking in the rearview mirror, making sure no one followed her.

She should've known it would only be a matter of time before the paparazzi found out where she lived. It's not like she and Elliot had been all that discreet, but she still didn't think about how intense it might be if and when they finally located her apartment.

She grabbed her phone and sent Elliot a text.

Hey. Sorry to bother you at work, but it looks like our secret's out. They found me. Cameras everywhere. I think they're still camped out in front of my apartment.

She tossed her phone onto the seat and started the ignition, trying to decide whether to follow through with her plan of going to the gym or head straight to Peyton's for some moral support. Before she could make a decision, her phone rang. Elliot's name appeared on the screen.

"You didn't have to call me back right away."

"Are you kidding? Of course I did. This is terrible. I'm so sorry."

Jessie could hear the concern in Elliot's voice and felt bad for texting her knowing that she was on set.

"It's okay, Elliot, I was just surprised. I'm not used to cameras in my face like that."

"Someone must've seen me leave your place this morning. They weren't out there when I left."

"So much for being stealthy, I guess."

"This is so messed up."

"Elliot, please don't feel bad."

"I can't help it. Are you sure you're okay?"

"I'll be fine. I think I'm just going to head to Peyton's and hang out there for a bit."

"Okay. I'll be out early today. Do you want to meet me for coffee around four?"

"Sure. Urth Caffé on Melrose?"

"Yeah. I'll see you then. And Jessie?"

"Yeah?"

"I'm really sorry."

"Babe, it's okay. I'm a big girl. I just panicked for a bit. I'm not used to this."

She didn't want to tell Elliot, but Jessie wasn't sure if she ever could get used to it.

*

"Jessie, my darling, my dear, you are far too tense." Peyton offered her a glass of whiskey as Jessie slumped in the comfortable chair in Peyton's living room.

"It's nine a.m., Peyton. Far too early to drink."

"Normally I'd agree, but this is an emergency. I can tell how rattled you are. Shit, just hearing about you getting blindsided like that has *me* all panicky." She took a sip from her own glass to show Jessie she wouldn't be drinking alone.

Jessie reluctantly took the glass and swirled the liquid around a bit before taking a drink. It felt weird drinking before noon, but Peyton was right. She needed to relax.

Peyton sat down on her couch and put her feet up on the coffee table in front of her.

"You want to watch a movie? It might get your mind off of everything."

Jessie shrugged. "Sure, just make it something light."

"Okay, so no *Virgin Suicides* or *Beaches*." Peyton dug through her DVD collection.

"Just throw on Netflix or whatever." Jessie took another sip and felt the warmth of the liquid trickle down her throat.

Peyton put on a random rom-com and sat back down on the couch.

"Wanna talk about it?"

"No."

"Okay."

After a few moments of silence, Jessie finally spoke.

"Do you think I made a mistake?"

"With what?"

"Breaking my rule. Sleeping with Elliot."

"No."

"You didn't even think about it," accused Jessie.

"I didn't have to. Hooking up with that girl was the best thing that could've ever happened to you, and the fact that you're still dating her is even better."

"But what about...everything that happened? The tape."

"Fuck the sex tape. I'm serious. Who cares? I know it was a terrible thing that happened to both of you. Neither of you deserve to have your privacy violated like that. But not for one second do I believe any of that negates the fact that Elliot is so damn good for you. God, Jessie, don't tell me you're thinking of ending it."

"No! No, not at all. Are you kidding me? I'd be an idiot to even consider that. I just can't help but think about how much simpler my life was before this whole thing happened."

"Oh yeah. Your simple life of work, the gym, and sleep. Not to mention your high protein diet complete with the most disgusting smoothies that've ever existed."

"Hey! You said you liked it and would've finished it if you weren't allergic to spinach."

"Oh honey, you're so cute and naïve."

Jessie shook her head. "You're such an asshole."

"Yes, I'm aware. My point is that this is the first time since you've moved here that I've ever witnessed you actually experience life outside of your work. You actually have fun now. You smile more. You're enjoying your life, which is what I've been trying to get you to do since you got here."

"I used to have fun."

"Yeah, back in Boulder until that bitch broke your heart."

"Can we not talk about Maggie, please? I'd like to keep my drink down."

"Fine. Let's talk about Elliot and the insanely hot sex I know you two have been having. Nice hickey, by the way."

Jessie brought her hand up to her neck and smiled at the memory of Elliot marking her in bed last night.

"She is pretty great, isn't she?"

Peyton clinked her glass against Jessie's. "I think you'd agree she's worth going through all that shit with the tape."

"She's worth even more than that."

Peyton stood up. "Good. I'm glad to know your head isn't up your ass. Now come on, it's a gorgeous day outside. Let's go hang out by the pool."

*

Elliot sat nervously waiting for Jessie to arrive at their agreed upon meeting place. It was a beautiful day, so she grabbed a seat outside and ordered them each an iced coffee. Even with her snapback and sunglasses on, she managed to get a few looks from fellow patrons. She could only offer them an acknowledging smile as she kept checking the time. Jessie was coming straight from Peyton's. With the exception of a couple texts, they hadn't spoken since their phone call earlier, and Elliot spent the majority of her day on set fluctuating between being worried about Jessie and being pissed off at the jerks camped outside her apartment building.

She nervously sipped her coffee and kept checking her phone, trying to avoid the prying eyes of the people around her. When she looked up, she saw Jessie approaching her table. She had to fight her instinct to get up and greet her with a kiss, but it didn't stop a genuine smile from forming on her face at the sight of the gorgeous girl.

"Hey you."

"Hey, sorry I'm late. My Lyft driver apparently didn't understand that Fountain is quicker than Sunset." She took a seat across from Elliot and sipped the coffee in front of her. "Mmm, honey vanilla. Thanks for ordering."

"No problem."

Elliot watched as Jessie took a few more sips and looked around the patio area.

"I see we have a bit of an audience," Jessie whispered as she leaned in closer.

"Yeah, sorry."

"Don't be. They love you. Besides, even without the fame, I'm pretty sure they'd all be looking at you anyway. You're quite good-looking, in case you weren't aware."

"Shut up."

Jessie feigned offense. "Rude."

Elliot giggled and rolled her eyes.

"Always so charming."

There was a quiet lull in their conversation as they enjoyed their drinks. A young girl came up to Elliot and shyly asked for her autograph, which Elliot happily gave her. Shortly after, a couple of girls asked to take a selfie with her. Elliot, never wanting to disappoint her fans, obliged, hoping that Jessie wouldn't mind the interruption. She didn't seem to.

After a few more moments of silence, Elliot noticed Jessie look across the street, angle her chair further from it, and face the door of the café. When Elliot finally noticed what Jessie was looking at, she was livid. A group of paparazzi snapped pictures of them from across the street.

"God damn it, they're relentless," muttered Elliot. She gave Jessie a concerned look. "I'm so sorry, Jess. You shouldn't have to deal with this paparazzi bullshit."

"It's not your fault."

"Still, I could've been more careful going to your place. If we'd gone to my house this whole time, they wouldn't know where you live."

Jessie shrugged and offered her a half smile. "We thought we were being smart."

Elliot nodded solemnly.

"Hey." Jessie put her drink down and reached across the table, her hand hovering over Elliot's. "Is this okay? Can I?"

Elliot took her hand in response. "Yes, of course."

Jessie's thumb caressed the top of Elliot's hand, which helped calm her down a bit. She knew the picture-happy assholes across the street were probably high-fiving each other at the gesture, but if Jessie was okay with it, then Elliot was definitely fine too.

"I don't want you feeling guilty over any of this. It's absolutely not your fault. None of this is, okay? I'm not going to lie to you, the fact that I no longer have my anonymity is something I'm struggling to come to terms with."

Elliot shifted uncomfortably in her seat. The words were like a punch in the gut.

"I know. I'm so, so sorry."

Jessie shook her head. "No. No more apologies from you. You've done nothing wrong. And none of this is going to change the way I feel about you. I just wanted to be honest with you. It's something I need to work on. Sex tape or not, cameras would still follow you—therefore follow me—and I have to get used to it. Today just really took me by surprise."

"You aren't required to do or say anything to anyone if they ask," informed Elliot. "If you do feel you want to respond, all that's needed is a simple 'no comment.' Your personal life is nobody's business."

"Neither is yours," argued Jessie.

"True, but it's pretty much a given that people will pry. It comes with the territory, and I knew that getting into this business in the first place. I definitely wasn't expecting to be outed like that, but I was well aware of the consequences when I went into acting." Elliot intertwined her fingers with Jessie's. "Look, I know that your anonymity is pretty much shot now, but I'm going to do everything in my power to protect you. I hope you know that."

Jessie grinned at her. "And here I thought I was the brave one. Has anyone ever told you you're kind of sweet?"

"Occasionally."

"Well, you are."

"Only kind of?"

"Kind of really."

Satisfied with Jessie's answer, Elliot took one last sip of her drink.

"What do you say we get out of here? Give ourselves some much-needed privacy."

"Where can we go?"

"Well, I think it's pretty ridiculous that you haven't seen where I live yet. So how about we go to my house?"

Jessie's eyes sparkled at the suggestion. "You mean I get to see the place *the* Elliot Chase calls home?"

"If you play your cards right, you might even get to see where she sleeps."

"Oh my." Jessie jokingly fanned herself.

"And where she eats, relaxes, goes to the bathroom."

"Wait, Elliot Chase goes to the bathroom? Wow, stars really *are* just like us."

Elliot threw her wadded up straw wrapper at Jessie.

"Shall we?"

"Yes, please."

Chapter 14

A few days later, Elliot found herself on the soundstage staring four stories up where Jessie and Kat rehearsed their stunt with the coordinator. This was not only their final stunt of the day, but also their final stunt of the film, which meant it was Jessie's last day on set. Elliot still had another week or so of shooting after this before her scenes were wrapped.

When she wasn't needed for filming, Elliot spent the majority of her day watching Jessie perform her fight scenes. Hayley teased her relentlessly about it, asking her why she'd want to watch her double when the real thing was standing right next to Elliot.

Elliot shrugged and told her, "if you looked like that while filming your scenes, maybe I'd pay more attention to you."

She was very obviously referring to Jessie's appearance. The way she looked in that tight, white ribbed tank top. The way the defined muscles in her arms flexed with each movement as she fought with Kat. The way her neck and shoulders glistened with sweat as the staged fight got more intense. Elliot knew she'd never get tired of watching Jessie work.

That coupled with the fact that this was Jessie's last day made her insist on staying behind to watch when Jessie and Kat set up for their final stunt: a 50 foot jump as an explosion went off.

"What are we all staring at?" Morgan came up behind Elliot and Hayley, throwing her arms around both of them and looking up to see what they were focused on.

"Elliot's girlfriend."

"Shut up, Hayley!"

"Am I wrong, though?"

"Hey, I don't blame you. Jessie's hot. Let's all stare at her," Morgan insisted.

Elliot playfully shoved her. "Don't you have an explosive to set off?"

"Hell yeah I do! The Morganator is all set up."

"You mean the detonator?"

"Bitch please. The way I set this up, it's going to look beautiful. A masterpiece. I deserve to have the button named after me."

Elliot rolled her eyes. "Fine, fine. Just make sure your 'work of art' doesn't endanger Jessie."

"You do realize Kat's up there too, right?" asked Morgan. "Who, by the way, looks even better than Jessie. Let's be real."

Hayley's mouth hung open. "Oh shit, Elliot, you're not going to let her get away with that, are you?"

Elliot was half tempted to wipe the smug look off Morgan's face, but decided to leave it. She knew Morgan had developed a little crush on Kat in the last few weeks and figured she'd offer up a compromise.

"We'll call it a tie. They're equally hot," offered Elliot.

Morgan shrugged. "Fair enough. Now if you ladies will excuse me, it's a beautiful day to blow some shit up."

She sauntered away with her typical overwhelming and almost annoying sense of self-confidence, leaving Elliot to continue watching Jessie set up for the stunt. This one wouldn't involve cables, so she'd free fall onto an inflatable stunt jump. Elliot knew Jessie was a professional, but she still worried. Kat's stunt, only having to hang on to the scaffolding as the explosion went off, was a little less daunting.

"Well, if you're really going to stay here and stare at the girl you literally stare at every day and night when you're *not* at work, I'm going to get some food." Hayley gave Elliot a forceful pat on the ass, causing Elliot to jump.

"Hayley!"

"Byeeee!"

She was gone before Elliot could even try to retaliate. That didn't matter, however, because they'd called for 'quiet on the set' and were about to film the stunt. Elliot made sure she staked out a prime location to watch the whole thing unfold. When the director called "action," Kat chased Jessie out of a hallway and onto the scaffolding. Jessie stopped on her mark, turned around to face Kat, struck a match, and threw it on the ground next to her. The match lit a trail of flames, and the explosion went off at the exact moment Jessie jumped over the scaffolding. Elliot watched her freefall onto the stunt jump as Kat, on her mark, clung to the scaffolding without falling. Once the director yelled cut, Jessie gave a fist pump, and the crew clapped for the stunt doubles upon completing their final stunt. Elliot clapped along with everyone else and watched as Jessie and Kat pointed at each other, smiling as a sign of solidarity and success.

Jessie rolled off the stunt jump and wiped the dirt and sweat from her face as she gave Elliot a sly smile and a wink. Elliot felt it everywhere.

She hung back, joining Hayley at the craft services table while Jessie and Kat spoke with the stunt coordinator to make sure everything was in order before they left. As they approached Elliot, she overheard Jessie telling Kat she hadn't secured her next job yet. Kat filled Jessie in on the job she had lined up and said she'd let Jessie know if anything was available on that film.

Elliot made some banal conversation with Hayley, hoping Jessie didn't think she was eavesdropping on her conversation with Kat, but made a mental note to call her agent and ask about any stunt work that needed to be done.

"Well, ladies. It's been real." Kat pulled Hayley in for a hug and then turned to Elliot. "It was such a blast working with you, Elliot. Hopefully we'll work together again soon."

"I'm counting on it. You did an amazing job." Elliot hugged her as Kat slipped a piece of paper in her hand and whispered, "Tell your friend Morgan to call me."

"I will do that." Elliot tried to hide her smile. She couldn't wait to share this news with Morgan.

Kat turned to Jessie and gave her a high five. "You and me. Drinks. This Saturday."

"I'll be there," assured Jessie.

"We're gonna get shit-faced! Bye ladies!" Kat blew them a kiss and left.

Elliot gave Jessie a teasing look. "Sounds like you're going to have an eventful evening on Saturday."

"Don't remind me. The last time Kat and I got drunk together…well, actually that's something we both swore we'd take to our graves. Maybe you and Morgan can join us?"

"I think I can arrange that. I'm pretty sure Morgan will jump at the chance to see her again."

Jessie looked over at Hayley. "You and Ashton want to join us, too?"

"Hell yeah. Sounds good to me." Once Hayley finished up the scone she was eating, she wiped her mouth and headed out toward her trailer. "I think we're wrapped for the day, so I'm going to change. See you tomorrow, Elliot. Good job, Jessie."

Jessie waved goodbye and turned to Elliot. "Good. Maybe with a crowd, Kat will actually behave herself on Saturday."

*

The blaring music reverberated through Jessie's entire body in what felt like an endless song of the same beat over and over. If it wasn't for the smoky atmosphere from the fog machines and people taking puffs from their vape pens, the lights would be blinding. Jessie chided herself for allowing Kat to pick the place they met for drinks. She pictured a low key bar with a jukebox and some bad fluorescent signs on the wall, but once Elliot, Morgan, Hayley, and Ashton were invited to come along, Jessie should've known Kat would choose some trendy club with a line out the door.

Not that they had to wait. Elliot didn't want to use her fame to get them in, but Hayley had no problem using hers. They were able to secure a VIP table without any issues.

It was too loud to even think, but Jessie was three shots in and feeling good, especially with Elliot right next to her looking every bit the bombshell the media made her out to be. Every time she looked over at Elliot, she felt her breath catch and the music became white noise. Every time Elliot returned her gaze, she cared less and less about the locale and her surroundings and thought more and more about getting Elliot out of the impossibly tight dress she was wearing.

Her eyes continually raked over Elliot's entire body. Really, she wasn't being subtle about it. If it weren't for their friends in the VIP booth with them, she probably would've lost her last remaining ounce of control. Her hand itched to move toward Elliot's thigh, but where they were wasn't exactly out of everyone's line of sight, including the people on the dance floor and at the bar. They definitely didn't need more attention than they already had. She noticed a few people snapping pictures of them from the dance floor, though she was pretty sure the quality came out dark and grainy.

Every time she went to reach for the soft expanse of skin just below the hemline of Elliot's short dress, Jessie managed to pull back and take a drink instead. Elliot, obviously sensing her desperation, reached for her hand, rested it on her thigh, and leaned in to whisper.

"If you want to touch me, you can touch me. If you want to hold my hand, you don't need permission." She nuzzled her nose ever so slightly against Jessie's ear. "If you want to kiss me..."

She pulled back and Jessie's mouth fell open, her eyes trained on Elliot's lips. She was desperate to taste them, and since Elliot gave her the okay, she moved her hand to Elliot's thigh and leaned in to capture her lips.

She felt the graze of Elliot's mouth, her breath hot on her face, but the moment was short-lived when Morgan appeared out of nowhere.

"More shots, bitches! Drink up!"

They pulled back, each with their own awkward smile. Jessie kept her hand on Elliot's thigh. She was pretty sure it'd have to be surgically removed.

"It seems the drunker Morgan gets, the louder she gets," observed Jessie.

Elliot giggled. "She's just showing off for Kat. I think she's got it pretty bad for the girl."

Jessie looked over to see Kat engrossed in conversation with Hayley and Ashton, all but ignoring Morgan. As much as she hated to do it, she moved away from Elliot to sit down next to Kat.

She listened as Kat told Hayley and Ashton all about her next gig. Jessie was happy that she booked something so quickly, but found herself feeling a little jealous about the fact that she still hadn't been able to line up her next job. As much as she tried not to think about it, Jessie was almost completely sure it was because of the tape. She tried to push the thoughts out of her mind. This was not the time or place to start dwelling on that.

She leaned in and whispered to Kat.

"What are you doing?"

"What?" Kat gave her one of her infamous innocent looks.

"You know what I'm talking about. Go dance with Morgan."

"All in good time."

"I think now is a good time," urged Jessie.

"I'm playing hard to get."

"I think you made your point. She obviously really likes you. Stop playing games and go dance with her."

"Okay, okay. Whatever you say, *Mom*."

"I don't think your mom would be encouraging you to drink and dance with an extremely sexy explosives expert."

Jessie playfully kicked Kat in the butt as she got up, nearly pushing her onto Morgan's lap. After a few exchanged whispers, Morgan got up, and they headed toward the dance floor. Morgan mouthed a quick "thank you" to Jessie.

Elliot took the opportunity to sit next to Jessie again, leaning up against her and playfully walking her fingers up Jessie's thigh.

"Now, where were we?"

"Elliot! Get your ass up and come dance with us."

This time it was Hayley who interrupted.

"I'm a little busy," she said without casting a glance in her direction, keeping her eyes on Jessie.

Hayley, not appreciating being rejected, pulled Elliot up and looked at her pleadingly.

"When was the last time we all went out dancing?"

"Okay, fine."

Jessie shifted in her seat. She knew what was coming next and wasn't nearly drunk enough for this. Elliot reached out her hand and gave her a little smirk, knowing it was going to take much more than this to get Jessie out on the dance floor.

Jessie, in turn, slapped her hand to give her a high five.

"I'm good here. You have fun."

Elliot gave her a pout, laying it on a bit too thick for such an accomplished actress.

"Jess, please. I'm not going to be the only one out there without someone to dance with."

Jessie had to fight the urge to pull Elliot down onto her lap. Instead, she took a sip of whiskey and mulled over Elliot's request.

Hayley nudged Elliot.

"Don't worry, Chase. I doubt you'll have any trouble finding someone to dance with. Pretty much all eyes have been on you since we got here."

Jessie slammed her glass down on the table and was up, pulling Elliot to the dance floor before Hayley even finished her sentence. She wasn't much of a dancer, but the thought of someone else grinding up against Elliot in the middle of a sweaty dance club was something she didn't like envisioning.

Jessie rolled her eyes at Hayley, who was obviously pleased with herself.

*

Elliot was actually quite impressed with Jessie. She thought it'd take a lot more to convince her to dance. Not only that, but for someone who claimed she didn't dance much, she moved extremely well. Almost too well, leaving Elliot to remind herself they were in a public place and she needed to chill.

Jessie's hips moved seductively with the music, and her body felt so sublimely perfect against her own. She wasn't even sure how long they'd been out there, but if the sweat dripping down her neck was any indication, it was a while. She couldn't seem to stop. She was tired and thirsty, and her high heels were killing her feet, but she couldn't pull herself away from Jessie's equally sweaty body for a single moment. From the look on Jessie's face, it seemed she was in the exact same predicament.

She indulged in the feeling of Jessie's hands around her waist, pulling her closer, moving her thigh between Elliot's legs while still dancing to the beat of the music. It was hot and sensual and at this point, Elliot didn't care who was watching. People had seen them do way more intimate things in way less clothing, and as affected as Elliot still was by the entire ordeal, she refused to stop living her life because of it.

She brought her hands up to cup the back of Jessie's neck, feeling little beads of sweat at the base. As the dance floor got more crowded, they were pushed closer and closer together. Jessie brought her hands up to Elliot's shoulders, then back down again, grazing the sides of Elliot's breasts. She brought her hands back up and repeated the same motion, only this time, Jessie lingered a bit longer on the swell of her breasts before trailing back down to grab her hips.

Elliot took a cue from Jessie and moved her hands from her neck down to her ass, which she'd been dying to touch all night. The tight jeans Jessie was wearing certainly accentuated its perfection.

The look on Jessie's face when she went for it was priceless—a combination of shock and lust that left Elliot craving more. She gave a firm squeeze as she continued grinding against Jessie's thigh, grateful for the much-needed friction.

All need for subtlety went out the window. By now, no one around them was fooled, so there was no point in even trying anymore. The prying eyes, the phones snapping shots of them dancing, the blatant whispers among the other club-goers—it was getting out of hand at this point. The photos were probably all over Instagram by now, but the only thing Elliot seemed to care about in this moment was getting Jessie home.

She looked to her left to see Hayley and Ashton making out, not even paying attention to the crowd taking photos of them. To her right, it seemed Kat and Morgan had crossed the line from flirtation to wildly inappropriate, practically humping each other in a way that made Elliot and Jessie's dancing seem PG rated.

Elliot decided this was their cue to leave. She pulled Jessie in closer and nuzzled along her jawline.

"This dress may look hot, but it's cutting off my circulation. Wanna take it off me?"

Jessie's widened eyes and emphatic nod were enough to make them say a quick round of goodbyes to their friends before slipping out the back entrance.

*

The silence in Elliot's bedroom was a stark contrast to the club. Jessie's ears rang from the pulsating, beat-laden music. Now, in the stillness of the bed, with a naked Elliot resting on top of her, she welcomed the quiet. She was content to stay this way until she felt Elliot push off of her and peruse her body.

"What?"

"I just really like you," admitted Elliot.

"I can see that." Jessie grabbed Elliot's hand and urged her back down on top of her. "Come here."

She pulled her in for a kiss while raking her hand through Elliot's wild sex hair. She felt the blonde's hand massaging her thigh as the kiss deepened. Jessie was sure Elliot was determined to wear her out, and she was completely okay with that.

Elliot hummed with contentment as she pulled away from Jessie and gazed down at her. Jessie could feel a lump forming in her throat, and she had no idea why. Suddenly, she was rendered speechless. She wanted to tell Elliot just how beautiful she looked in this moment. She wanted to tell her how much she means to her. She wanted the words "I love you" to roll off her tongue and fill Elliot's ears, assuring the girl that her heart belonged only to her. But all she could do was stare at the stunning woman on top of her who, at this very moment, looked at her with so much adoration and wonder.

Elliot opened her mouth to say something, but it appeared she was having the same struggles as Jessie. Her shoulders slumped, and her head lowered as she took a deep breath. When her eyes met Jessie's once more, they contained a newfound confidence that wasn't there a moment ago.

"Jessie?"

"Hmm?" It was the only sound she could muster at the moment.

Elliot's lips parted slightly. Her chin lifted, and her hand rested on Jessie's cheek, but she never lost eye contact.

"I love you."

Jessie had no idea Elliot could make her feel any higher than she already had, but hearing that declaration pour from her lips took her to new heights. Higher than any altitude she'd ever jumped from. It made her heart race faster than any stunt car or motorcycle she'd ever driven. This wasn't stunt work. This was real life. These were real emotions. There was no net, no safety harness, no landing mats, nothing to catch her. Only Elliot. And in this moment, she knew that Elliot could very well be the one to catch her if she needed it. Elliot loved her and that thought was the most pulse-pounding thing she'd ever experienced. She never felt more alive.

She rested her hand on Elliot's and finally found her voice.

"I love you too."

Chapter 15

The next few weeks were fairly uneventful, for which Elliot and Jessie were both grateful. The days Elliot didn't have to film, she'd stay in bed all morning with Jessie.

The days they actually got up before noon, Elliot was either at the studio or in meetings about her next project, and Jessie headed to the gym for her vigorous workout regimen. Whenever Elliot told her she worked too hard, that her body was already in amazing shape, Jessie reminded her that just because she was between jobs, didn't mean she should neglect her routine.

On the mornings when Elliot had to be at the studio, Jessie woke up early and made them breakfast. In the evenings, Elliot brought Jessie her favorite hot tea with a kiss on her forehead as she curled up on the couch and read. Elliot would cuddle up next to her and go over scripts her agent sent to her. At times, she'd find herself looking over at Jessie, loving how it felt to have her there and thinking to herself how easy it all was. It shouldn't be, especially after they'd been through, but it was. She had to force herself to go back to her scripts so as not to jinx the moment.

They weren't living together. Not technically. But they may as well have been. Jessie still had her apartment, which she'd go back to every few days to check her mail and pick up some fresh clothes, but the majority of their time was spent at Elliot's. They'd fall asleep together every night and wake up entangled in each other. Elliot couldn't remember the last time she had anything this good.

*

"Where are we going?"

"I told you, it's a surprise."

Jessie huffed and pouted while Elliot chuckled and took her hand as she drove down the freeway. It was a perfect day. A blue sky scattered with a few white, puffy clouds. Sia played on the radio, and the most beautiful girl sat in Elliot's passenger seat holding her hand, humming along to the music.

"Hmm...we're heading south, so I know we're not going to Vegas."

Elliot laughed at the suggestion.

"Wouldn't that be nice, though? We could have a little repeat of our last Vegas getaway."

Jessie smiled and brought Elliot's hand up to her lips.

"We'll make it back there someday. Next time with less drama."

"Agreed. But definitely a hotel with a pool table."

Jessie nodded before she ventured another guess.

"San Diego?"

"Stop trying to guess. We're not actually going that far."

Elliot exited the freeway and made a left.

"I swear if you're taking me to the art exhibit where that woman in body paint eats only sugar cubes and lives in a cage, I can tell you right now, I'm not paying admission to see that. I can see it on YouTube for free when it's over."

"Why on earth would I take you to that? How little do you think I know you?"

"I'm just trying to get you to at least give me a hint."

"No need. We're here." Elliot pulled into a parking lot and put the car in park. They got out and looked up at a rather large warehouse in front of them.

"Where exactly is here? What is this place?"

Elliot placed a kiss on Jessie's cheek and grabbed her hand.

"Come on. I'll show you."

*

Inside, the building looked and felt a lot warmer and more welcoming than the nondescript outside. Jessie stood in the lobby and looked around at the freshly painted walls, new carpet, and the sparkling clean glass that divided small offices. The place looked huge.

"Welcome to the official space of my non-profit women's center. I don't have a name for it yet, but at least we've secured a building and made some good headway on the interior."

Jessie continued exploring as she walked past the lobby and down one of the corridors while Elliot followed closely behind.

"This is what you've been working on? What you told me about that night at the bar?"

Elliot didn't respond, but Jessie could see her nodding from her peripheral.

"It's so much farther along than I expected. I thought you were just sort of talking about it."

"Well, I was, but I was also acting on it. They found this space right before I left to film in the desert and had been working on securing it for a while. The lease was signed a few weeks ago."

"This is incredible." Jessie made her way to a large kitchen area.

"We're hoping to hand out meals to women and children who are struggling financially," Elliot explained.

Jessie smiled and excitedly continued to explore, taking in her surroundings.

"I like the color scheme on the walls. It's welcoming. And there's no harsh fluorescent lighting."

"I didn't want to make it feel like a doctor's or a lawyer's office, even though we'll have doctors and lawyers volunteering their time here."

"This is so impressive. So much has already been done."

Elliot shrugged.

"Well, the foundation hired some great people. I knew I wouldn't be able to oversee a lot of things because of my schedule, so I had to really trust that they'd get the ball rolling."

Jessie made her way down another corridor lined with private offices.

"This is amazing."

Elliot took her hand.

"Here, I want to show you a few things. Obviously there's still a lot of work to be done. I'm hoping most of it will be completed by the time I wrap my next film. I just hate that I can't be here for a lot of it, so I've been doing what I can while I'm in town."

"Wait, so those meetings you've been going to?"

"Were with my agent, yes. But then last week, I started coming here afterward to take care of any issues that needed to be worked out. I didn't want to show it to you until there was actually something to show. A week ago, everything was a mess. The crew and some volunteers have been working their asses off. They actually just went home not too long ago, so we have the place to ourselves."

"I'm just...this is...wow." Jessie was truly at a loss for words.

"Better than Vegas?"

Jessie smiled at her and nodded.

"Better than Vegas. What you're doing here is so inspiring."

Elliot took Jessie from room to room, showing her the various components of the women's center, including a large room stacked with bunk beds for any woman in need of escaping a dangerous domestic situation without a place to go. She showed her the area designated for the day care center for single moms who can't afford childcare. Around the corner was the fitness room and through that door was a large studio space.

"This is what I really wanted to show you. It's going to be a training room for martial arts. This is where I was hoping you'd volunteer to teach women self-defense."

Jessie walked to the center of the studio and took a moment to familiarize herself with the place.

"I can't think of a more perfect location for a more perfect cause. I'd be honored to teach self-defense here." She walked over to Elliot and put her hands on her shoulders. "Next time you sneak off to one of your meetings, can you take me with you? I'd love to help in any way I can. Even if it's just to get coffee for all the staff putting this place together. I can totally be a gopher."

Elliot chuckled.

"I think we can find you a more dignified position."

"You never cease to amaze me, you know that?"

Elliot's crooked smile and slight blush were so endearing to Jessie. She wanted to kiss her right then and there.

Elliot nervously ran her fingers through her hair.

"I got a little sidetracked for a bit. I had some pretty intense phone calls with the other board members after the tape was leaked. They wanted me to steer clear of the foundation and the center for a while until it blew over. I agreed and stayed away for a bit. Everything was too overwhelming anyway. But then I realized that this was my idea, my vision, and my money that went into this. I'm only in town another couple weeks until my next film starts, so I decided screw it. I'm here."

Elliot's passion, the fire in her eyes, the way her entire body moved when she talked about this place—it all captivated Jessie.

"I've never known anyone like you. How are you even real?"

"I often ask myself that about you."

Jessie pulled Elliot into her and placed a chaste kiss on her lips.

"You're beautiful."

If Elliot turned any redder, she'd match the crimson color of her shirt.

"Jessie, I hate to break it to you, but I think you might be gay."

"Damn, I've been found out."

"I won't tell a soul."

"Way to ruin a perfectly sweet moment by the way."

Elliot smirked playfully.

215

"I wouldn't call it ruined."

Elliot pulled her in for a kiss, deeper and more intense than their earlier one. Jessie was thankful that Elliot was right: the moment certainly wasn't ruined, and Jessie was definitely very gay.

*

"God, I can't believe I'm reliving that bridge scene. Do you know how terrifying that was for me?"

Jessie paused the video on the laptop and looked at Elliot.

"I was there. You were physically shaking."

"It was windy!"

"You were so adorable."

"And you were so sweet to make me feel safe."

Elliot hit play again as they sat back on the couch and continued watching the electronic press kit for *Best of Enemies.* Elliot needed to approve any footage they used of her.

She'd just wrapped on the movie. They were still in production and had more scenes to shoot, but Elliot's scenes were now all officially completed. They wouldn't need her again until post-production to film any pick-ups or record dialogue.

"Wow, they got some great shots of you," observed Elliot.

"I know, it looks like they included all the biggest stunts. You don't think the studio will release the motorcycle crash footage, do you? I don't need that thing up on YouTube."

"Not if I have anything to say about it. Plus, they have no reason to release it."

Jessie cuddled into Elliot and rested her head on her shoulder.

"I should add this footage to my reel. Though I'm not sure it'll do any good."

"Still haven't heard anything?"

"I've sent my reel out to every stunt coordinator I know. No one will get back to me. I can't even remember the last time I've had to send my reel out."

Elliot leaned her head against Jessie's and sighed contemplatively.

"My offer still stands. I can get you work on my next film. As the star, I think it's safe to say I have pull, and I know they need stunt work."

"And my answer still stands. I appreciate the offer, babe, I really do. But I want to get work on my own merit. Not by someone doing a favor for you."

"I wouldn't hate having you on set with me."

Jessie smiled and moved her hand up under Elliot's shirt, playfully tickling her side.

"I'd be a distraction and you know it."

Elliot giggled and feigned trying to push Jessie's hand away.

"A very welcomed, sexy distraction."

"Oh, so you think I'm sexy?" Jessie teased.

Elliot's laugh grew louder the more Jessie tickled her.

"Not when you torture me like this. Stop!"

"I think you deserve to be tortured a bit. You can be bratty sometimes."

Jessie moved to straddle Elliot and started attacking her with both hands. Elliot turned red, unable to control her laughter. She was too weak to stop Jessie from continuing her assault on her most ticklish areas.

"I've been so nice!" argued Elliot.

"So the other day when you untied the string from my bikini top before I jumped in the pool?"

Elliot tried fighting back, but Jessie flexed her abs, steeling herself against Elliot's onslaught.

"Can you blame me for wanting to see your boobs?"

"It was broad daylight, Elliot!"

"And no one can see into my yard, Jessie!"

"Ugh! Such a brat! You are infuriating."

Jessie redoubled her efforts, and Elliot howled with laughter.

"Babe, you know I wouldn't do that unless I knew it was safe. Forgive me? Please? I can't take anymore!"

"Make me." Jessie challenged her, hoping she'd accept.

Elliot grabbed Jessie's wrists and pulled her down into a searing kiss. Jessie nearly lost her balance, but Elliot steadied her as she brought Jessie's hands up to wrap around her neck. They fell deeper into the kiss, Jessie growing exceedingly happy that Elliot accepted her challenge.

Both completely forgot about the EPK footage they were supposed to be watching. There were more important matters to attend to.

Jessie grabbed the hem of her shirt and pulled it off over her head.

"You still want to see my boobs?"

*

The following week, they enjoyed a lazy Sunday in bed together watching Netflix. Neither had anything to do that day, and Elliot was just a few days away from leaving for Vancouver for her next film. They wanted to take advantage of the time they had together before Elliot was gone for three months.

Elliot was curled up practically on top of Jessie, resting her head on her stomach with a leg draped over Jessie's legs for good measure. She was happy—blissfully happy—and didn't want it to be interrupted for any reason. She sighed in contentment, a little louder than she expected.

"Everything okay?" Jessie ran her fingers through Elliot's hair.

"Yeah. Just...I could get used to you being in my bed every day."

"You mean you're not used to it by now?"

"You know what I mean. It's going to suck waking up without you next to me."

"I know. I'm not looking forward to it, either." Jessie trailed her fingers from Elliot's hair down to her arm, then her back, and up to her hair again.

"I hate hotel rooms."

The statement hung heavily between them, both fully knowing the implication.

"I still think you should make the studio pay for a private house. It'll make you feel more comfortable."

"I don't want to be isolated from the rest of the cast and crew. But don't worry, they'll be diligent about who's allowed on our floor, and I definitely won't throw or attend any parties."

"Don't let one bad experience ruin your fun." Jessie gave Elliot's arm a little squeeze.

"No, it's fine. This is a more serious role, so I'll need to focus and rest." She nuzzled further into Jessie's stomach. "I'm really going to miss you."

Upon hearing Jessie's sigh, Elliot sat up.

"I'm not going to ask again. Don't worry," assured Elliot.

Jessie chuckled. "Was that your way of bringing it up without bringing it up?"

"Maybe. Sorry. I know—you want to stay in LA and find work. I understand. I'm just pouting a bit."

Jessie sat up and pulled Elliot onto her lap until she was straddling her. Elliot couldn't help but give a little grind against her, causing Jessie to pause a moment before remembering what she was about to say.

"You'll have some days off. Once you get the official schedule, we'll set a time for me to come visit you. It'll be okay."

Elliot intertwined her hands with Jessie's and leaned down to kiss her.

"I want you to feel free to stay at my house while I'm gone. Maybe keep my bed warm for me?"

Jessie brought her in for another long kiss, and Elliot wondered how she'd go so long without feeling those lips against her own. She felt herself getting worked up again but knew they should probably get some food before even thinking about going another round.

"I don't know how much I'll be around," confessed Jessie.

Elliot pulled back, head cocked in confusion.

"What do you mean?"

"Since you'll be gone, and I can't seem to find work, I was thinking of going back to Colorado for a few months. Just to clear my head and regroup. Maybe put some distance between me and the sex tape. After some time away, maybe they'll forget and my reputation will be restored."

Elliot froze. She could feel the blood drain from her face.

"Are...are you breaking up with me?"

Jessie's eyes went wide, and she wrapped her arms around Elliot, pulling her against her skin.

"Oh babe, no. God no. The thought never even crossed my mind. Shit, I probably should've led with that."

Elliot's heart beat erratically, but she began to calm down as Jessie rubbed her back and held her tighter.

"I just figured there's not much for me to do out here while you're gone. I haven't been back to see my family in a while. Peyton said she could sublet my apartment since she's looking for a new place. I would've brought it up earlier, but I swear this was all a recent notion. I thought about it yesterday, and it just makes sense."

"So it's just a visit. You're not moving back?"

"It's just a visit."

"And you're still going to come visit me in Vancouver?"

"I'm still coming to visit you in Vancouver. I wouldn't miss that for anything."

Elliot started to feel a little better about the situation, so she tried her luck.

"And you're going to let me take your Buffy hoodie with me?"

Jessie paused to think for a moment.

"Colorado is awfully cold this time of year."

"So is Vancouver! Jessie, please? You know I love that hoodie, and it smells like you."

Elliot pulled back and placed Jessie's hands on her boobs, then seductively moved her hips against Jessie's core before giving her a playful grin. She knew Jessie's resolve was fading fast, so she threw in a few sexy moans until she finally relented.

"Okay. You can take my Buffy hoodie with you."

Chapter 16

Two months later…

It was a slow night, and Jessie hoped to close up a little early this evening. A snowstorm was expected soon. Likely the last one of the season, but the late season storms were usually the worst. She didn't want to be caught in it. Even from back behind the bar, she could feel a chill from the outside air as a few patrons walked out.

She'd give anything to be back in Vancouver with Elliot. Visiting her had been the highlight of the last two months. She got back to Boulder three weeks ago. They'd only gotten to spend five days together, but it was a perfect five days. Much warmer despite the fact that they were in Canada, though that was most likely because they barely left Elliot's room.

Before Jessie went to visit her, they texted, emailed, and Skyped when they could. The day Jessie left Vancouver to come back to Boulder, she cried for an hour on the flight back, but she never told Elliot. Elliot had enough to worry about with filming, and Jessie was just being a hopeless gay.

Other than those five days of bliss with Elliot, not much else had happened in Jessie's life since coming back to Colorado two months ago. She continued sending out her reel to try and secure a job by the time Elliot finished filming, but only received one return call saying they'd keep her reel on file if they had any upcoming projects for her.

In the meantime, she rented a studio apartment because she wasn't about to live with her parents again. She got a job tending bar at the place where she used to work before moving to LA. When she wasn't working, she was working out, hiking, or spending time with her family. Thankfully, no one ever mentioned the tape. It was a sort of unspoken agreement. She also saw a couple of old friends that were still in town, but most people had moved away after high school. Nothing really felt the same here. She started to regret coming back, but she needed to clear her head and put some distance between herself and Hollywood for the time being.

Finally, the last two patrons left the bar. Jessie was getting ready to close up so she could duck out early and beat the storm when she heard the door open.

"Where can a girl get a stiff drink to warm up around here?"

Jessie paused. She knew that voice. It was connected to a distant memory from long ago, but the pain still lingered the moment she heard it. Jessie turned to face the woman and was greeted by a ghost from her past.

"Maggie. What are you doing back in town?"

"I could ask you the same thing." She sidled up to one of the stools at the bar and sat down.

"We're closed."

"I used to work here, remember? This place doesn't close until one a.m. Now how about that drink and you tell me all about what you've been up to these past few years."

Jessie wasn't in the mood for this. She had a warm bed waiting for her and a scheduled Skype call with Elliot.

"Like I said, we're closed. You can show yourself out."

Maggie reached over the bar to grab a bottle of whiskey and a shot glass. She took it upon herself to pour a drink, completely ignoring Jessie's icy dismissal of her. Jessie watched as she threw back the shot and poured another before grabbing a second shot glass for Jessie. She filled it and slid it across the bar, but Jessie just looked down at it, uninterested in partaking.

"Come on, Jess. Consider it a peace offering."

"You plan on paying for these?"

"You plan on being nice to me?"

Jessie scoffed. "What do you want?"

Maggie stared at the whiskey in her glass before swallowing it, squinting her face as if it were too strong for her liking.

"I heard you were back in town. I wanted to see you."

"Why?"

Maggie shrugged. "Because I miss you."

Jessie was silent, contemplating. Maggie had been so far from her thoughts for so long now that seeing her again was the last thing she ever expected. She certainly never expected those words to come out of Maggie's mouth. Not after the way she left. Suddenly the shot of whiskey looked rather inviting, so she relented and took it. The slight burn in her throat was a welcome feeling.

"How's Emma?"

Jessie watched as Maggie's face fell.

"I don't know. That didn't end well."

Jessie nodded, almost feeling sorry for the girl, but she caught herself before the empathy took hold of her.

"Well, it's one a.m. now. We're officially closed. You better leave before the snow gets any worse."

Looking dejected, Maggie pulled a $50 dollar bill from her pocket and tossed it onto the bar.

"Good seeing you, Jess."

Jessie didn't respond. She didn't even look at her as she exited.

Yep, coming back to Boulder was definitely a bad idea.

*

Jessie's blunt response to Maggie casually walking back into her life didn't seem to faze Maggie in the slightest. Every night Jessie worked, her ex-girlfriend would stop by around closing time and order two shots of whiskey—one for herself and one for Jessie as a sort of olive branch. Jessie refused the drink every time after that first night. She wanted nothing from the girl who broke her heart all those years ago.

After a couple weeks, Maggie's presence wasn't as cumbersome. She was just sort of there. At first, it bothered Jessie. There was still some bitterness towards her, but eventually it faded away to the point where she genuinely felt nothing for the girl. Time seemed to have healed those wounds, and Jessie wasn't as hurt as she remembered. She was pretty sure that was mainly because of Elliot. Any feelings she ever had for Maggie were nothing compared to what she felt for Elliot. Maggie was her first love, but Elliot was her forever love. Knowing that made it a little easier to deal with seeing Maggie every night. She was part of the background. One patron among many. It was pretty clear though that she was trying to make amends. Maggie was relentless seeing as how Jessie ignored her every night.

One night, no other customers were in the bar. Everyone was home watching the football game. The bar had one small TV, but it didn't carry the channel the game aired on. Jessie constantly tried to tell the owner their business would double if he invested in some new TVs, but he was too stubborn to listen.

Tonight, it was just her and Maggie, and since it was obvious the girl wasn't going to leave any time soon, Jessie finally decided to be cordial and at least attempt another conversation.

"Why do you insist on coming here every night?" Jessie opened a couple of beers and handed one to her.

"I thought it was obvious. To see you."

"Believe it or not, I don't particularly feel like seeing you. I'm glad we got a chance to catch up, but..."

"We didn't catch up. After that first night, you've barely said anything to me other than to take my order."

"Well, you seem to be doing okay. I'm glad you're doing well, but there's nothing more to say."

"Nothing? We used to be so close. What happened?" Maggie got up and walked around behind the bar, trying to get closer.

Jessie kept her distance and hopped up on the counter behind her.

"What happened? Well, let's see. You cheated on me with one of my best friends and then ran off together with no warning. I had no idea where you were, if you were okay. I mean, I knew we were over, but it didn't mean I didn't worry about you."

Maggie leaned back against the bar and folded her arms.

"For what it's worth, I'm sorry. I know it's years too late, but I really am sorry. It was a shitty thing to do."

"It was."

"And like I said, she and I are not together anymore."

"I don't care."

"Fair enough. Well, it seems like things aren't so terrible for you. I mean...Elliot Chase. Damn."

Jessie felt her fists clench at the sound of Elliot's name in Maggie's mouth.

"We're not talking about this."

"It had to suck. That whole sex tape thing. How are you doing with all that by the way?"

"I told you, we're not having this conversation."

"Must be hard. Her career is still thriving while you're stuck here."

Jessie knew it was a bad idea to attempt a conversation with her. She should've followed her instincts.

"I'm only here temporarily."

"That's a shame. I'm back for good. Officially. You should come see my place. It's not too far from here."

"I'm sure it's nice, but no thank you."

"You should stay, Jess. This is your home."

"My life is in LA, and my home is with Elliot.

Maggie took a few steps until she was face to face with Jessie, but still smart enough to keep a bit of distance.

"Seems like your life and home are here. Seeing as how you're...you know...here."

Jessie jumped off the counter and pushed past Maggie.

"I came here to get some clarity, and I got it. I'm only here another week or so."

"Oh."

She could see the look of disappointment on Maggie's face.

"I appreciate your apology. I really do. It helps with the whole closure thing, so thank you."

They stood in an uncomfortable silence for a few moments before Jessie opted to put an end to the awkwardness.

"I should get ready to close up. Drive home safe, okay?"

Maggie nodded in defeat.

"Okay."

*

The only thing Elliot wanted more than a shower and a 12 hour nap was to see her girlfriend's face on her iPad screen. She didn't even change out of her clothes after closing the door to her hotel suite and crawling into bed after an 18 hour day on set.

In a matter of moments, Jessie's face appeared before her. Every ounce of fatigue, stress, and soreness escaped her body at the sight of Jessie's smile.

"Hi, baby."

"Hey, you."

"Sorry I was late calling you."

"It's okay. You sound exhausted."

Elliot stifled a yawn.

"I am."

"We can make it a short conversation tonight. I just wanted to hear your voice and see your face," offered Jessie.

"No. No short conversations. We've had too many conversations cut short lately. I might rest my eyes from time to time though."

She reveled at the sound of Jessie's laughter.

"Okay."

Elliot hated that they hadn't Skyped in over a week. Her schedule made it too difficult to find a time when both of them had more than a few minutes to spare, so they resorted to texts and emails.

Elliot rolled over onto her side, propping herself up on her elbow.

"I miss you in my bed."

"I miss being in your bed."

Elliot buried her face in her pillow and groaned.

"Come over."

"Okay. I'll be there in five minutes."

"You're mocking me."

"Maybe a little. Besides, I'm comfy in my bed. You look like you're not even in your pajamas, so you should come to me."

"Mmm…five minutes," Elliot mumbled.

"You're really cute when you're tired."

"And you're really cute when you're you."

Jessie chuckled.

"You're also surprisingly smooth when you're tired. I'll give that a 10 out of 10."

"That's what I give your body."

Elliot was feeling playful, almost high. She wasn't sure if it was the fatigue or the fact that she was finally talking to Jessie, but she embraced the delirium. She also enjoyed the sight of Jessie blush.

"Stop making me miss you so much," replied Jessie.

"Stop being so far away," Elliot countered.

"Jesus, we're fucking hopeless."

Elliot rolled over on her back, holding her iPad above her.

"I know. We're in the home stretch. One more week, and I'm free. Then we can enjoy the warmth of the LA sun. It's so freaking cold here, Jess."

"You think it's not cold here?"

"I'm sure it's very cold without me next to you."

"Indeed it is."

They were quiet for a moment, simply looking at each other. Elliot took the time to trace the contours of Jessie's face, longing to kiss that epic jawline of hers. She closed her eyes and let out a sigh.

"So how was your day?"

"Pretty uneventful compared to yours, I'm sure. But guess who's back in town."

"Who?"

"Maggie."

This caught Elliot's attention. She sat up and crossed her legs.

"What?"

"Yeah. She's been stopping by the bar the nights I work."

Elliot was quiet for a moment, trying to process everything.

"I...are you okay?"

"Yeah, I'm fine," answered Jessie. She looked genuinely concerned. "Are you?"

"I don't know. I feel like I should be jealous, but that's ridiculous, right? I have no reason to be jealous."

"No, you really don't. Trust me."

"I do trust you, but I also feel kind of angry. She just barged back into your life like nothing happened?"

"Sort of. Words were exchanged. She sort of wore out her welcome, but I think it's good that it happened. I'm able to completely put it all behind me now. I know I probably should've told you sooner, but I just didn't want to worry you."

Elliot plopped back onto her bed.

"I have this uncontrollable need to wrap you in a hug right now, and I can't, and it sucks."

"I know, but I'm really okay. I think she was trying to initiate a reconciliation, but I shut that down real fast."

"And here comes that jealous feeling again."

"Elliot…"

"I know. Don't worry. It'll pass. I just don't like that she's in the same town as you, and I'm so far away."

"I'm really in love with you."

Jessie's words managed to quell any doubts or pangs of jealousy Elliot had.

"Yeah?"

Jessie nodded.

"Yeah. Now get some sleep. You have an early day tomorrow."

Elliot could already feel sleep take over her body.

"I have to change."

"Somehow I don't think you'll get that far."

Jessie was right. Elliot was fading fast, and her adrenaline from the day was dropping fast. She closed her eyes and rested the iPad next to her.

"Jessie?"

"Hmm?"

"Will you stay with me until I'm asleep?"

"I'll stay with you until you wake up."

*

The following night, Jessie worked at the bar again. It was another slow night, and she tried to remember if it was like this when she used to work here or if people got tired of the lack of flair in the place. It was the kind of bar built for people who want to get good and drunk. The occasional group of hipsters would stop in and order a few rounds of Pabst Blue Ribbon before posting photos of the cheap beer to their Instagram pages, but for the most part it catered to an older crowd, people stopping in for a drink and a bite to eat on their way home from work.

Maggie hadn't shown up yet tonight. She was glad their conversation last night actually seemed to stick with Maggie. All Jessie wanted to do was finish out the rest of the week drama-free before leaving this place for good and heading home to Los Angeles.

Once the placed emptied out, Jessie was left alone. In this moment of solitude, she found herself really missing Elliot. She knew their relationship was still fairly new and that there'd be a lot more obstacles ahead of them, especially with Elliot's heavy filming and travel schedule, but she didn't care. She was willing to endure all of it as long as she and Elliot always came home to each other. Next week couldn't come fast enough.

She brought out a case of beer from the back when the door opened and footsteps pounded on the wooden floors.

Frustrated, she dropped the case on the back counter and lowered her head. She didn't have the patience to go through this again with Maggie.

"This place is exactly the way I pictured it. It's very you."

Jessie's breath quickened. *That wasn't Maggie's voice.* She turned around, and her jaw dropped.

"Elliot."

She was greeted with a bright smile and those sparkling blue eyes she'd missed so much.

"Hey, you."

The words barely left Elliot's mouth before Jessie practically jumped over the bar to get to her. She wrapped her arms around the small of her back and kissed her. Their lips slid against each other and immediately, Jessie was taken back to their last night in Vancouver when all they did was make out and watch bad movies on cable. She'd dreaded the next day because she knew she had to leave. She couldn't stop kissing Elliot that night, and Elliot didn't seem to want to stop kissing her either.

Now, Jessie couldn't believe Elliot was finally in her arms again, her lips against her own, their tongues gliding so deliciously against each other. She brought her hands up around the back of Elliot's neck, pulling her closer, and delving her tongue deeper, loving every little sound that escaped Elliot's throat. Elliot's hands rested firmly on Jessie's ass. She made it well-known how much she missed it while she was away. She pretty much ended every email describing in detail just how perfect Jessie's ass was.

Jessie pushed forward, needing to be closer still. Elliot stepped backward and almost knocked a table over, but their kiss remained intact. Jessie needed a bit more leverage, so she turned them around and guided Elliot to the bar, pushing her back against it and deepening the kiss even more. She fisted Elliot's shirt before moving her hands underneath it and running her fingers along Elliot's warm skin. They both sighed at the contact.

Elliot pulled her as close as she possibly could, but really, there was no more room between them. They'd practically melded together as one.

Elliot broke the kiss first, but only so she could kiss down Jessie's jawline before sucking at her pulse point, biting down where her shoulder met her neck. Jessie groaned at the sensation, nearly losing her footing.

Her hands trailed up Elliot's stomach to her chest as her fingers floated along the silky bra Elliot was wearing. She couldn't stop the moaning that escaped her mouth; Elliot did wonders with those lips on her neck.

"I've missed you so much," said Elliot.

"I've missed you too."

Elliot ran her tongue along Jessie's neck from shoulder to jaw, and Jessie felt her legs start to give out from under her. It felt incredible.

"How did you get here?" she asked breathlessly.

"By plane."

"Very funny. I mean why? You're not done filming until next week."

Elliot pulled back to look at her, and Jessie wanted to kick herself for asking stupid questions when they could be making out.

"I'm done. I finished my last scene today. Some things got switched around, and the rest of my scenes were all filmed this morning. As soon as I was done, I caught the first flight I could out to Boulder. I wanted to surprise you."

"But we were supposed to meet back in LA."

"I couldn't wait that long, so I came here to get you. To take you home. I know you were expecting to stay another week, but…"

"No, no. This is good. I'm ready to get out of here."

Elliot smiled and rested her forehead against Jessie's.

"Good. Let's go home."

Chapter 17

Six months later…

Elliot was thankful she wore her sunglasses. Not just because the Los Angeles sun beat down on her, but also because it kept her from being painfully overt about ogling her girlfriend. She watched Jessie wielding two swords in front of the camera, nailing the stunt choreography perfectly. The fight scene could've been done in one take if it wasn't for the other double constantly missing his mark. A couple times he even came close to catching Jessie with his sword. It could've been bad if Jessie's agility and reflexes hadn't kicked in as she ducked. If she was frustrated, Elliot couldn't tell. She remained as poised and stoic as she always did in a professional setting, but Elliot was tempted to pull the director aside and tell him to fire the other double for putting someone in danger. Even if she was just a guest on the set and not in the movie, Elliot didn't care. Thankfully, she didn't have to say anything. The stunt coordinator came in and did the stunt himself with Jessie, and the rest of the fight scene went smoothly.

Jessie only had a minute to come say hi to Elliot before her next stunt. Elliot found it rather comical that whenever Jessie was working, a crowd suddenly formed— the actresses in the film, the men and women on the crew, the other stunt doubles. All were conveniently in the vicinity whenever Jessie had to do a stunt. This next one was going to be big. Jessie told Elliot all about it. There'd be a long shot of her jumping from a two-story roof, then a close-up stunt fall onto the concrete (from a much lower height, of course), and finally a jump onto a motorcycle to drive away.

As the some of the guys and girls on set watched Jessie set up for the stunt, Elliot side-eyed them behind her sunglasses, throwing them as much shade as possible without being too obvious. Her jealousy easily subsided because whenever Jessie wasn't completely focused on her job, she snuck glances at Elliot, seeing only her and no one else.

Seeing Jessie once again in tight leather, performing a dangerous stunt, made Elliot feel suddenly very thirsty again, not unlike the first time they met. At least today was a bit cooler than it was in the desert. Still, she found herself needing an ice cold beverage. She loved watching Jessie like this, completely in her element. Cool, confident, and unbelievably sexy. Elliot was overjoyed when Jessie finally started getting work again.

A month after they got back to LA, Jessie got a call for some stunt work on a new HBO show which then led to more offers. Jessie was called into a meeting with the stunt coordinator who hired her. She'd worked for him several times before. He explained that she was, in a sense, blacklisted. No one wanted the negative publicity or to risk working with a stunt double who unprofessionally slept with the actors. Jessie tried to explain, but he stopped her, saying he knew she wasn't like that. He'd always been impressed with her work ethic and that obviously things with Elliot were different. He said he'd truly never met anyone more professional than Jessie. He explained he'd have booked her sooner—not caring about what had happened—but that he'd had no projects she would've been right for until now.

Once the scandal died down a bit and word got around that someone took a chance on Jessie, she received more and more calls. At this point, she hadn't had more than a few days off between jobs.

Elliot took a few steps back as the director called for quiet on the set. Once "action" was called, she held her breath while watching her girlfriend leap off the makeshift roof, land a stunt roll on the ground, shed her harness, and ride off on the sleek, red motorcycle until the director called "cut." Elliot could finally breathe again once she knew Jessie was safe. She still sometimes had flashes of Jessie's motorcycle crash in the desert, and while she knew Jessie was a pro, Elliot still worried any time she had to ride one.

The audience around her clapped, cheered, and even swooned, but the second Jessie hopped off the bike, she ran to Elliot and picked her up.

"See? I told you there's nothing to worry about," assured Jessie.

She lowered Elliot to the ground and kissed her. Elliot was too dazed to come up with any kind of witty comeback, so she kissed her back.

*

A couple months later, Jessie looked out among the sea of women who hung on to her every word and followed every direction she gave them. They were 8 weeks into a 10 week self-defense course that Jessie had been teaching ever since the Polis Center for Women officially opened two months ago. Elliot decided to name the place after the first film she was ever cast in, and Jessie, true to her word, began teaching self-defense classes once a week since the day it opened. The number of participants grew every week.

Jessie would have to add another class soon, but she was happy to do it.

"Okay, everyone in your fighting stance. Remember lefties, keep your right foot forward. On my count!"

Jessie moved around the room helping those who needed it and adjusting forms as she continued to count. The women in the class varied in age, some as young as 20 and some as old at 60, but she tried to keep the same pace for everyone since most of them were beginners anyway.

"Good. Back in your fighting stance. And again, on my count."

Jessie continued to make her way through the room checking everyone's form when she spotted a rather sweaty, red-faced blonde in the back corner out of breath but throwing perfect punches. Jessie shot her a grin, and Elliot returned a wink as Jessie moved back to the front of the class. She loved when Elliot attended her classes. Sometimes it was a distraction, but she didn't care. It was too cute watching her, always in the same spot in the back corner, watching as some of the younger women asked Jessie for extra help or attention. Elliot brought it up once after her second class, making it quite clear that there were three very cute and very obvious culprits vying for Jessie's attention.

Jessie knew exactly the girls Elliot was speaking of. Most of the women here came from broken homes or abusive relationships; this was the main point of teaching these women self-defense. But the center and the classes were open to all women, no questions asked. When these girls signed up, they weren't seeking shelter or in need of help. They just wanted the free self-defense classes advertised on the flyer one of them received. Jessie welcomed them, always happy that more women wanted to learn how to protect themselves. The cause was very important to her, and Elliot was thrilled with the turnout. When the girls started flirting with Jessie, she noticed Elliot make her jealous face. A face she'd seen many times on set when everyone watched her perform different stunts.

The girls may have been overly flirtatious, but they were also eager to learn, so Jessie couldn't refuse them help if they asked her for it.

"Great work, everyone. Okay, we're going to partner up now for some floor work and ground techniques. I need a volunteer to help me demonstrate."

Immediately, multiple hands shot up, three of which belonged to the girls Elliot stared daggers at. Jessie watched her girlfriend try to hide her jealousy, but Elliot didn't fool her for a second. She had a tendency to wear her emotions on her sleeve and was terrible at hiding how she really felt. It was one of Jessie's favorite qualities about her.

Today's floor work techniques required everyone to be up close and personal with their partners. As cute as "jealous Elliot" was, Jessie refused to miss an opportunity to get sweaty on the ground with her beautiful girlfriend.

"Elliot, you want to help me demonstrate? These are techniques I've shown you before."

Elliot smiled and made her way to the front. Jessie grinned, ready to take her down to the ground.

"You ready?"

"Yes."

Jessie addressed the class.

"If your attacker approaches you, knocks you over and pins you down, this is a way to try to get out of it." She turned back to her girlfriend. "Elliot, I need you on your back."

She could tell Elliot was trying to stifle a giggle as she got down on the ground face up. Jessie was able to remain all business, at least from an outsider's perspective. She straddled Elliot and turned to the class.

"If your attacker holds you down with his or her weight on your hips, you have the ability to gain some leverage by bucking your hips upward like this."

She turned to Elliot and nodded. Elliot's hips bucked and shot Jessie forward a bit so she now straddled her chest. Elliot's playful smile and quirked eyebrow almost threw Jessie off her balance. They were both sweating, and Elliot's face was bright red, but Jessie didn't know if it was still from the intense physical exertion of the class or the fact that she was practically being topped by Jessie in front of the class. In this position, Jessie couldn't help but feel a little turned on. If it weren't for the room full of people watching them, she'd definitely try to find a way to keep Elliot under her. But since this was a demonstration on how to get out of this position, Elliot had to end up on top of her, which Jessie was also perfectly fine with.

"So, Elliot is now going to collapse my arm at the elbow and use the force of her hips to turn me over and pin me."

Elliot pulled off the move flawlessly. Jessie was quite proud as Elliot slammed her down onto her back, gaining the upper position and straddling her.

"Now, you'll want to back away, but while doing so, use your elbows to dig into their thighs as you crawl off them. It'll hurt like a bitch and make it more difficult for them to get up right away. Once you're up, you run. The most important thing is to get away safely."

Elliot demonstrated that part, but only mimicked her elbows digging into Jessie's thighs so as not to inflict any damage. Then she came back to straddle Jessie. With Elliot still on top of her, Jessie instructed the class to start working on the move.

"Everyone pair off and give it a try. I'll come by to answer any questions," instructed Jessie. She looked up at Elliot and whispered, "You're really good at that."

"I learned from the best."

"I only showed you the move a couple times."

"What can I say? When you're on me, I pay attention."

She continued looking up at Elliot, watching as the sweat glistened from her neck, her chest heaving with each breath. Her face looked almost purple because that's what happened whenever Elliot tried to work out. It was the cutest shit Jessie had ever seen.

"I kind of don't want you to get off me, but I have to go help the class."

"Can I maybe get a private one-on-one lesson after class today?" Elliot gave a very subtle roll of her hips against Jessie, and Jessie felt all of it.

"God, yes. Very private. Very one-on-one."

With that, Elliot allowed Jessie to get up and help out the students. As professional as she tried to remain, Jessie spent the rest of the class watching the clock, waiting for it to be over so she could finish what she started on the ground with Elliot.

Elliot Chase always had a way of making Jessie lose all rationale, and she wouldn't have it any other way.

*

A few weeks later, all their friends gathered in Elliot's backyard for a goodbye party to see Elliot and

Stunted

Jessie off. They were leaving for a four month shoot in London—Elliot as the lead actress and Jessie working as a stunt coordinator on the film. They were both ecstatic to work together again, especially since the shoot was so long. They wouldn't have to worry about spending time apart.

Elliot invited everyone over for a barbeque and some beers before being bogged down with work thousands of miles away. The party was well underway and everyone had a decent buzz going.

"We're gonna miss you, Chase," declared a rather drunk Morgan as she put her arm around Elliot's shoulder. "Who's gonna keep this one in line with our mom friend off in London?"

Morgan gestured towards Hayley who replied with a middle finger.

"Fuck off, Morgan. We all know you're the troublemaker of the group." Hayley turned to Elliot. "But she is right. We are going to miss you."

"It's only four months, you guys. I think you'll survive."

Elliot spotted Jessie sitting next to Kat, both deeply engrossed in conversation.

"Hey!" snapped Morgan. "You have the next four months to stare at your girlfriend. Tonight is about us."

"Is that so? Then why have you been staring at Kat every ten seconds?" asked Hayley.

Morgan shrugged. "Because she's hot. Look at her. Wouldn't you want to stare at that every 10 seconds? Hey babe! You're really hot!"

Kat glanced over at Morgan and rolled her eyes, obviously used to her girlfriend's antics by now.

Morgan smiled proudly.

"Oh yeah. I know that look. I'm definitely getting laid tonight." If her slurred speech was any indication, Elliot knew Morgan would probably pass out before she saw any action.

"Pretty sure that was a look of annoyance and disgust, but whatever you need to tell yourself," teased Hayley.

Elliot was tempted to leave the two of them to bicker with each other and join Jessie and Kat, but James and Ashton came charging out of the house with bottles of champagne.

"A toast!" Ashton exclaimed as he put his arm around Hayley. "To the second cutest couple in all of Los Angeles—next to Hayley and me, of course—and the soon to be cutest couple in London. I know you guys will kick some serious ass out there."

Everyone cheered as the corks were popped, and the champagne was poured. By the end of the night, Elliot had to call cabs for everyone, making sure they all got home safely. By the time everyone was gone, she found Jessie in the backyard, sitting at the edge of the pool with her bare feet underwater. Elliot kicked off her sandals and joined her.

Jessie put her head on Elliot's shoulder as Elliot wrapped her arm around Jessie's waist.

"Tired, babe?"

"Yeah."

"You want to go to sleep?"

"In a minute. I just want to sit here with you for a while, if that's okay."

Elliot smiled and kissed the top of Jessie's head.

"That's more than okay."

They sat together in silence for a while, hearing only the sound of the water splashing as their feet dangled into the pool.

Elliot couldn't help but think back on everything that brought them to this moment. The movie, the sex tape, the aftermath. Somehow the worst thing that ever happened to her also resulted in the best thing that ever happened: the girl sitting next to her with her head resting on her shoulder. When they heard about what happened to Lucy and Cassie after they were found guilty of invasion of privacy, Elliot thought that was the best possible outcome of the entire debacle. Both Lucy and Cassie were forced to pay restitution, which Elliot and Jessie agreed to donate to Elliot's women's shelter. After that, Lucy moved to Phoenix once her probation was up, and the last they had heard of Cassie was that she was trying to make a living working as an extra in film and television. Hayley noticed her on the set of the new TV series she starred in and had her banned from the set permanently.

As deliciously sweet as all that karma was, nothing was better than having Jessie by her side every single moment, from the dark early days after the tape was leaked through the triumphs and successes they'd shared after. She truly couldn't believe how lucky she was.

"Are you nervous?" asked Jessie, breaking the silence.

"About London? No, I'm excited."

"Excited for the movie?"

Elliot couldn't hide her smile. She pulled Jessie closer to her and looked out at her dimly lit yard.

"No, I'm excited for my next great adventure with you."

About the Author

Breanna Hughes' passion for writing began in high school. She went on to graduate with a BFA in Theatre Performance from Chapman University where she took screenwriting, fiction writing and play-writing classes. Her debut novel, *A Fine Mess*, was released in 2016. Breanna is also a singer/songwriter who has performed everywhere from Los Angeles to New York to Nashville, and she has been working in the entertainment industry for over ten years. She was born and raised in Fullerton, California and currently resides in Los Angeles.

Other Titles Available From Triplicity Publishing

Mission Compromised by Graysen Morgen. Natalia Moreno is thrilled when she arrives in Fiji for a relaxing vacation. However, she soon discovers the overwater bungalow she's staying in has been double booked for the entire stay, and the resort is full. Annoyed and frustrated, she has no other choice but to share her hut with a stranger. Christian Garnier is sent to Fiji for what she refers to as a working vacation, until she finds out she has an ornery roommate for the next two weeks who is dead set on making her job twice as hard. Soon, all hell breaks loose and the two women are sent around the world on a wild goose chase.

Stargazing by Kathy L. Salt. Lissa stared open-mouthed at the GIF that played over and over on the screen in front of her. Heat flushed to her face, igniting her skin. Her heart started pounding in her chest. *Stupid internet, it should really come with a warning label.* She's never been interested in relationships or sex and as the years have gone by she has retreated more and more into her work. Everything changes when she meets Star, a porn actress with a heart of gold and a troubled childhood. *They say that opposites attract, but how much of that is true? What chance do they have when one of them is a virgin and the other one star in pornography?*

A New Beginning by KD Rye. There's a quietness, an empty space, that surrounds your life after losing someone you love. Autumn lives in that empty space, day after day, following the same routine, in unresolved angst. She doesn't know how to keep her head above water until the arrival of May, a mysterious dream-like girl who just moved in. Autumn finds refuge in their quickly defined friendship. As her mother falls deeper into depression, Autumn doesn't see a way out of her current situation, until May shows her that anything is possible. However, nothing is what it seems and Autumn has to decipher if the relationship she has built with May is real.

I Belong with Her by Domina Alexandra. Tajel Pierce loves the thrill of being a paramedic. Every call she goes on gives her a rush. She makes no time for a personal life. No one can ruin her love for her career. Then there is Arianna Castaldi, who just transferred to her new paramedic position in a whole new state. All she needs is a new start without any distractions. Arianna and Tajel's relationship doesn't start off perfect. Embarrassed of the one night stand Arianna believes she had with Tajel, she wants to pretend they never met and make their relationship strictly business. The only choice they have to keep from strangling each other is to go from denying their feelings to accepting them as they work through intense 911 calls.

Awakened by Fate by Lynn Lawler. Jackie is a woman living life according to her own rules. She's married, but it's the unspoken, open kind. She can have as many female lovers as she likes; she just can't talk about them. After a bizarre encounter turns her world upside down, things slowly begin to change. She finds herself in desperation as she searches for answers. What she discovers is nothing is delivered in a neatly wrapped box. Now that everything has been brought out into the open, she finds she can't run away from her truth anymore. With her new life, comes new responsibilities and a different outcome than what she was expecting. Jackie isn't alone in the story. She meets several new people who help her along her journey.

Nautical Delights by S. L. Gape. Lady Elizabeth Barrington has spent her entire life trying to please her family; constantly opting for a quiet life, she utilises her profession as a doctor to keep out of her families' clutches; bar the annual two-week Caribbean private cruise, where there is simply no budge. Confined to two weeks on board the Iconica super yacht, she intends on keeping her head down and enjoying as much of the holiday as she can, whilst keeping her family at arm's length. Until a crew member catches her eye.

Whispers of the Heart by KA Moll. Days after completing her fellowship in pediatric ophthalmology, thirty-five-year-old Aki Williams travels from her home in Los Angeles to a small town in Illinois, interviewing for a job that she doesn't want. What she does want is to meet her biological sister, Jack Camdon, a sister whom she didn't know existed until she dreamt of her. Three years ago on Sunday, forty-three-year-old professor of archaeology, Carsyn Lyndon, lost her parents and her wife in a tragic accident. Since then, she's suffered from PTSD and loneliness. She's kind-hearted and handsome but dates no one. When she meets Aki at her four-year-old Godson's birthday party, they're incredibly attracted to one another, and those feelings intensify during a family camping trip—a particularly interesting development for Aki since prior to that she'd never considered that she might be a lesbian.

Worlds Apart by S.L. Gape. Hollywood A-lister Heidi Spencer-Brady is everything you'd expect of an Idol. Loved by all, the British Beauty is graceful, talented, humble and so far removed from the 'typical' LA scene. When her husband's infidelity with his new 'leading lady' is leaked, Dawn, Heidi's best friend and manager, goes all out to protect her. She arranges for Heidi to go back to the UK and stay on her cousins farm they had visited as children, much to the disappointment of the animal fearing Heidi.

Castor Valley (Law & Order Series Book 2) by Graysen Morgen. Jessie Henry is torn when she reads about the capture of the Doyle brothers, two young men who were part of her old gang. Unable to let them hang for a crime she's sure they didn't commit, Jessie leaves her wife and the Town of Boone Creek behind, and sets out on a journey back to the one place she thought she'd never see again, *Castor Valley*. Ellie Henry watches the love of her life leave, not knowing if she will ever return. When she gets an odd telegram, nearly a week later, she fears Jessie is in trouble. With no other choice, she goes to the one person who can help her.

Close Enough to Touch by Cade Brogan. Joanna Grey injects the deadly poison into the chamber of the syringe—time after time. She's murdered before and she'll do it again. She's intelligent, educated, and beautiful. Rylee Hayes is a respected homicide detective. Her best friends are her grandparents, her coonhound, and her partner—in that order. Kenzie Bigham is the single mom of a thirteen-year-old, a church secretary, and a woman who's struggled much of her adult life with her own sexuality. Their paths will cross when Rylee's new investigation involves members of Kenzie's congregation. Will Rylee have what it takes to meet the challenge of a serial killer who's proven herself to be a more than worthy opponent?

Fight to the Top by S. L. Gape. Georgia is a forty year old, single, Area Director from Manchester, UK who is all work and definitely no play. Having no time to socialise or spend time with her family she prides herself on being fit and well-polished. Erika is an Area Director for the same company, but in the United States. Whilst she is concentrating so heavily on the promotion she has been fighting for, she's starting to feel like her life outside of work is falling apart. The two women are exceptionally different, and worlds apart. Both of their lives are turned upside down when their jobs are snatched from under their noses, and they are suddenly faced with being thrown together by their bosses for one last major project...in Texas.

Boone Creek (Law & Order Series book 1) by Graysen Morgen. Jessie Henry is looking for a new life. She's unknown in the town of Boone Creek when she arrives, and wants to keep it that way. When she's offered the job of Town Marshal, she takes it, believing that protecting others and upholding the law is the penance for her past. Ellie Fray is a widowed, shopkeeper. She generally keeps to herself, but the mysterious new Town Marshal both intrigues and infuriates her. She believes the last thing the town needs is someone stirring up trouble with the outlaws who have taken over.

Witness by Joan L. Anderson. Becca and Kate have lived together for eight years, and have always spent their vacation in a tropical paradise, lying on a beach. This year, Becca wanted to try something different: a seven day, 65-mile hike in the beautiful Cascade Mountains of Washington state. Their peaceful vacation turns to horror when they stumble upon a brutal murder taking place in the back country.

Too Soon by S.L. Gape. Brooke is a twenty-nine year old detective from Oxford, who has her life pretty much planned out until her boss and partner of nine years, Maria, tells her their relationship is over. When Brooke finds out the truth, that Maria cheated on her with their best friend Paula, she decides to get her life back on track by getting away for six weeks in Anglesey, North Wales. Chloe, a thirty three year old artist and art director, owns a log cabin on Anglesey where she spends each weekend painting and surfing. After returning from a surf, she stumbles upon the somewhat uptight and enigmatic Brooke.

Blue Ice Landing by KA Moll. Coy is a beautiful blonde with a southern accent and a successful practice as a physician assistant. She has a comfortable home, good friends, and a loving family. She's also a widow, carrying a burden of responsibility for her wife's untimely death. Coby is a woman with secrets. She's estranged from her family, a recovering alcoholic, and alone because she's convinced that she's unlovable. When she loses her job as a heavy equipment operator, she'll accept one that'll force her to step way outside her comfort zone. When Coy quits her job to accept a position in Antarctica, her path will cross with Coby's. Their attraction to one another will be immediate, and despite their differences, it won't be long before they fall in love. But for these two, with all their baggage, will love be enough?

Never Quit (Never Series book 2) by Graysen Morgen. Two years after stepping away from the action as a Coast Guard Rescue Swimmer to become an instructor, Finley finds herself in charge of the most difficult class of cadets she's ever faced, while also juggling the taxing demands of having a home life with her partner Nicole, and their fifteen year old daughter. Jordy Ross gave up everything, dropping out of college, and leaving her family behind, to join the Coast Guard and become a rescue swimmer cadet. The extreme training tests her fitness level, pushing her mentally and physically further than she's ever been in her life, but it's the aggressive competition between her and another female cadet that proves to be the most challenging.

For a Moment's Indiscretion by KA Moll. With ten years of marriage under their belt, Zane and Jaina are coasting. The little things they used to do for one another have fallen by the wayside. They've gotten busy with life. They've forgotten to nurture their love and relationship. Even soul mates can stumble on hard times and have marital difficulties. Enter Amelia, a new faculty member in Jaina's building. She's new in town, young, and very pretty. When an argument with Zane causes Jaina to storm out angry, she reaches out to Amelia. Of course, she seizes the opportunity. And for a moment of indiscretion, Jaina could lose everything.

Never Let Go (Never Series book 1) by Graysen Morgen. For Coast Guard Rescue Swimmer, Finley Morris, life is good. She loves her job, is well respected by her peers, and has been given an opportunity to take her career to the next level. The only thing missing is the love of her life, who walked out, taking their daughter with her, seven years earlier. When Finley gets a call from her ex, saying their teenage daughter is coming to spend the summer with her, she's floored. While spending more time with her daughter, whom she doesn't get to see often, and learning to be a full-time parent, Finley quickly realizes she has not, and will never, let go of what is important.

Pursuit by Joan L. Anderson. Claire is a workaholic attorney who flies to Paris to lick her wounds after being dumped by her girlfriend of seventeen years. On the plane she chats with the young woman sitting next to her, and when they land the woman is inexplicably detained in Customs. Claire is surprised when she later runs into the woman in the city. They agree to meet for breakfast the next morning, but when the woman doesn't show up Claire goes to her hotel and makes a horrifying discovery. She soon finds herself ensnared in a web of intrigue and international terrorism, becoming the target of a high stakes game of cat and mouse through the streets of Paris.

Wrecked by Sydney Canyon. To most people, the *Duchess* is a myth formed by old pirates tales, but to Reid Cavanaugh, a Caribbean island bum and one of the best divers and treasure hunters in the world, it's a real, seventeenth century pirate ship—the holy grail of underwater treasure hunting. Reid uses the same cunning tactics she always has before setting out to find the lost ship. However, she is forced to bring her business partner's daughter along as collateral this time because he doesn't trust her. Neither woman is thrilled, but being cooped up on a small dive boat for days, forces them to get know each other quickly.

Arson by Austen Thorne. Madison Drake is a detective for the Stetson Beach Police Department. The last thing she wants to do is show a new detective the ropes, especially when a fire investigation becomes arson to cover up a murder. Madison butts heads with Tara, her trainee, deals with sarcasm from Nic, her ex-girlfriend who is a patrol officer, and finds calm in the chaos of police work with Jamie, her best friend who is the county medical examiner. Arson is the first of many in a series of novella episodes surrounding the fictional Stetson Beach Police Department and Detective Madison Drake.

Change of Heart by KA Moll. Courtney Holloman is a woman at the top of her game. She's successful, wealthy, and a highly sought after Washington lobbyist. She has money, her job, booze, and nothing else. In quiet moments, against her will, her mind drifts back to her days in high school and to all that she gave up. Jack Camdon is a complex woman, and yet not at all. She is also a woman who has never moved beyond the sudden and unexplained departure of her high school sweetheart, her lover, and her soul mate. When circumstances bring Courtney back to town two decades later, their paths will cross. Will it be too late?

Mommies (Bridal Series book 3) **by Graysen Morgen.** Britton and her wife Daphne have been married for a year and a half and are happy with their life, until Britton's mother hounds her to find out why her sister Bridget hasn't decided to have children yet. This prompts

Daphne to bring up the big subject of having kids of their own with Britton. Britton hadn't really thought much about having kids, but her love for Daphne makes her see life and their future together in a whole new way when they decide to become mommies.

***Haunting Love* by K.A. Moll.** Anna Crestwood was raised in the strict beliefs of a religious sect nestled in the foothills of the Smoky Mountains. She's a lesbian with a ton of baggage—fearful, guilty, and alone. Very few things would compel her to leave the familiar. The job offer of a lifetime is one of them. Gabe Garst is a police officer. She's also a powerful medium. Her work with juvenile delinquents and ghosts is all that keeps her going. Inside she's dead, certain that her capacity to love is buried six feet under. Anna and Gabe's paths cross. Their attraction is immediate, but they hold back until all hope seems lost.

***Rapture & Rogue* by Sydney Canyon.** Taren Rauley is happy and in a good relationship, until the one person she thought she'd never see again comes back into her life. She struggles to keep the past from colliding with the present as old feelings she thought were dead and gone, begin to haunt her. In college, Gianna Revisi was a mastermind, ring-leading, crime boss. Now, she has a great life and spends her time running Rapture and Rogue, the two establishments she built from the ground up. The last person she ever expects to see walk into one of them, is the girl who walked out on her, breaking her heart five years ago.

***Second Chance* by Sydney Canyon.** After an attack on her convoy, Marine Corps Staff Sergeant, Darien Hollister, must learn to live without her sight. When an experimental procedure allows her to see again, Darien is torn, knowing someone had to die in order for this to happen.

She embarks on a journey to personally thank the donor's family, but is too stunned to tell them the truth. Mixed emotions stir inside of her as she slowly gets to the know the people that feel like so much more than strangers to her. When the truth finally comes out, Darien walks away, taking the second chance that she's been given to go back to the only life she's ever known, but she's not the only one with a second chance at life.

Meant to Be by Graysen Morgen. Brandt is about to walk down the aisle with her girlfriend, when an unexpected chain of events turns her world upside down, causing her to question the last three years of her life. A chance encounter sparks a mix of rage and excitement that she has never felt before. Summer is living life and following her dreams, all the while, harboring a huge secret that could ruin her career. She believes that some things are better kept in the dark, until she has her third run-in with a woman she had hoped to never see again, and gives into temptation. Brandt and Summer start believing everything happens for a reason as they learn the true meaning of meant to be.

Coming Home by Graysen Morgen. After tragedy derails TJ Abernathy's life, she packs up her three year old son and heads back to Pennsylvania to live with her grandmother on the family farm. TJ picks back up where she left off eight years earlier, tending to the fruit and nut tree orchard, while learning her grandmother's secret trade. Soon, TJ's high school sweetheart and the same girl who broke her heart, comes back into her life, threatening to steal it away once again. As the weeks turn into months and tragedy strikes again, TJ realizes coming home was the best thing she could've ever done.

Special Assignment by Austen Thorne. Secret Service Agent Parker Meeks has her hands full when she gets her new assignment, protecting a Congressman's teenage daughter, who has had threats made on her life and been whisked away to a Christian boarding school under an alias to finish out her senior year. Parker is fine with the assignment, until she finds out she has to go undercover as a Canon Priest. The last thing Parker expects to find is a beautiful, art history teacher, who is intrigued by her in more ways than one.

Miracle at Christmas by Sydney Canyon. A Modern Twist on the Classic Scrooge Story. Dylan is a power-hungry lawyer who pushed away everything good in her life to become the best defense attorney in the, often winning the worst cases and keeping anyone with enough money out of jail. She's visited on Christmas Eve by her deceased law partner, who threatens her with a life in hell like his own, if she doesn't change her path. During the course of the night, she is taken on a journey through her past, present, and future with three very different spirits.

Bella Vita by Sydney Canyon. Brady is the First Officer of the crew on the Bella Vita, a luxury charter yacht in the Caribbean. She enjoys the laidback island lifestyle, and is accustomed to high profile guests, but when a U.S. Senator charters the yacht as a gift to his beautiful twin daughters who have just graduated from college and a few of their friends, she literally has her hands full.

Brides (Bridal Series book 2) by Graysen Morgen. Britton Prescott is dating the love of her life, Daphne Attwood, after a few tumultuous events that happened to unravel at her sister's wedding reception, seven months earlier. She's happy with the way things are, but immense pressure from her family and friends to take the next step, nearly sends her back to the single life. The idea of a long engagement and simple wedding are thrown out the window, as both families take over, rushing Britton and Daphne to the altar in a matter of weeks.

Cypress Lake by Graysen Morgen. The small town of Cypress Lake is rocked when one murder after another happens. Dani Ricketts, the Chief Deputy for the Cypress Lake Sheriff's Office, realizes the murders are linked. She's surprised when the girl that broke her heart in high school has not only returned home, but she's also Dani's only suspect. Kristen Malone has come back to Cypress Lake to put the past behind her so that she can move on with her life. Seeing Dani Ricketts again throws her off-guard, nearly derailing her plans to finally rid herself and her family of Cypress Lake.

Crashing Waves by Graysen Morgen. After a tragic accident, Pro Surfer, Rory Eden, spends her days hiding in the surf and snowboard manufacturing company that she built from the ground up, while living her life as a shell of the person that she once was. Rory's world is turned upside when a young surfer pursues her, asking for the one thing she can't do. Adler Troy and Dr. Cason Macauley from Graysen Morgen's bestselling novel: *Falling Snow*, make an appearance in this romantic adventure about life, love, and letting go.

Bridesmaid of Honor (Bridal Series book 1) by Graysen Morgen. Britton Prescott's best friend is getting married and she's the maid of honor. As if that isn't enough to deal with, Britton's sister announces she's getting married in the same month and her maid of honor is her best friend Daphne, the same woman who has tormented Britton for years. Britton has to suck it up and play nice, instead of scratching her eyes out, because she and Daphne are in both weddings. Everyone is counting on them to behave like adults.

Falling Snow by Graysen Morgen. Dr. Cason Macauley, a high-speed trauma surgeon from Denver meets Adler Troy, a professional snowboarder and sparks fly. The last thing Cason wants is a relationship and Adler doesn't realize what's right in front of her until it's gone, but will it be too late?

Fate vs. Destiny by Graysen Morgen. Logan Greer devotes her life to investigating plane crashes for the National Transportation Safety Board. Brooke McCabe is an investigator with the Federal Aviation Association who literally flies by the seat of her pants. When Logan gets tangled in head games with both women will she choose fate or destiny?

Just Me by Graysen Morgen. Wild child Ian Wiley has to grow up and take the reins of the hundred year old family business when tragedy strikes. Cassidy Harland is a little surprised that she came within an inch of picking up a gorgeous stranger in a bar and is shocked to find out that stranger is the new head of her company.

Love Loss Revenge by Graysen Morgen. Rian Casey is an FBI Agent working the biggest case of her career and madly in love with her girlfriend. Her world is turned upside when tragedy strikes. Heartbroken, she tries to rebuild her life. When she discovers the truth behind what really happened that awful night she decides justice isn't good enough, and vows revenge on everyone involved.

Natural Instinct by Graysen Morgen. Chandler Scott is a Marine Biologist who keeps her private life private. Corey Joslen is intrigued by Chandler from the moment she meets her. Chandler is forced to finally open her life up to Corey. It backfires in Corey's face and sends her running. Will either woman learn to trust her natural instinct?

Secluded Heart by Graysen Morgen. Chase Leery is an overworked cardiac surgeon with a group of best friends that have an opinion and a reason for everything. When she meets a new artist named Remy Sheridan at her best friend's art gallery she is captivated by the reclusive woman. When Chase finds out why Remy is so sheltered will she put her career on the line to help her or is it too difficult to love someone with a secluded heart?

In Love, at War by Graysen Morgen. Charley Hayes is in the Army Air Force and stationed at Ford Island in Pearl Harbor. She is the commanding officer of her own female-only service squadron and doing the one thing she loves most, repairing airplanes. Life is good for Charley, until the day she finds herself falling in love while fighting for her life as her country is thrown haphazardly into World War II. Can she survive being in love and at war?

Fast Pitch by Graysen Morgen. Graham Cahill is a senior in college and the catcher and captain of the softball team. Despite being an all-star pitcher, Bailey Michaels is young and arrogant. Graham and Bailey are forced to get to know each other off the field in order to learn to work together on the field. Will the extra time pay off or will it drive a nail through the team?

Submerged by Graysen Morgen. Assistant District Attorney Layne Carmichael had no idea that the sexy woman she took home from a local bar for a one night stand would turn out to be someone she would be prosecuting months later. Scooter is a Naval Officer on a submarine who changes women like she changes uniforms. When she is accused of a heinous crime she is shocked to see her latest conquest sitting across from her as the prosecuting attorney.

Vow of Solitude by Austen Thorne. Detective Jordan Denali is in a fight for her life against the ghosts from her past and a Serial Killer taunting her with his every move. She lives a life of solitude and plans to keep it that way. When Callie Marceau, a curious Medical Examiner, decides she wants in on the biggest case of her career, as well as, Jordan's life, Jordan is powerless to stop her.

Igniting Temptation by Sydney Canyon. Mackenzie Trotter is the Head of Pediatrics at the local hospital. Her life takes a rather unexpected turn when she meets a flirtatious, beautiful fire fighter. Both women soon discover it doesn't take much to ignite temptation.

One Night by Sydney Canyon. While on a business trip, Caylen Jarrett spends an amazing night with a beautiful stripper. Months later, she is shocked and confused when that same woman re-enters her life. The fact that this stranger could destroy her career doesn't bother her. C.J. is more terrified of the feelings this woman stirs in her. Could she have fallen in love in one night and not even known it?

Fine by Sydney Canyon. Collin Anderson hides behind a façade, pretending everything is fine. Her workaholic wife and best friend are both oblivious as she goes on an emotional journey, battling a potentially hereditary disease that her mother has been diagnosed with. The only person who knows what is really going on, is Collin's doctor. The same doctor, who is an acquaintance that she's always been attracted to, and who has a partner of her own.

Shadow's Eyes by Sydney Canyon. Tyler McCain is the owner of a large ranch that breeds and sells different types of horses. She isn't exactly thrilled when a Hollywood movie producer shows up wanting to film his latest movie on her property. Reegan Delsol is an up and coming actress who has everything going for her when she lands the lead role in a new film, but there one small problem that could blow the entire picture.

Light Reading: A Collection of Novellas by Sydney Canyon. Four of Sydney Canyon's novellas together in one book, including the bestsellers Shadow's Eyes and One Night.

Breanna Hughes

Visit us at www.tri-pub.com

www.ingramcontent.com/pod-product-compliance
Lightning Source LLC
Chambersburg PA
CBHW030241200626
46816CB00002BA/455